FORGIVEN

ANN El-NEMR

To Patricia
Love to see you the
always.
Best Your Ann El Nem
2014

FORGIVEN

ANN EL-NEMR

Published May 2014
Little Creek Books
Imprint of Jan-Carol Publishing, Inc
All rights reserved

ISBN: 978-1-939289-40-7
Library of Congress Control Number: 2014939762

You may contact the publisher:
Jan-Carol Publishing, Inc
PO Box 701 Johnson City, TN 37605
E-mail: publisher@jancarolpublishing.com
jancarolpublishing.com

Jan-Carol
Publishing, Inc
"every story needs a book"

This book is dedicated to the memory of my nephew,
Luc Arsenault.

You are in our hearts and will never be forgotten.

LETTER TO THE READER

Here we are again—back with the Rian family of *Betrayed*. But this time—the story of *Forgiven*—it's all about Tom Smith, the security expert once hired by patriarch Ron Rian. Tom has spent the last ten years in prison, and he wants his revenge on Ron, the man who put him there. As the author, I faced many difficult questions while writing *Forgiven*. Should I let Tom get caught again, or should he find the love he needs to quench his thirst for revenge? Enter Chantal—a dear friend of Gabrielle Rian and woman who labors to teach others how to forgive. Can Tom accept Chantal's love as long as he has a mission to fulfill? Can there ever be forgiveness between Ron and Tom? By the end of *Forgiven*, these questions (and more!) are answered, but not without many twists and spins—which actually changed my mind about the final outcome! Enjoy visiting Boston and the beaches of Hyannis while reading *Forgiven*, and then go to my website (www.annelnemr.com) to tell me how you liked it.

Yours truly,

Ann El-Nemr

ACKNOWLEDGMENTS

I would like to thank my family and friends (you know who you are) who encouraged me and believed that I could write another book. I especially thank Patricia Peterleitner, who has always provided me with great advice.

Thanks to my children—Fouad, Badih, and Amiranour—and funny 'go-to girl' Becca Shurtleff: you are always the ones I turn to when I need help with my computer. Thank you for being so patient and understanding.

And last but not least, I thank Janie Jessee and her staff at Jan-Carol Publishing, Inc, for helping me to go forward with this book.

INTRODUCTION

Picking up where *Betrayed* left off, *Forgiven* begins with Tom Smith's release from a ten-year prison term. Tom is determined to seek revenge from Ron Rian—his former employer, a man he respected as a father figure, and the one (Tom believes) betrayed him and ultimately sent him to prison. In making his plans, Tom spies on the Rian family and becomes captivated by Gabrielle Rian's closest friend, Chantal. But for Tom and Chantal's love to have a future, forgiveness must overcome pride, fear, and hate—not only in Tom's life, but in Ron's life and even Gabrielle's as well. Can all truly be *Forgiven* to win the love of a lifetime?

CHAPTER 1

On the outskirts of a small town in the western part of Massachusetts, an ex-convict named Tom Smith was on parole after serving ten years for attempted murder. He was an ex-Army sergeant from the Special Ops department, he had served two tours in the Middle East, and he was a veteran of the war in Iraq. He had been dishonorably discharged for disobeying orders several times. He used to be Bernard Rian's father's right-hand man and enforcer for many years of his life, but Ron had betrayed him. He had lost years while incarcerated in prison for trying to murder his employer.

Tom was a bitter man, and he was consumed by evil. There was nothing he wouldn't do for the right price. He had counted the days until he would be released from prison and he would be able to bring his wrath upon Ron's family for the pain that he had suffered for being a loyal servant. He had had a long time to plot his retaliation, every day waiting with anticipation to put his plan into action. Now, it was time for his revenge.

Tom had been 'on the outside' for the last month. To protect himself, he had bought an old, run-down farmhouse in the town of Ashburnham under an assumed name. The house was located down a long dirt road near the woods. The house needed work, but Tom had always been good with his hands, and he didn't mind repairing the house as a way to spend time.

It was secluded and tranquil, despite what he had planned for the near future. He worked diligently on the house, reinforcing the doors of one room and installing bars on the windows. Tom had found a job as a janitor, cleaning an office building at night. It gave him his alibi if his parole officer checked on him. The job also provided him with free time during the day. In addition, Tom was renting a room in a boarding house in Worcester, so that his parole officer would not become suspicious of anything. The law required that the parole officer have a record of Tom's address, and it was essential that he project a perfect image until he could execute his plan. He just needed a few more days of preparation, and then he would have everything ready.

"Are you sure this plan will work?" Neil asked Tom. He was sitting on a rundown couch with sagging seats and rips here and there. As he watched Tom, Neil bit the nails on one of his hands and held a beer in the other.

"Don't worry. Everything is under control. Just do what I tell you, and we'll be good. You'll be well taken care of, and you'll be able to buy and do whatever you want after we're done," Tom answered. He needed a partner who would take the fall should something go wrong with his plan. Neil had served seven years for armed robbery and had been Tom's cellmate during prison.

Neil wasn't an educated man. He was a follower and wet behind the ears, which was what had gotten him caught in the first place. Neil followed Tom without question because Tom had protected him numerous times from other inmates who had wanted to hurt or control him. Little did Neil realize, however, that Tom himself had been manipulating Neil to gain his trust. Tom knew that he could use Neil to his advantage once they were released. Neil had gotten out of prison nearly a year ago and had been working as a handy man, fixing houses whenever he could.

"Okay, I've got it." Neil took another sip of his beer.

"I need you to go in town and pick up a few things. Don't buy everything at the same store. I need to see someone. I'll meet you back here in a few hours," Tom said, then handed Neil a slip of paper with a list. Neil looked at it and then extended his hand for cash. Tom placed several $100 bills Neil's hand. Neil slipped the money into his pocket and got up from his seat.

"Get going. Meet you back here around six o'clock—and be discreet. If I'm not back by six, stay put. Don't leave the house and don't talk to anyone. Understood?" Tom asked, staring at Neil with slanted eyes, his lips tight as he pointed his finger toward the door. "Go."

"All right, boss." Neil got up and slowly walked to the front door. He took one last gulp of his beer, pushed the screen door open, and left. From the door, Tom watched Neil carefully as he got into his old, battered car and took off. He did trust this guy—but only to a certain degree. He needed someone to help him with his plan. Once it was over, Tom would decide what to do with Neil. Tom took his cellphone out of his pocket and dialed a number.

"Hey! It's me. Did you find what I needed?" Tom asked.

"Yeah! I did, but it's going to cost you. I'm taking a big risk here, giving you this. Just meet me in the parking lot behind The Red Zone in fifteen minutes," his associate replied.

"I know—I appreciate it. I'm on my way. I'll be there in ten minutes," Tom replied and then hung up the phone.

He grabbed his keys from the coffee table and walked to his truck, started the engine, and started for his destination. As he drove, Tom opened the center console to make sure that his 9-mm gun was there. He smiled, looked at it, caressed it with the tips of his fingers, and then slowly closed the center console. He reached for the volume button on his iPod and turned it up. His favorite album was playing—*Trilogy* by The Weekend. He listened to the music as he continued down the highway, lost in his own world as he drove.

A few minutes later, Tom parked his truck behind The Red Zone, a strip club, and waited for his friend to arrive. He kept his eyes peeled and on the lookout for anything suspicious. It was in his nature to not trust anyone completely. His eyes scanned the area until he saw a figure coming toward him. It was his pharmaceutical friend, Richard—an ex-Army comrade who owned him a favor.

Tom had made a lot of money working as chief of security for his former employer. He had stashed it in a Swiss bank account long before he had gone to prison. Because of this, he was financially secure. Not too many people knew this, and he worked a part-time job to keep his friends in the dark. The side door of the truck opened, and his friend sat down. Small beads of sweat were running down his neck, and his eyes were darting everywhere.

"I hope you know how difficult it was to get this stuff," Richard said, taking the small bottle from his pocket. His hand shook as he looked at it.

"I understand. I am sure this will compensate for it and your silence." Tom handed him a white envelope with ten $100 bills. He observed as Richard opened it and his eyes bulged out. He handed Tom an 8-oz brown bottle with clear liquid in it. Tom examined it and placed it in the glove compartment.

"Make sure not too use too much. It could kill a person," his friend warned him, and then stretched his hand toward the truck handle, pulled it, and opened the door.

"Thanks a lot," Tom said, then watched Richard walk quickly back into the strip club. Tom started his truck, turned it around, and headed back to the farm. As he drove, he contemplated the last small details of his plan. He only had a few hours left before he headed south toward Newport, Rhode Island.

***

"Hurry up, Junior! Your father is waiting in the truck! We're late!" Gabrielle, his mother, yelled down the hall at her son, her hands on her hips, her foot tapping the floor. She looked at her wristwatch again.

"I'm coming!" Junior answered. He ran down the hallway with his backpack full of Transformer toys and other games.

"Here I am," he replied and looked at his mother with a wide smile and puppy eyes. Junior was ten years old, and he looked exactly like his father, with black hair, piecing blue eyes, and high cheekbones. He was the heir to The Rian Empire, a billion-dollar hotel conglomerate that his grandfather had inherited. His father, Bernard, had inherited the company and had built it over the years. "Let's go," Gabrielle said. They walked hand in hand to the front entrance, where the chauffeur was holding the car door open. Junior hopped into the Range Rover, clicked his seatbelt on, grabbed his Transformer from his backpack, and started to battle an imaginary enemy.

"Hey, Buddy! You ready to go swimming and have some fun in Newport?" Bernard held his hand up and high-fived his son. Bernard winked then smiled at his son.

"If only he could hurry. This child is so slow," Gabrielle said as she sat beside her husband. She was happy the whole family finally was going to their summerhouse for a well-deserved vacation. She could not wait!

She expected her longtime friend, Chantal, to visit them for a few weeks. Gabrielle had been feeling homesick, so she had called Chantal and invited her to come spend time with her. Gabrielle wanted to catch up on all the gossip from her hometown and have a few good laughs.

Gabrielle and Chantal had known each other since high school, and they had kept in touch over the years. Chantal was a petite woman with long, curly, blonde hair and a bubbly personality. She was a first-grade teacher at the local elementary school in her village. Chantal also was a bit naïve when it came to men—which was why at the age of thirty-five she was still single and searching for a man. Chantal loved children, and she was Junior's godmother.

"A few weeks of fresh air by the beach will be relaxing," Gabrielle said to Bernard. She reached over and took his hand in hers.

"I agree. I have been so busy at work lately that I have not been able to spend much time with my little man here or especially you," Bernard said, looking at his wife from head to toe and then grinning. She gave him a small slap on his hand, her face turning pink. Even after these years, he still made her blush. Gabrielle was looking forward to spending quality time with her husband.

Bernard worked long hours as CEO of The Rian Empire. He travelled for weeks on end but always came home to her and their son. She had chosen to move to Boston from her small French town in Canada to help care for Bernard's father, who had been shot ten years earlier. Gabrielle was in a good mood, and she had been humming a tune for the past week.

"Will you built a sand castle with me, Papa, like you always do?" Junior tapped his father's shoulder as he bounced on the edge of his seat.

"Absolutely. And maybe we can have your friend Brian come along and help," Bernard answered and smiled at him again. Brian was a neighborhood friend of Junior's. Junior had met the boy three years previously while at the beach. The boys, who were the same age, had become chums and shared similar interests.

"That will be so much fun! Can we do it this afternoon?" Junior asked. He looked at his father in the rearview mirror. Bernard nodded his head up and down.

"I will talk to Brian's mother," Gabrielle said. Every year in July for the last ten years—since their son—had been born, the family had made a point of leaving everything behind and spending quality time together.

They drove down the highway toward Newport, Rhode Island while Junior bombarded them with questions and played with his toys.

Two hours later, they were driving down Ochre Point Avenue, where Bernard and Gabrielle had spent their first weekend together visiting The Breakers Mansion. This town brought back memories of when they had first fallen in love with each other. Gabrielle loved this town. It was so much quieter than Boston. The days passed slowly and she was able to fully unwind. It reminded her of her hometown of Shediac, which was located on the east coast of Canada, where the people were friendly and you could smell the fresh ocean air. She could leave her worries of everyday life behind and fully enjoy the little things in life. "Here we are!" Gabrielle exclaimed when Bernard parked the vehicle in the front yard of their small cottage on the east side of the island. The cottage had three bedrooms, with a great view of the ocean and its sandy beach. Gabrielle did not have time to even get out of the truck before Junior jumped out and opened his father's door. He was tugging on his father's arm and pulling him toward the front door.

"Can we go down to the beach now, pleaseeee? Hurry," the boy said.

"Let me bring the bags into the house first, then we can go," Bernard laughed at his son. Bernard looked at Gabrielle and mouthed "Sorry!" while his son was trying to drag him out of his seat. They headed toward the back of the truck to get the bags.

"Great! I'll help." Junior snatched his bag and started running toward the front porch of the cottage.

"I wish I had half his energy," Gabrielle said as she walked up the path to the bungalow and unlocked the door. She watched as her son ran to his bedroom to change into his bathing trunks. Bernard dropped the bags in the bedroom and then walked slowly to the kitchen, where Gabrielle was standing. He wrapped his muscular arms around her waist, pulling her close to him.

Bernard bent his head down and kissed Gabrielle softly on the lips. She could feel his heartbeat beating fast against her chest. She brought her arms up around his neck and let her fingers play with the hair at the nape of his neck. Every time she was near him, she still could not believe he was her husband. He was gentle with their son and always so understanding. He made her feel like she was the only one. How she loved this man!

"I cannot wait until we are alone this evening," Bernard whispered near her ear and nibbled on her earlobe. A chill went down her spine to her toes. He rubbed his bulge against her as he brought his hands down toward her butt and squeezed it.

"Well, I think you should go off to the beach before—" Gabrielle said, as she tried to wiggle away from him.

"The sooner you leave, the sooner he will get tired, the sooner he will go to bed, and the sooner we will be alone," Gabrielle said in a low voice, and then she laughed and slowly walked away. She watched Bernard make a sad face at her, then turn and hurry toward the bedroom to change into his swim trunks. He grabbed two towels from the closet on the way out, and Bernard and Junior strutted toward the beach.

Gabrielle waved to them from the entrance of the cottage until they were out of sight. Bernard had bought the small house many years ago for his first fiancée, Danielle, but she had died in a car crash right before their wedding. He had not returned to the house until he had met Gabrielle. It was now Gabrielle's favorite spot to relax and spend time with her family. She loved to sit on the veranda in her rocking chair and watch the sailboats go by as she listened to the sound of the ocean and the birds. She adored how secluded the cottage was, with its wrap-around porch, large windows, and the intimate atmosphere she felt when she was here. She turned and walked to the kitchen to prepare lunch for her boys to eat when they returned from their afternoon at the beach.

CHAPTER 2

Ron Rian was Bernard's father. Ron was a middle-aged man with gray hair, a strong mind, and impeccable attire. He was also a paraplegic. A team of medical personnel lived on the premises, addressing all his physical and personnel needs. He had built and inherited his fortune in his younger days, but now his only son, Bernard, sat at the head of his company and had taken charge of his father's corporation and his well-being after his accident.

Ron was sitting quietly in the library of his home behind a huge mahogany desk. This room served as Ron's office. His desk sat in front of two large patio doors that overlooked the manicured grounds of his estate. On the far right was a large stone fireplace that went all the way up the ten-foot mahogany panel walls to the beamed ceiling. Books lined the walls, but most of the rest of the room was bare, except for two leather chairs in front of the fireplace. The floors were made of marble and were clear of rugs so that Ron could maneuver his wheelchair freely. A small bar stood in one of the corners and held an assortment of bottles of fine scotch and crystal glasses.

Pictures of a small child and his parents hung on the opposite wall, bringing warmth to the room. Ron sat in a state-of-the-art motorized electric chair, where he was destined to live the rest of his life. He had been shot years ago by a man that Ron called a lunatic and whom he unfortunately had employed at the time. Ron was paralyzed from the waist down;

it had taken him a long time to adjust to his condition, but he had finally accepted it—more or less—after many years of denial.

Ron was using a gold-letter opener to casually open business correspondence when he noticed a particular yellow envelope on the right side of his desk. It was from a friend at the Department of Probation and Parole. He reached for the envelope, opened it, removed the letter, and read it carefully. It was a copy of a notification of a parole board hearing regarding the release of Tom Smith. It was dated a month ago. Ron sighed and pursed his lips together. His face turned red from anger as he ripped the paper into pieces and threw them into the wastebasket beside him. He clenched his hands into fists. He had to do something! But what? He had to calm himself. He took a deep breath, and let it out. He did this several times until he had cleared his mind.

Think, Ron. Think.

He just hoped Tom wouldn't go after him or his family again. How was he going to defend himself or them? He had to tell them Tom was out. Maybe Tom was a changed man, but Ron doubted it. Tom had just spent ten years in prison because of him. Ron picked up the receiver of the phone next him, dialed a familiar number, and waited impatiently while it rang. Ron was drummed his fingers on the top of the desk. There was no answer from the other end.

***

Chantal sat in seat 2A on the second row of an Air Canada flight bound for Boston. She was excited to see her best friend Gabrielle. They hadn't seen each other in a year. She gripped her armrests tightly, her knuckles white as she clenched her hands. Her heartbeat pounded in her chest. She hated to fly, but it was a lot faster than driving down to Massachusetts. They were in the process of landing at Logan Airport. As the wheels touched down, the plane bumped a bit. She heard the flaps of the wings open as the aircraft slowed to a crawl and approached the entrance of the terminal.

Finally the plane stopped, and the flight attendant welcomed them to Boston. Chantal unbuckled her seatbelt, stood, opened the overhead compartment, grabbed her small bag, and exited the plane. She hurried down the hall, her feet not moving her toward the immigration department quickly enough. When it was her turn, she approached the station with a smile on her face.

"Good afternoon," Chantal said as she passed the officer her Canadian passport. He looked at her, nodded, scanned her passport, and then examined her immigration form.

"How long will you be in the United States?" he asked.

"For ten days to two weeks," Chantal answered and smiled. She shifted her weight from one leg to the other. She was trying to not show how anxious she was. She didn't like going through Immigration for some reason.

"Where will you be staying?" The officer asked with a stern look, not smiling as his eyes focused on her.

"With a friend in Newport." She tried to smile, but she couldn't bring herself to do it.

"Thank you." The officer stamped her passport, returned it to her, and looked away, saying, "Next!" as he waved to the following person in line. Chantal gladly accepted her passport and walked toward the exit. At the end of the corridor, she could see two large doors through which other passengers passed. She trailed behind them, figuring they knew their way, and *voila!* She found herself in the main lobby of the airport. Chantal sighed with relief and gazed at the people waiting anxiously on the other side of the railing, eagerly seeking their loved ones. Gabrielle had told her she had sent a car for her. Chantal saw a tall man in his mid-thirties wearing a black suit and hat. He held a sign with her name written on it. *That must be it,* she thought. She walked toward him.

"Miss Chantal Arsenault?" he asked, smiling.

"Yes, that's me," she said excitedly, almost jumping up and down.

"Welcome. Nice to meet you. My name is Steve, and I'm your chauffeur. I'll take your bag, and if you'll follow me, we'll get going." He reached over for her bag. Steve led the way while she followed him—like a child—to the car. He opened the back door of the vehicle, and she smiled as she got in. She could get used to this service. Steve opened the trunk and laid down the suitcase. He came back, sat in the driver's seat, started the car, and proceeded to leave the airport area.

"We should be in Newport in about two hours, so enjoy the ride," Steve said to her.

"Thank you." Chantal didn't know what else to say. The man was so formal, and she wasn't used to this. She glanced at him in the rear view mirror; his eyes were on the road. She decided to take a nap until she got to Newport, so she closed her eyes and stretched out her legs. It had been an early flight, and she was tired.

She was looking forward to relaxing with a glass of wine with Gabrielle—lying on the beach, soaking in the rays, and not having a worry in the world. She had been counting the days. She hadn't had a vacation in two years because she had been so busy with her career. If only she could meet someone like Gabrielle's husband. How blessed she would be! *Don't fool yourself, Chantal! You're dreaming*, she told herself. She drifted into a light sleep, the sound of music in the background as she thought about meeting her future Prince Charming. She longed to have a relationship with a man who would take care of her. Time passed without her noticing.

"Miss Arsenault, I'm sorry to wake you, but we're almost there," Steve said while looking in the mirror at her. Chantal opened her eyes and extended her arms, trying to wake up. She scanned her surroundings. *How beautiful*, she thought, as they passed the mansions of Newport.

"Thank you. I must have dozed off." Chantal felt her face heat up. She knew it must have been turning pink. She looked at the driver, and he had his eyes on the road. She had slept the whole way. Unbelievable! Chantal straightened her shirt and sat up. She opened her pocketbook, fishing for her lipstick. She could see a white house at the end of the road. She noticed a woman coming out the front door, waving at the black sedan as it approached. It was Gabrielle!

Chantal's heart swelled to see her friend. When the car stopped, she couldn't wait for the chauffeur. She grabbed for the door handle and opened it. She ran toward Gabrielle, extending her arms and enveloping Gabrielle in them. Chantal kissed Gabrielle's cheeks and then stepped back to embrace Junior, who was standing next to her.

"Well, well, how is my favorite little man? You have grown since I last saw you. You're almost the same height as me," she joked as she kissed the top of his head.

"I am so happy you are here. How was your flight? Good, I hope," Gabrielle said while leading Chantal inside. She motioned to Steve, who was holding Chantal's bag, to follow them inside.

"Thank you, Steve. You can put the luggage in the guest bedroom." Gabrielle smiled at him, and he disappeared down the hallway.

"Where is your loving husband?" Chantal asked, scanning the room.

"He went to Newport to see a buddy of his. He'll be back later." Gabrielle gently took Chantal's arm and sat by her in the living room.

"How about a glass of wine? I have a nice Pinot Grigio chilling if you'd like. I already started before you," Gabrielle said, laughing.

"Well in that case, sure!" Chantal responded, "that would be great." She watched as Gabrielle went to the counter. She pulled a bottle from a wine bucket and then poured the wine into a crystal glass, filling it to the halfway mark. She placed the glass on a tray that had cheese, crackers, fruit, and dips. She began walking toward Chantal but stopped. She turned her head and quickly looked outside, then back at Chantal.

"Hey! Why don't we sit on the porch? It is such a nice day, and we can watch the boats go by," Gabrielle suggested.

"That is a good idea so far, but first—" Chantal got up from the couch, walked to Gabrielle, and took a sip of wine. Lifting her glass, Chantal said, "Now I am ready! Let the good times begin!" The two friends both started to laugh as they walked toward the veranda.

***

Tom had arrived in Newport an hour ago. He had a full view of the Rians' cottage. He had climbed into position—behind some trees and bushes on the far side of the home. The sun was going down, and the crickets had begun chirping. It was now dark enough that the people in the house wouldn't be able to him. Wearing a camouflage shirt and pants, Tom was lying flat on his stomach on the ground. He had black and green paint on his face and was watching the house through Steiner Predator binoculars.

Tom had great vantage point from which he could watch the comings and goings of the house's occupants. He had been here before ten years ago when he had tried and failed to assassinate one of the Rians. This time he would succeed or die trying. He wanted his revenge. Ten long years he had spent in prison. Ten long years he had had time to think of how and who he would kill. This would be his last mission, his destiny.

The woman who had arrived a half-hour ago had caught his attention. Tom had watched her get out of the car, walk up to Gabrielle, and embrace her. He had noticed her small breasts and the way her hips moved from side to side as she walked. He wondered what color her eyes were and how her long curly blonde hair would feel between his fingers. He observed as she disappear behind the front door with Gabrielle. He decided to wait and see if he could get another glimpse of her.

A half-hour later, the front door swung open, and the new woman appeared again. The overhead light illuminated her body. She sat on the porch with Gabrielle, drinking a glass of wine. Tom examined the new woman. For some reason, she intrigued him. He scrutinized her every move—how she laughed, how refined her posture was, how her curls bounced when she nodded her head. He was mesmerized by her. He couldn't keep his eyes off her.

He was captivated by how her dainty, small hands held her wine glass and how she so delicately crossed her legs. *This cannot be happening*, Tom thought, but it was, and he could feel a bulge growing between his legs. This had never happened to him before! He had always had control of his senses when he was on an assignment. He licked his lips, his mouth feeling like sandpaper. He wondered how she would taste and if her skin was soft. She was the most beautiful woman he had laid eyes on in years, and he had to find out who she was. He wanted to meet her.

Stop it. You need to focus, Tom murmured to himself.

He shook his head, trying to refocus his attention. He put his binoculars on the ground, laid on his back, closed his eyes, and took a long breath. He let it out slowly and repeated the action several times, but to no avail. He grabbed his bottle of water and took a long drink. He was totally enthralled by her. She would destroy his mission if he didn't keep his sexual desire for this woman in check.

Tom opened his backpack and stowed his binoculars. He took out his camera with its long-range zoom lens and aimed it at the woman. His hands trembled a bit, and he had to force himself to focus. He couldn't help himself; he needed a photograph. He pushed the button on top of the camera, clicking it once, twice, and a third time.

Tom looked at her one last time through the lens, and then carefully put the camera away in his knapsack. He stood behind a large oak tree and took one last look at her before he turned and walked through the bushes. He moved back to his truck as quickly as he could, keeping his eyes open for anything unusual. When he made it to the other side of the woods, he scanned the area before he quickly walked to his truck. He opened the door, sat on the front seat, opened his bag, and removed several wet wipes so that he could clean his face. He brought the wipes to his face and rubbed off the paint as fast as he could. Then he put the key into the ignition, turned it, and started the vehicle. He moved the gear into drive and he drove away, all the while thinking about the mystery woman he had seen on the porch.

Forget her. She was just a passing ship in the night, he told himself.

He couldn't shake the desire to see her again, even though it might cost him everything he had planned for years. She was a distraction, one he didn't need at the moment. He still saw her image in his mind. Why the hell had he taken pictures of her? There was something special about her, and if he wasn't careful, he would fail because of her. The hair on the back of his neck stood up.

He would return tomorrow, refocus all his energy on his assignment, and stop thinking about her. Tom drove north, concentrating on the road, his hands on the wheel and his eyes straight ahead, trying to clear his mind. He headed back to his hideout in silence, planning his next move as he drove. He still needed more time before he executed his plan. He had to get to his night job because he couldn't afford to skip work and have his parole officer find out about it. He would never return to prison. He had to keep his cover. He would be able to think clearly while he did his work tonight.

CHAPTER 3

R on wouldn't go to bed or eat until he talked to his son and told him what he had learned. Hours had passed, and he was still sitting behind his desk in his study. A tray stood nearby, its crystal glass of water and fine china plate holding a filet mignon with hollandaise sauce, red potatoes, and asparagus sat untouched. Ron drummed his fingers on the top of his mahogany desk. He kept staring at his damn phone. *Why doesn't Bernard answer his phone?* he thought. *Maybe I should send someone over to Newport to check on him and Gabrielle. My God!* He was going out of his mind. He placed his hand on the phone again, then pulled it away. He had just dialed Bernard's phone five minutes ago. *They're fine. If there was something wrong, I would have heard,* he thought, trying to convince himself. His fingers went back to the phone. He punched in his son's number one more time and placed the phone to his ear. He heard one ring, then two. *Answer the phone,* he thought. *Please answer.* Suddenly he heard an angel.

"Hi, Grandpa! How are you?" Junior said.

"Oh! Thank God! How are you, love?" Ron said, relieved. A smile came to his lips.

"I'm fine. We were at the beach all day. We had lots of fun," he answered in a soft voice.

"That's great. Where is your father? I need to speak to him. It's important." Ron was trying to sound normal, but he was going to lose it at any

15

second. His heart was still pounding in his chest, and his blood pressure was rising. He heard his grandson's voice. "Papa, Grandpa wants to talk to you. It's important."

"Hello, Father. Is everything all right?" Bernard answered, concerned.

"Where have you been all day? I have been trying to call you!" Ron was trying hard not to scream. He sighed loudly.

"We were at the beach. I had left my phone in the truck. I just retrieved it a few minutes ago. I saw you called, but I hadn't had time to return your call. Why?" Bernard questioned.

"Listen, I don't want you to mention this to Gabrielle and get her agitated, but I received a letter today from a friend at the parole office. It said Tom got out last month, and he's on parole. I was worried about you guys. Have you seen anything abnormal?" Ron said.

"Calm down, Father. Everyone is fine. Tom wouldn't chance coming here again. I'll keep my eyes open, but I wouldn't lose sleep over it. He learned his lesson, and I was told he had changed over the past few years. He has had counseling and has been rehabilitated," Bernard said confidently.

"Well, I hope you're right, but I would feel better if you allowed me to send security to stay with you for the time you are out there." Ron passed a shaking hand through his gray hair.

"Absolutely not. We are fine. I'll keep my eyes open, and I'll let you know if I see something strange," Bernard answered sternly.

"I really don't like it, but as you wish. Be vigilant while you're there. I'll talk to you soon. Bye." Ron pursed his lips and held his tongue. He wasn't content. He ended the call and threw the phone onto the desk. He would never believe that Tom had changed in prison. Ron knew him better that anyone. Tom had worked under him for more than ten years. Tom had never questioned his orders, even if he hadn't agreed with them. He was a mercenary, and he had no remorse. He had been trained to be a killing machine in the Army, and that was why Ron had employed him.

Ron didn't want to cause his family any more hardship than he had already, but he was going to keep his ears open. If he heard anything—even a whisper!—that Tom was near his family, Ron would act. First, he needed information, and he knew the guy for the job. Ron picked up his phone again and dialed another friend in the police force.

"Hello, Raymond. This is Ron Rian. How are you?" he asked.

"Good evening, Mr. Rian. I'm fine. What can I do for you?" Raymond Roberts answered. He was a retired police sergeant who had served the city of Boston. He was a longtime friend and had always been loyal to Ron. Twenty years ago, Ron had met Raymond one night at an event that the Rians had been hosting. Raymond had been doing security to earn some additional cash to buy a home for his family. They had talked that night, and the two men made a bargain. Ron would give Raymond money if Raymond provided him with a few favors every now and then. Raymond had been faithful to him since that night.

"I'd like you to get some information on a man named Tom Smith. He was released from prison about a month ago. He was the man who put me in this chair. I need to know his whereabouts, as well as his coming and goings. Anything you can find would be greatly appreciated," Ron said. He was optimistic that Ray would find Tom for him. Raymond had yet to fail him.

"I'll get on it right away, sir. I'll call you as soon as I find out something. Anything else, sir?" Raymond asked.

"Thank you, but that will be all," Ron answered and hung up the phone. He was calmer now, but tired. At least he would have details about this evil man soon. He pushed a button on his desk for his nurse to come help him get ready for bed. He closed his eyes, laid his hands on top of each other on his lap, and waited. There was nothing else he could do at this point, and Ron needed his rest if he was going to fight Tom.

***

Chantal woke to the sound of birds, as a breeze came through the open window. A headache vibrated in her temples from all the wine they had consumed the previous night. She lifted her hands and rubbed her temples, trying to appease the pain. *Just what I need on the first day of vacation!* She turned her head slowly and looked at the clock on her night stand. It was nine-thirty.

She didn't want to get up. Chantal turned to her left side and faced the window. From her bedroom, she could see the whitecaps on the waves as they moved through the ocean. The sight didn't help her stomach. She started feeling queasy, so she lay on her back again and didn't move.

Chantal closed her eyes, hoping that she could fall asleep again, but the bombardment in her head wasn't stopping.

She heard a light knock on the door. "Chantal, it's me. Are you awake yet? Can I come in?" Gabrielle asked quietly. Chantal turned her head toward the door.

"Sure, come on in," she replied. The door handle moved, and then Gabrielle walked in and sat on the edge of her bed. Gabrielle smiled at Chantal.

"Having a bad day?" Gabrielle chuckled and then lightly tapped Chantal's foot with her right hand.

"I think we had too much wine last night," Chantal replied, forcing a small smile. She pushed herself up against the headboard so she could sit. Her head hurt even more.

"Well, I just wanted to let you know we are going to do some shopping on Thames Street. I wanted to know if you wanted to come, but if you don't feel like it, I understand." Gabrielle laughed even more.

"Would you mind terribly if I didn't go? I think I'll just stick around here. Maybe I'll go for a walk on the beach or something," Chantal answered, trying to sound upbeat. Her head still felt like a train wreck.

"That's fine. We should be back later this afternoon. Junior wants to go to the Pier for a boat ride. There's Tylenol in the bathroom cabinet and food in the fridge. I made coffee. Eat something. Make yourself at home." Gabrielle smiled at her again.

"Thanks, I appreciate it. I'll do that. Don't worry. By the time you come back, I'll be in tip-top shape," Chantal answered, although she wasn't so sure. "Go and have fun. I'll be just fine."

"Okay, then. See you later." Gabrielle got up, leaned over, and kissed her friend on the cheek. Chantal watched Gabrielle leave the room. Chantal heard the doors of their vehicle shut and the engine start. For a few minutes, she sat there, unmoving, her head against the wall. She decided she couldn't stay in bed all day. With the stroke of her hand, she pushed off the blanket and sat on the edge of the bed, looking down at her toes for a minute.

Finally, Chantal pushed herself up and stood. Pain throbbed through her head as she walked toward the bathroom. She opened the cabinet door, scanned the shelves, reached in, and grabbed the bottle of Tylenol.

She shook two pills into her hand. She replaced the bottle on the shelf, turned around, and took small steps toward the kitchen.

She poured herself a cup of coffee and took the pills. As she felt the pills going down, she hoped for the best. Chantal sat on the stool in the kitchen and waited for the medication to take effect while she drank her coffee. An hour later, after she had eaten some toast, her stomach had settled, and her headache diminished. She walked to the large window facing the ocean, looked out, and decided to go for a stroll on the beach after all. The sun was shining, the sky was blue, and a walk would get her out of the house for a while. Chantal found her bikini in her suitcase, put it on, and tied her hair in a ponytail. *Not bad. It could be worse*, she thought when she saw herself in the mirror. She grabbed a towel, her sunglasses, sunscreen, and a bottle of water and packed it all in her beach bag.

She locked the front door with the key Gabrielle had given her the night before and started walking toward the golden sand. There was a pathway that led down to the beach, so Chantal decided to follow it. She gazed at a sailboat out on the horizon—so small she could barely see it. There were all kinds of pebbles scattered at the line where the water met the sand. She sauntered along the border, the cool water lightly splashing against her feet.

Her feet sank into the warm sand with every step she took. The rays of the sun gave her life as she strolled across the endless shoreline. The further she walked, the fewer the people there were on the beach. Finally, she found the perfect spot. Chantal stopped, reached into her bag and took out her towel. She lifted her arms and spread it on the ground. After dropping her bag beside the towel, she applied sunscreen to her exposed skin and laid down to soak up the sunshine. Listening to the sound of the waves, she was completely oblivious to the fact that someone was watching her—and had been watching her every move since she had left the house. She also didn't know that he was headed her way.

***

Tom had worked at his janitorial job as usual the previous night, but he hadn't been able to concentrate on any of his work. All he could think of was the vision of the woman who was at the Rian's house. Because of her small suitcase and the fact that she had been driven by a chauffeur, he had concluded that she must be a friend of Gabrielle's from Canada.

Tom had tossed and turned in his bed in the early hours of the morning, trying to sleep, but after only a few hours, he had decided to get up. His body was accustomed to being deprived of sleep ever since he had served in the Army. He had decided to drive back to Newport to continue surveying the area. He needed to know every inch of this property before he could put his plan into action. Maybe if he got lucky, he would get another look at this woman.

He had arrived at his hiding spot by the trees at approximately the same time he saw the three Rians drive off in their Range Rover. He hadn't seen the woman with them, so she must still have been in the house. Tom was dressed in black shorts and a black t-shirt that hugged his muscular body perfectly. His black hair was slicked back with gel, showing off his manly jaw. His blue eyes made him look harmless, but looks were deceiving.

He waited until he couldn't see the Rians anymore, then he picked up his backpack and tossed it over his shoulder. He came out of his hiding place, his eyes darting, looking for anything suspicion along the way. He quickly arrived at the back wall of the cottage. He crouched near one of the windows, breathing normally despite his run down the hillside. He dropped his bag next to him, lifted his head cautiously to the edge of the windowsill, and peeked inside, his eyes registering everything in a flash.

He lowered himself again. His back was glued against the wall. He had seen that woman inside. She had been tying her hair in a ponytail in front of a mirror. She was wearing a bathing suit that made her look like a model. One peek at her told him she was preparing to go to the beach. His heart began beating faster, and he could feel his pulse in his ears. He hadn't expected to have this reaction. He was a soldier on a mission. He had to clear his mind, otherwise he might fail to accomplish what he had dreamed about for so many years. He sat there immobile for a few minutes, listening to every sound around him. *Calm down. This isn't you*, he told himself.

Suddenly, he heard the sound of a door closing to his right. Through the leaves of the bush in which he was hiding, he watched her walk down the path to the beach. He didn't move until she was out of sight. He carefully stood up, swung his bag over his shoulder, and proceeded to follow her at a safe distance. She was walking by the edge of the water. His eyes were riveted on her. He watched her hips move from side to side as she strolled farther away from the entrance to the beach. He walked couple of hundred feet behind her, afraid that he would scare her or that she would notice him.

She dropped her bag just as he had sat down on the sand. He watched her apply sunscreen lotion on her legs and arms. When she placed her hand on her belly, he could feel himself getting an erection. His shorts had become tight, and he tried to look away. He wanted to feel her touch on his body. Never before had he wanted to meet anyone as much as he wanted to meet her. He couldn't move from where he was sitting. He turned his head toward her. He rubbed his palms together, trying to get the nerve to introduce himself to her. He wondered what her voice sounded like and if she had a man in her life. Minutes passed, still he was frozen to the spot. His eyes were the only part of him that just moved.

She sat up and searched for something in her bag. She took out a bottle of water, brought it to her lips, and swallowed. She stood up and walked up to the water. Bending down, she splashed the water against her skin. She took handfuls of water and spread them all over her body.

She finally dove in, the ocean engulfing her. She was just floating around. Tom stood up, grabbed the bottom of his shirt, pulled it off, and threw it beside him. He then unlaced his hiking boots as fast as he could, fumbling to get them off. He ran into the water and submerged himself. He came up for a gulp of air and started swimming in her direction.

With long strokes, he pushed himself through the water. Within seconds, he had closed the ten-foot gap between them. He came up in front of her. He pushed his hair back from his face and pretended to be surprised to see her. He stood still, water dripping from his body. It was now or never. Thank God she couldn't see his shaking legs!

"Oh! Hi, I didn't see you standing there," Tom said as casually as he could. He noticed she had blue eyes and full lips. He couldn't stop staring at her.

"Hi! Enjoying your swim? You're a good swimmer," she replied.

"Thank you. I hope I didn't startle you," he said. He detected a slight French accent in her voice. Now he knew for sure she was a friend of Gabrielle's from Canada.

"No, no," she said, then looked away from him for a moment, returning to face him a moment later.

"It's a great day for the beach. I noticed a slight accent when you spoke. Are you from the area?" He had to find out her name at least.

"No, I'm here visiting a friend of mine. I'm from Canada. What about yourself?" she asked.

"Oh! I'm from the Boston area. I drove up for the day. Just trying to stay cool." He smiled at her, and she gave him the most gorgeous smile, her eyes sparkling. Tom almost lost it. He wanted to grab her at that moment and kiss her, but he kept his hands underneath the water.

"My name is ... John Baker. And you are?" He raised his arm from the water and extended his hand to her, not taking his eyes off her face. She looked at his hand for a second, and then extended her hand.

"I am Chantal, Chantal Arsenault. Nice to meet you, John," she said. The touch of her skin against his sent a shock right between his legs. He gently took her hand and squeezed it as he caressed her soft hand with his thumb. From the second that their skin met, he knew he was in trouble. Nothing was ever going to be the same again. He looked into her eyes and finally realized he had to let go of her hand. She was blushing, her eyes downcast as she looked away again

"Sorry, it's just rare that I meet such a beautiful who is as stunning as you."

He was making a fool of himself. He was expecting her to run away any moment. She just looked at him again and said, "Thank you."

"So, how long are you here for? Have you visited the area before?" he asked her, all the while aware that they had started walking back to shore. Should he follow her or go his separate way? He couldn't resist—he wanted to at least accompany her to the shoreline.

"I'm just here for ten days or so. And no, this is my first time in Newport." They were almost to the edge of the water. He didn't want to return to his place. He wanted to stay with her for while.

"Here, give me your hand. These small pebbles are tricky and slippery. You could fall." He extended his hand to her again, and she took it immediately. Her small, delicate hand fit perfectly in his. He held it like it was as fragile as a china doll's hand.

"Thanks again. Would you like to sit with me for a while?" she asked him. He couldn't believe his ears. This was not a good idea. He really was in big trouble. There was no way he could execute his plan as long as she was here staying with the Rians. He did not want her to get hurt.

"Sure, I'd love too." He followed her to her towel, all the while scanning the perimeter of the beach for someone suspicious, like one of the Rians. She sat down, leaving enough space on her towel so that he could sit beside her. He watched as she patted the top of it and said, "We'll have to share. I only have one towel." She looked up at him with her blue eyes as if to say, *Don't leave just yet.* Or was he imagining things?

"I can't stay too long—but for a few minutes, okay." He sat down next to her and dug his feet into the sand. Looking out at the ocean, he hoped she didn't notice how nervous he was. He kept playing with the sand between his feet.

"What do you do for work in Canada?" He wanted to know as much as he could about her. He loved to hear her voice.

"I teach children at a grade school in my town. I enjoy being with children they keep me going and guessing. They always have tons of questions and I love to try to answer them. What about yourself? What kind of work do you do for a living?" she asked. Tom was caught off guard for a moment. He had to think fast.

"Well, I ... I'm an engineer." That was not too far from the truth—he could engineer things that exploded. He grinned at himself. "I was just wondering, are those curls natural?" He fingered one that had fallen out of place and tucked it behind her ear.

"As a matter of fact, they are natural. Do you like them?" Chantal sighed. "I can never keep them in place" she whispered and then blushed.

"Yes, I do." They talked about her. He didn't realize the time was slipping away so quickly. Minutes had turned into hours, and they were laughing at nothing. He was caught up in whatever she had to say. He listened, and she told him stories about herself.

He turned his head, and her face was so close to his. He wanted to kiss her. He could feel the heat from her body against his skin. She tilted her head to the right slightly, and her lips were beckoning him. Tom lost all control. He placed his hands around her cheeks. She didn't resist, so he pulled her face closer to his and let his mouth touch her lips. She placed her hands on his chest and she pressed her lips against his harder. She tasted incredible. Their tongues danced together, and for a moment Tom forgot everything he had ever learned and concentrated on this kiss. He didn't want it to end, but he knew it wasn't right to lead her on. He pulled away slowly. He stopped and looked into her eyes. He wanted to remember them.

"I'm sorry, I shouldn't have done that, but you looked so—" He couldn't speak, afraid she might reject him. He had to leave now, or he might not be able to later.

"I didn't mind at all," Chantal answered, and they started to laugh together. They sat on the beach for another hour, just talking. Tom hadn't been so at ease with someone in a long time. But he knew he wouldn't see her again, so he savored all that he could in that short period of time. He still had a mission to complete. He still needed his revenge. Maybe later after he escaped, he would find her again.

"Would you like to come meet my friends and maybe stay for dinner? They have a house right up there." She was pointing in the direction of the Rians'. Tom was brought back to reality.

"I'm sorry, but I have to return to Boston. I am already late. Maybe some other time." He had to lie and leave her.

"I understand. I did have a very nice afternoon, thanks to you. Would you mind giving me your phone number so maybe I could call you sometime—just to talk, I mean," she said, and then she bowed her head. He closed his eyes. He didn't want to hurt her.

"Sure, that would be fine." He quickly wrote his number on a piece of paper she had found in her bag. He handed it back to her. He leaned over, picked up his bag, and kissed her softly on the lips one last time. He stood up and started walking away without another word. He couldn't turn around to wave goodbye to her or even to steal one last glance at her because he couldn't trust himself. He hurried because he didn't want her to follow him up the trail. Now he would have to wait ten days before he could continue with his plan.

She had to leave and go back home. He wouldn't chance her getting hurt. Tom wanted to stay with her, but he knew he could not. Maybe after all was done with his plan, he would travel to Canada and find her, but now it was impossible for him to be near Chantal or have any contact with her. He had just made the biggest mistake of his life. He had gotten too close to one person who could jeopardize his mission—or worse, get him caught.

CHAPTER 4

As Chantal watched John walk away, she was on the verge of running after him. She watched him until she couldn't see him anymore. She finally had met someone she wanted to spend time with, and this might be the end. Would she ever see him again? *Yes, I will,* she told herself. He had left his phone number with her. That had to mean something—right? She couldn't believe he had left such an impression on her. She stood up, folded her towel, and picked up her bag.

Stop thinking that way, you idiot. You'll see him again.

The sun was setting, and Chantal was sure Gabrielle must be wondering where she was. She had been gone the whole afternoon. She walked slowly back up the beach, dragging her feet in the water. She was in a good mood. She kept jumping up and down, splashing her feet in the ocean, and letting the sun's last rays warm her back. A little while later, she could see the house and Bernard's Range Rover parked in the front yard. They were back from their Newport boat trip.

Chantal could still feel John's lips on hers. She brought her finger to her lips and touched them. It sent a chill down her back just remembering it. This mystery man named John Baker—would she ever see him again? Yes, she would, or hoped she would. She would make sure she would call him tomorrow. Hopefully he felt the same as she did. Maybe they could meet for lunch. But would he drive all the way back here from Boston just for lunch? She had to believe that there was still hope for her to find love after all.

She really didn't know much about him. For some reason, she had done most of all the talking. She should have asked more questions. She had better not tell Gabrielle about him just yet, because Gabrielle would think she was out of her mind—first for spending all afternoon with him on an almost-deserted beach, and then for letting him kiss her like he had.

She chuckled just like a teenager thinking about him. God! She was a grown woman. What was she doing? It would be her little secret until she saw him again. She thought he was absolutely sexy with his mysterious answers. What a perfect body he had, with his strong arms and his abs just like a washboard. But what drew her in was his blue eyes. When he had glanced at her, she could have melted away in a second. She would never forget those eyes. She had to see them again.

She usually wasn't attracted to that type of man, but this one she wanted. She bet he would be a great lover, being very attentive to what his woman needed. The way he had looked at her like there was no one else around. She was getting aroused just thinking about him. Well, that was new. She giggled again like a schoolgirl as she approached the front steps of the porch. This would be her private affair if she ever saw him again.

"Hey! Where have you been? I was about to sent a search party for you," Gabrielle said as she pushed the front screen door open with her hand.

"Oh! I went for a walk on the beach, and then soaked up some of those rays," Chantal replied as casually as she could. "I didn't notice the time, I was just relaxing."

Chantal looked away from her friend. She didn't like lying to her—but it really wasn't lying, just not adding anything or telling her everything. Chantal looked up at her and smiled.

"So how was your day?" Chantal asked, trying to change the subject.

"Great. We had a nice boat ride around the bay. Are you hungry yet?" Gabrielle asked her. Chantal sat on the step of the porch, took her towel out of her bag, and started to rub off the leftover sand from her feet.

"Sure, but first let me take a shower. What did you have in mind for supper?" Chantal asked, trying to divert the conversation away from her.

"Well, we can either barbeque, or we could order pizza," Gabrielle said. Junior came running out on the porch and tugged on his mother's arm.

"Pizza! Pizza! Pizza!" Junior yelled, jumping up and down.

"It sounds like pizza, if that's okay with you," Gabrielle said. Chantal nodded. Gabrielle turned her head and nodded toward Junior. He had a wide smile on his face.

"Fine by me, but first I need a shower." Chantal got up, shook her towel out, folded it, and headed inside with Gabrielle and Junior not far behind her. She still was in her small little world, thinking about the afternoon rendezvous.

***

The sun went down, and the stars came out over the waters in Newport. Chantal was in her bedroom getting ready for bed. She pushed her bed covers aside, and then she slid under them. She pulled the blanket up to her waist. Her night stand light brightened her the room, and she could see shadows on the wall, but her attention was elsewhere.

She bent down, grabbed her beach bag, and fumbled to find the small piece of paper she had hidden in the side pocket. She found it and let her finger stroked the numbers that he had written just a few hours previously. *I'll see you again*, she told herself. She reached over to the night stand drawer, opened it, placed the note inside, and closed the drawer. She lay down on her back, her pillow enveloping the sides of her head, and closed her eyes, hoping to dream of the man she had met today.

Chantal woke up the next morning before anyone else in the house had arisen. Eyes closed, she listening attentively for any sound from the other rooms. She sat up in her bed, stretched her arms toward the ceiling, and then rubbed her eyes with her fists. She yawned once, and then remembered the man she had met. She turned her head and looked at the clock on her night table. It read eight o'clock. She couldn't wait until mid-morning to call him. Well, maybe it was too soon, but she didn't care. She wanted to see him again. *If I don't try, how will I know what will happen? The worst he can say is no.* She opened the drawer and peeked at the note. It was still there. She took it in her hand and looked at it once more. She put it back to its original place.

She got out of bed as quietly as she could and walked on tiptoe to the bathroom to shower. Gabrielle would probably be up by the time she finished and got dressed. Maybe she should call him early? Maybe she could go into town to meet him? What if he didn't want to see her again. But why would he give her his number? Her mind was in a whirlwind. She had to relax and think this through.

She opened the door of her bedroom and heard, "Good morning, sleepyhead." It was Gabrielle talking to her from the kitchen. She was making pancakes.

"Good morning. I thought everyone was still sleeping," Chantal said as she approached the kitchen counter. She noticed Junior was busy eating pancakes. She saw coffee, so she went to the cabinet, grabbed a cup, and poured some for herself.

"Where's Bernard?" Chantal scanned the open area of the living room, but didn't see him.

"He left early to go golfing with some friends. Pancakes?" Gabrielle flipped two pancakes on a plate and passed them to her. Chantal took them from Gabrielle and sat beside Junior.

"So, what are your plans for today?" Chantal asked before shoving another bite of pancake in her mouth. All of a sudden, she was famished.

"Well, my dear son here wants to go to the movies, and I did promise him. If you don't want to join us, I can drop you off in town and you can browse the stores on Thames Street. I can call you when we're finished and come pick you up. What do you think?" Gabrielle said.

"That sounds perfect. What time were you planning to go?" Chantal asked. She was pleased. Now she would not have to make an excuse to go to town. She could call him when she got there.

"How about we go to the twelve o'clock movie, Junior?" Gabrielle looked at her son, who nodded, his mouth full of pancakes, and gave her a thumb's up.

"Perfect! Then it's a plan. I can pick up lobster from the pier for supper, if you want." Chantal said. They had finished eating, and she was helping Gabrielle clean up.

"I think I'll go for a short walk on the beach before we leave, if that's okay with you," Chantal said. She was trying to find some time alone so she could call John in private. "Sure, go right ahead. It will give me time to straighten up the place a bit before we leave," Gabrielle replied, wiping the counter where they had just eaten.

"Thanks." Chantal walked to her room to retrieve the note and her cell phone. She placed the note in her jeans pocket, walked out the door, and made a beeline toward the beach.

***

Tom couldn't get her out of his mind. He still could feel her soft lips touching his. He needed to see her one more time. He had driven straight from work to Newport in the early hours of the morning. He was hiding in the treeline by the house again, hoping to see her once more. He knew that getting involved with her would be disastrous for his plan, but then why had he given her his number? He couldn't think straight when she was near him. Why had he come back? That was the million-dollar question. It was stronger that he. His emotions were pulling him back here. This had never happened in his life. He had always been in complete control of a situation and his emotions.

A shiver passed over him. There she was, going toward the beach. His eyes followed her every step, her every movement. He observed her until she was behind the hillside and out of sight. Should he go find her? No, definitely not. It wasn't right to lead her on, and then leave her later.

He felt a vibration in his pocket. His phone was buzzing. He slipped his hand into his pocket and looked at the caller ID. It said unknown. It had to be her calling him. With the exception of a few people, no one had this number. He was transfixed by the number on the screen. He could not answer it. *Let it ring*, he told himself. *Don't answer*. It was the right thing to do. It stopped buzzing. She had hung up. Maybe he should have answered, but it was too late—and too dangerous for her to be with him. What did he have to offer her? He was an ex-convict who was on a mission to harm her friends.

It was done now. It was over. He hung his head low, his eyes closed, and didn't move for a minute. He made the decision to leave the area. He got up slowly walked back to his truck, started the engine, and drove away.

***

Ron had waited patiently for two days, but now he was at the end of his rope. He hadn't heard from Raymond yet. What could be taking him so long?

He was sitting in his study, looking at the landscaped grounds. He couldn't wait any longer. His right hand moved to the remote control on the armrest of his electric chair. He moved himself behind the desk. He snatched his cell phone off the top of his desk and dialed Raymond's number. Holding the phone to his ear, he waited, all the while biting the inside of his lip. It rang once. No answer. Then it rang again. "Come on. Answer the damn phone," Ron said between his teeth.

He heard a click, "Hello, this is Raymond."

"Finally. This Ron Rian. Do you have any information for me?" he said, trying to stay calm and not raise his voice. His knuckles were white from holding the phone so tightly.

"Mr. Rian, I checked with his parole officer—a friend of mine, as a matter of fact—and he said Tom is working as a janitor cleaning an office building in Worcester at night. He is renting a room at a boarding house on Main Street. He has been reporting to him regularly, and so far he hasn't done anything illegal. He's walking a straight line," Raymond answered him.

"What does he do during the day?" Ron asked.

"Umm, I don't know exactly, but I can find out if you want me to. It might take a few days."

"Please. Find out, and call me as soon as you know," Ron said and threw the phone on the top of his desk, not even bothering to say goodbye. He clenched his right fist into a ball and slammed it on the desk.

"Goddamn it! I know you are up to something, but what? I know you too well." Ron took his hand and swept away every item from the desktop, from right to left. He hurled them to the floor. His breathing quickened, and his face turned from white to pink. He was so furious. He didn't have any in-depth information on Tom.

He had to calm down. He stared at the mess on the marble floor below him, not caring. He told himself to take deep breaths—in through the nose and out through the mouth. Ron did this several times to calm himself. He hated this man with his whole being. He had ruined his life. He was chair-bound for the rest of his life, with no chance of ever walking again on his own because of a bullet that was stuck in his back. Tom might have served his time in prison, but Ron was damned if he'd allow him to have a normal life—free to roam the streets while he was confined to this awful wheelchair.

CHAPTER 5

Chantal sat on the sand near the water, holding her cell phone in her hand. She couldn't take her eyes off her phone. She didn't budge from her spot for ten minutes, her mind going through various scenarios that might explain why John hadn't answered her call. Was he busy, or did he not want to talk to her? Maybe he was sleeping, maybe he was working—or worst, maybe he didn't want to see her again! She gazed out at the ocean, looking for a response, and came to the conclusion that she was over-analyzing the situation.

Chantal stood up and brushed the sand off her butt. She would wait and try to call John once more, later in the day. If he didn't answer, then she would have the answer to all her questions: he wasn't interested in her and had only given her the number out of politeness. She started walking back to the cottage, trying to not over-think the situation. She wanted to go, enjoy her day of sightseeing, and do some shopping in Newport.

"Everyone ready? Let's go!" Gabrielle said and started driving toward the center of Newport.

Chantal smiled at her, then turned her head toward the window of the truck, looking at nothing in particular. Her heart was heavy. She had hoped that maybe John would be 'the one.' She really liked him and had hoped for more.

"Where do you want me to drop you off?" Gabrielle asked her.

"Oh! Wherever is easiest for you, I suppose," she answered, uninterested.

"How about I drop you off at The Marriot Hotel? That way you can walk up to the wharf area or continue up Thames Street to visit the boutiques," Gabrielle replied.

"Sure, that sounds good. How long do you think you will be?" Chantal asked as they drove up America Cup Avenue. Gabrielle turned the vehicle right and stopped in front of the hotel to drop off Chantal.

"A few hours at least. I'll tell you what, don't worry about time. Just call me when you are ready to come home, and I'll come pick you up."

"Okay. I'll do that. Have fun, and I'll see you later. Bye!" Chantal reached out for the door handle and jumped out of the truck. She waved goodbye to them as they started to roll out of the hotel's driveway.

Now what? she thought. She swung her pocketbook over her shoulder and started walking toward the waterfront area. She admired the yachts that were docked nearby. She noticed a park bench not far away and decided to sit for a few minutes. She was still a bit disappointed with the call she had made this morning. She placed her purse in her lap and opened it. She fished for her cell phone and the note with John's number.

Looking straight ahead at the floating boats, she said, "I'm going to try one more time." She brought the phone to her chest, said a silent prayer, and then pushed the ten digits of his number. It rang and rang and rang. No answer, not even a voicemail. She shut it off, closed her eyes, and let the small piece of paper fly from her fingers.

It wasn't meant to be, that's all. Move on. Chantal stood and walked slowly toward the wharf area, stopping to window-shop along the way and observing the other tourists as she continued down the avenue. She felt her stomach growl and decided to go eat. She walked into the first restaurant that she saw—The Black Pearl. It was a casual dining restaurant on Bannister Wharf, known for its splendid food, high-gloss black walls, and old nautical maps that hung on its walls.

She pushed the door open and entered the establishment. She was looking for the hostess when a young girl approached and greeted her. Chantal followed her to a small table near a window and sat down. The girl gave her a menu and told her that the waitress would be with her in a few minutes. Chantal thanked her and started to read her choices. She took a few minutes to scroll through the menu, and then she was ready to order her meal. She closed her menu and laid it in front of her. She turned her head toward the window, watching the tourists come and go in and out of the small stores. She saw people having a cold beverage on the patio and a child eating an ice-cream cone. The scene brought a smile to her face despite her gloomy day.

Chantal's stomach reminded her that she needed food, so she focused on trying to find her waitress. As she glanced up, she got the shock of her life. Coming through a door at the back of the restaurant was John! He was dressed all in black. His tight jeans fit him beautifully, the muscles of his arms strained against the sleeves of his t-shirt. Man, he looked good enough to eat! He was coming her way, walking toward her with long strides.

She wanted to hide under the table, but there was no time, so Chantal quickly grabbed her menu and hid her face behind it. Her heartbeat pounded in her chest like a child's who had been caught with his hand in the cookie jar. She was embarrassed. She had called him twice. She could feel the heat rising to her face. She sank as low into her chair as she could. She didn't dare look up but instead cast her eyes downward and cringed. She wanted to be invisible. He was here.

"Hi there, gorgeous," John said to her. She slowly brought the menu down so only her eyes were showing. He was grinning at her from ear to ear. Chantal was speechless. All she could do was stare at him. She tried to gave him a smile, but she was too surprised. She just couldn't do it! She just sat there with her mouth half-open.

"Hi," was all Chantal managed to utter. He was standing so close that she could smell his cologne and feel the heat from his body. She placed the menu on the table and folded her hands on her lap. She was mortified. She ran her fingers back through her hair. He was still staring down at her. He pointed to the chair next to her.

"Anyone sitting here?"

All Chantal could do was shake her head from right to left. He pulled the chair out then sat down next to her. His knee gently bumped against hers. She tried to ignore it, but it was fruitless. She noticed everything about this man. His blue eyes pierced right through her.

"Did you order yet? Apparently the clam chowder here is delicious," he said casually. Her tongue was like a dried twig. She swallowed hard. She shook her head. He kept grinning at her. *Get it together, Chantal. Say something!* she thought, but her brain was not cooperating at the moment. Her hormones had overtaken her common sense.

"Do you mind if I look at your menu? I haven't gotten one yet."

He reached over and took the menu from her, and then opened it and started to examine it. Chantal saw the waitress coming toward them with two glasses of water. She placed them in front of them. Thank God! Chantal gripped the glass and immediately brought it to her mouth. She drank, hoping the water would heal her parched throat.

"What are you doing here?" she asked, but was instantly sorry at how harshly she had blurted the words out. He lifted his eyes from the menu winked at her, and then returned to the list of dishes.

"I mean, here in Newport again," she was trying to fix her sentence but nothing was coming out.

"I came to see you," he answered, and then smirked at her. She had definitely not expected that answer. She started playing with the utensils on the table, trying to clear her head and compose herself.

"I tried calling you today, but you never answered." *I shouldn't have said that either,* she thought, but she needed to know why he had not answered her phone calls.

"Well, the first time you called I was taking a shower, and the second time I was parking my truck and didn't get to the phone on time. Then I got hungry. What about you? Why are you here?" he asked, at the same time reaching out and tucking a curl that had escaped from her ponytail behind her ear. She reached up and caught his hand in hers. He pulled her hand to his lips and gently kissed her knuckles. Goosebumps went down her back. She hadn't anticipated that from him either. This man was full of surprises, and he was comfortable with himself.

"Oh! Well, I was just window-shopping and got hungry too, so—let's share that menu so we can order faster," she replied. She felt like she had overreacted about the phone calls. She was having lunch with him, wasn't she? That had been the point of calling him, right?

She felt his knee rub against hers. She tried to ignore it, but it was hard. He then laid his strong hand on her knee and rubbed it gently. In her eyes, he could do no harm, but she was a little disillusioned. She noticed how his eyes were on her all through lunch. He made her laugh, with his funny jokes and the faces he made. Chantal was falling for this man. She didn't know much about him, but his touch melted all her worries and uneasiness about him.

"I'm going to order chocolate cake for dessert. That's my favorite. What about you? Dessert?"

He leaned forward and whispered in her ear. "You can be my dessert." She was caught off guard again. She could sense her face heating up again.

"We can share if you want," John said, then raised his hand to attract the attention of their waitress.

"Ask for two forks," Chantal told him. The cake arrived quickly. She took her fork and fed him the first bite. He smiled at her and opened his mouth. They ate it quietly until she licked the chocolate frosting off her lower lip. He was watching her every move. He leaned in and kissed her on the mouth in front of everyone in the restaurant. A hot surge washed over her, and when their tongues met, she almost forgot where she was. He tasted like chocolate. *He's a very good kisser,* she thought to herself. She pulled away slowly, looked up at him, and smiled, then took a quick look around her to see if people were scrutinizing them. As far as she could tell, no one cared.

"That was unexpected—but sweet," Chantal told John.

"What are you doing for the rest of the day?" he asked in a low voice. She leaned against him, her small hand on his shoulder. She pulled him nearer, brought her lips near his ear, and whispered to him. "I am not that type of girl, but if you want, you can stroll down Thames Street with me." She pulled back and sat up straight, her eyes locked on him. He laughed loudly, and so did she.

"Let's get out of here." He flagged the waitress and paid the bill. He stood up and offered her his hand. Chantal placed her tiny hand in his. He squeezed it lightly, and they left the restaurant—hand in hand—for an afternoon of adventure.

***

Tom had been astonished when he had walked out of the bathroom at The Black Pearl and had seen Chantal sitting at the table next to the window. It must have been fate, because he hadn't been able to get her out of his mind. He couldn't believe his luck. What were the chances he would run into her again? It had taken him all his effort to not answer the second call from her. He had just wanted to get a bite to eat before he went home to prepare his strike against the Rians, but now his plan was on hold one more time.

This woman had a grip on him that he could neither deny nor understand. He was unable to resist when she was near. As hard as he tried to escape, he was drawn to her. It could not have this woman in his life right now. He was an ex-con, and he wanted his revenge. He didn't want her to cloud his mind or interfere with his judgment, but here she was again.

What would she do when she found out he had lied to her about himself and had manipulated her in believing in him? Each time she was near him, he experienced a sensation that he had never known with anyone else. All of his defenses were cast to the wind. Nothing else was of any consequence. There was only Chantal. The minute he had seen her azure eyes looking up at him, she could have demanded hell, and he would have gone through fire for her—even though they had only just met.

Now, in a strange twist of fate, he was holding Chantal's hand and walking down Thames Street—window-shopping without a care in the world except to please her. He usually had no patience or time for this sort of thing. They were strolling quietly down the street when Chantal started pulling him toward the other side of the street. She was almost running blindly across the street.

"Where are you going?" he asked her, laughing as he ran along with her and trying to keep them both from getting hit by a passing car.

"Come on," Chantal replied, still tugging on his hand. They made it and were standing on the other side of the street on the sidewalk catching their breath and cracking up. Finally, she took both his hands, cocked her head toward the store on her right, and giggled.

"You want Ben & Jerry's ice cream," he said looking up at the sign. "Aren't you still full from lunch?"

She shook her head like a child and made a sad face, sticking out her lower lip at him. It made Tom grin. "Okay. I'll buy, but first you have to pay for it. Follow me." She looked at him, puzzled. He pulled her by the arm to the side of the building where it was a little more private. He turned her around and placed her back against the brick building. He gently planted his hands around her waist and lowered his head until he felt his lips touch hers. She didn't resist. Instead, she wrapped her arms around his neck. She played with the hairs at the nape, and he felt a hot sensation between his legs. Their tongues intertwined and swayed like dancers. She moved her hips forward to rub against his growing erection. He pulled away and gazed into her blue eyes, trying to regain control of his body and his emotions. He pushed her hair away front her forehead. He wondered how it would be to make love to her. How he wanted this woman now!

"How much do I have to pay?" she asked and smiled up at him. Tom bent down and quickly kiss her on the mouth once more.

"You more than paid your share. Let's go before we get arrested for indecent behavior or something." They laughed and, as much as he did not want to, separated. She led the way into the store, where she ordered a scoop of Chunky Monkey in a sugar cone. Tom gladly paid, and they marched out of the store. They saw a bench not far away, walked over, and sat down.

"Would you like to taste?" Chantal asked him. Tom took the cone from her, bit into it, and then gave it back to her.

"Not bad," he said, watching her tongue as she licked the ice cream. He wanted that tongue on his body instead of on the ice cream. *Stop it!* he thought, otherwise he might have to go find a cold shower.

"It's the best. Banana ice cream with walnuts and chocolate chunks," she replied and then resumed licking. He was intrigued by her. She piqued his interest; again he wondered if she would be good in bed. He had no doubt she would be a great lover.

Suddenly, his thoughts were interrupted by the sound of a phone ringing. It was coming from Chantal's pocketbook. She gave him her ice cream to hold and unzipped her bag. She reached inside her purse pocket.

"That must be my friend Gabrielle. She's suppose to pick me up," Chantal said as she grabbed her phone and brought it to her ear. Tom felt a cold chill run through his body.

"Don't answer it," he said, taking the phone from her hand and shutting it off.

CHAPTER 6

Gabrielle was getting worried about Chantal. It had been five hours since she had dropped her off, and she still had not heard from her. She had tried calling, but Chantal hadn't answered. She would try again in half an hour, or she would drive down to Newport to look for her on Thames Street.

"She didn't answer. Do you think she's all right?" Gabrielle asked her husband, who was sitting next to her on the couch, playing cards with their son.

"She's probably shopping up a storm. Stop worrying. She's a grown woman. If there were something wrong, she would call. It must be your motherly instinct kicking in," Bernard said, teasing her as he poked her in the side and then laughed at her.

"That's not funny. Do you think I should go look for her?" she replied with a troubled look on her face. She knew he was right.

"No, I don't think you should go looking for her just yet. She'll call. Now, come here." Bernard reached over, dragged Gabrielle into his lap, and kissed her on the cheek.

"I'll wait another hour then. Maybe she didn't hear the phone or she was busy doing something. That's got to be it." Gabrielle said. She leaned against him, kissed him on the lips, and then watched as Bernard and Junior resumed their game.

"Good girl," Bernard said as he went back to playing with his son.

***

"Why did you do that? I need to talk to her, otherwise she will be worried and she'll come looking for me," Chantal said, looking annoyed as she took her phone back from him.

"I'm sorry. Don't get mad. It's just—I don't want you to leave so soon." He lifted his hands up over his head, as if he were surrendering to her, and winked at her.

"I thought maybe I could charter a boat, and we could go for a ride around the islands and have dinner on board. How does that sound?" he asked her, hoping she would agree. It was still early, and he had the night off from work.

"Well, I suppose it would be fun, but I still have to call Gabrielle and let her know where I am," she answered and then lightly slapped him on the arm and started to giggle.

"That's fine. I tell you what—let's walk back to the wharf area. I'll go find a boat and dinner for us while you call your friend and tell her not to expect you for dinner—or maybe longer." He quickly kissed Chantal on the mouth.

Tom wanted to spend a little more time with her, plus he really couldn't do much until she returned home to Canada. He definitely was not going to do anything to the Rians while she was still with them. He didn't want to endanger her. In the back of his mind, Tom knew he shouldn't even be near this woman because of her relationship with the Rians, but he was fond of her. He really wanted to spend more time with her so he could get to know her.

He also understood that he ran the risk of being discovered by her and rejected, but when he was near her, all his rational thinking blurred. Tom took Chantal's hand in his, and they started walking back toward the wharf. He was happy that he would have her to himself for a little while longer.

They arrived near the boats a half-hour later. "Have a seat here, call your friend, and I'll be back in fifteen minutes," Tom said to her, delighted that Chantal had decided to stay. She sat on the bench and nodded at him. He bent down, placed both his hands on her cheeks, and planted another passionate kiss on her mouth. He closed his eyes and savored the taste of her lips. He was so close to her he could smell her perfume. It was making him delirious. He let go of her, and she smiled up at him. He turned around and started moving toward the boats on the pier, stopping midway to look at her sitting by herself before continuing to his destination.

***

Chantal could not believe that she had agreed to go sailing with John. She felt calm and content with this man. She wasn't afraid of him hurting her, even though she had just met him the previous day. She wanted to be here with him so she could get to know more about him. What was she going to say to Gabrielle? She wasn't going to think about it. She didn't want to brood too much about what she was about to do, otherwise she might back out and not go. She opened her phone and punched in her friend's number. It rang once, and then she heard a familiar voice.

"Hi, I thought you got lost. I tried to call you earlier, but you didn't answer. Are you all right? " Gabrielle said, very upbeat. How was Chantal going to explain this to her friend?

"Hi, I know you called before, and I'm not lost. As a matter of fact, I'm having a great time," Chantal replied, trying to sound cheerful, though deep down she knew they were going to argue a bit.

"So, are you ready for me to come pick you up? Just give me ten minutes, and I'll be there," Gabrielle said enthusiastically.

"Umm, I'm not ready to come home just yet. I'm going sailing with a friend." Chantal cringed, shut her eyes tight and waited for her response.

"What are you talking about? A friend?" Gabrielle replied slowly.

"Well, I met this man named John Baker yesterday on the beach, and I bumped into him again today. We had lunch, I've been with him all day, and he invited me to go sailing and have dinner with him tonight." There— she had said it. Now she was bracing herself for the blowup. Chantal knew Gabrielle wouldn't agree.

"Are you out of your mind? What do you know about this man? He could be a rapist as far as you know!" Gabrielle was getting agitated.

"He is not! He's very nice and a complete gentleman, if you must know." Chantal didn't know what else to say. Her adrenaline was spiking;

41

she could feel her temperature rising, and her ears were getting hot with anxiety.

"Let's talk about this rationally. This is not a good idea," Gabrielle said.

"Gabrielle, I am a grown woman. I do believe I can make this decision. You did the same thing when you met Bernard, for God's sake. I'll be fine—don't worry." Chantal was trying to sound confident, but Gabrielle could be stubborn.

"That was different," Gabrielle answered.

"No, it was not. I like this guy, and I'm going. I'm in my thirties. I should be able to judge who I date. If I don't take chances, I will never find a man." Chantal was trying hard to make Gabrielle see her side.

"What is his name? Where's he from?" she inquired.

"His name is John Baker, and he's from Boston." Chantal told her flatly.

"All right, then promise me that you'll be careful and that you'll keep your phone close. I will wait up for you." Gabrielle emphasized.

"Yes, Mom, I'll be careful! Anything else?" Chantal knew she had won her friend over. They were both laughing.

"No, just be careful," Gabrielle said again.

"I will. Love you! Bye!" Chantal smiled to herself. She was going to have a splendid time. *Hopefully*, she thought. *Stop it—everything will be fine!* She could see John coming toward her. He was waving at her. He was almost running. This man was handsome and had a manly body that would drive any woman wild. She liked him; she just hoped he wouldn't break her heart.

"So, is everything all set? Did you talk to your friend?" he asked her, smiling from ear to ear. She could jump for joy.

"Yes, I did. We're all set. Let's go sailing," Chantal answered and stood up. She was so excited that he wanted to spend more time with her. He offered her his arm, and she looped hers into his without hesitation. They strolled leisurely down to the pier, enjoying each other's company as if they had been a couple for a long time. She could see that the sun was beginning to set. The red, orange, and gold that streaked the sky were beautiful, and she loved the smell of the ocean breeze. Tom unexpectedly stopped walking in the middle of the quay. He took Chatal's hand and pointed to one of the yachts that was docked in the harbor.

"Your ship awaits. Would you care to board?" He asked her with the biggest smirk on his face.

"Are you serious? This is the boat you chartered?" Chantal was stunned, her eyes bulging with surprise at what he had done.

"Yes, it is. Anything wrong with it?" he asked, tilting his head and looking at her.

"Oh! My God! No, no, there is absolutely nothing wrong at all, but –" For once in her life, Chantal was speechless. She kept peeking at the yacht behind him and then gazing back at him. Tom kept nodding at her. She took a step toward him and gave him a huge hug. She could not believe her eyes. This wasn't a boat, but a ship that was two-stories tall and had to be at least seventy-five feet long. She had seen boats like this in magazines, and now she was about to have dinner on one!

"Do you want to go on board? I even hired a chef to cook us dinner. Now, shall we proceed, my lady?" Tom asked in a debonair tone. He took her hand and guided her across the bridge to the boat's deck. Chantal was overwhelmed. She didn't know where to look or what to look at. She kept turning her head, her eyes darting back and forth. She was in awe.

"Are you sure it's ours for the evening? You didn't steal it or hijack it, did you? How did you manage to get this boat on such short notice?" Chantal had so many questions.

"The answers are yes, no, and money." Tom had a wide smile on his face. She was exhilarated by all that surrounded her. She heard the sound of the engine starting and felt it begin to slowly push the vessel away from the dock.

"It has its own crew?" She was amazed that he could managed to afford to rent this ship. He must be well-off to be able to pay for this on such short notice. She would have to ask him about that later on, but right now she was going to relish this experience and try to not jinx it. She was overjoyed by the prospect of spending the evening with this man. He was so generous and altruistic. She had never done anything like this in her life on the spur of the moment. She wondered what else he might have up his sleeve that would shock her. She loved his spontaneity, and moments like this made her heart skip a beat.

"Do you want to see the rest of the ship?" he asked, but all she could do was nod at him. He led the way into the main room, a convertible lounge that was furnished with long white leather couches, beautiful white drapes, and pine floors. She noticed that a glass table in the middle of the deck was set for two. On either side of the table was a white chair covered in white linen, and the table itself was decorated with china and crystal dinnerware. A mirrored bar stood at the far end of the room, stocked with crystal glasses and multiple bottles of liquor. Tom guided her toward the bar area. Chantal followed him without a word, soaking it all in.

"Would you like a drink?" Tom asked her, taking two tumblers from the cabinet.

"Yes, maybe I should have one, because right now I cannot believe how I ended here on this ship with you," Chantal uttered, and then perched herself on a stool. She put her hands on the counter in front of her.

"Is that good or bad?" he questioned, but before Chantal could answer, he continued. "What can I get you? Wine or something stronger?" He inched closer to her and covered her hands with his, holding them in place. He leaned over the counter and kissed her ever so lightly, generating a feeling she hadn't felt in years. He then passed his tongue across her upper and lower lips. She closed her eyes, intensifying the sensation that his kisses had caused in her core. He pulled way, but Chantal wasn't ready for him to stop just yet.

She opened her eyes and said, "I think I need something stronger than wine. How about Grey Goose vodka with cranberry juice, if you have it?"

She watched him find the bottles he needed and began making her drink, all the while keeping an eye on her. He also poured himself vodka neat. He slipped her drink between her fingers, lifted up his own, and said, "To a great evening. Cheers," and tapped her glass against his. She brought the cocktail to her mouth and took a huge gulp. She could feel a burn as her drink went down to her stomach. It brought her back to reality. She gave him a smile.

"Wow! That's better," Chantal said to him.

"Do you want to continue the tour, or sit outside and enjoy the view?" he asked her. Chantal looked out to the ocean, and then pointed at the outside couches.

"Come sit with me for a while. I can see the rest later." She got up, picked up her drink, and moved toward the sofas to look at the sights. She turned around, but John was nowhere to be seen. She sat down and waited. He emerged a few minutes later with a red blanket. As he came forward, he opened the blanket and wrapped it around her shoulders.

"I thought you might be cold because of the wind out here," he said to her. He then tucked the blanket around her.

How considerate of him to think of her! "All I need is you, and I'll be warm enough." She reached over to him with her free hand, pulled him close, and sat him down next to her. She cuddled next to him. She was in a good place at the moment.

Hours passed by like lightning. They devoured a surf-and-turf dinner of steak with lobster tails that the chef had presented after they had been at sea for about an hour. Everything was so romantic! This man she barely knew was sweeping her off her feet, but Chantal didn't care. She was having a good time, and right now, that was all she was concerned about.

They talked about her childhood and her experiences throughout her life. Chantal explained how she loved to teach her students and considered them her own children while they were in her class. He listened attentively to every word she said and asked many questions along the way. She noticed he didn't talk much about himself, but she guessed that must be his way and that he might open up when he knew her better. She hoped that she would be able to see him again during her stay. She noticed they were approaching the marina area of Newport. She really didn't want this absolutely marvelous evening to end.

They were back sitting in the lounge, all snuggled together on the couches. His kisses had left her wanting more, but she decided she would wait. She didn't want to get hurt or to scare him off by moving too fast. She had never wanted to make love to someone as much as she wanted to make love to John. A few minutes later, the ship docked at its original port. A feeling of sadness swept over Chantal. She really didn't want this journey to end just yet.

"Well, here we are again. Back where we started." She struggled to move from her comfortable place. His arms were wrapped around her, their feet next to each other on a tabouret. All his kisses and nibbles on her neck and ears had brought her desire to new level. She didn't want to leave.

"Are we going to see each other again?" She couldn't believe she had asked it, but in her heart, she really wanted to know. She sat up straight beside him and lowered her chin, not wanting to look at him when he let her down. He took his hand and lifted her chin up so their eyes could meet. She raised her eyes and watched as a smile came over his face. Then he kissed her so hard that she could taste him as their tongues twisted together. His hand slid down the small of her back and up again. He cupped his big hands around her cheeks. She couldn't deny the sexual attraction that she felt toward him. She had to pull away from their kiss to take a breath; her heart was throbbing against her chest—her body felt alive.

"Does that answer your question?" he asked her.

"Yes, it does." Chantal laughed out loud. She bent down and picked up her pocketbook, found a pen and a piece of paper, and wrote her cell phone number on it. She passed it to him. He looked at it. "This time, you call me."

He looked at it again, and for a second she thought she saw the saddest look in his eyes. She must be mistaken! Not after the embrace they had just had!

"Thanks. I'll call you soon," he answered as he lifted his hip and placed the number in the pocket of his jeans. They debarked the ship and walked across the wharf to the end of the street.

"I'm parked at the other end of this street. It's kind of far, so I'll flag you a cab. That way you can get home sooner so that your friend doesn't send a search party for you," he told her.

"I don't mind walking with you." She wanted to stay with him as long as she could.

"This will be easier, and I still have to drive back to Boston." His arm went up as a cab passed by. It stopped in front of them. He reached for the handle of the door and opened it. As she went to sit in the car, he took her arm and pulled her toward him one last time.

"I had a great time. I'll talk to you soon," he said and then kissed her on the mouth. She leaned into his body so that she could feel him against her. He held her close, and then let her go as he planted one last kiss on her nose. She felt a surge of speechless passion but turned around and sat in the taxi. He closed the door and waved to her. She gave the cabbie the address and watched John, as he stood on the curb, until he disappeared from her sight.

CHAPTER 7

Ron hadn't slept all night. He had tossed and turned for hours. He kept looking at the clock ticking away the minutes. He now had dark circles under his eyes and wasn't in the mood for pampering. Morning had not come fast enough for him.

At the break of dawn, Jacob, his nurse, had knocked on his bedroom door. When he came into Ron's room to bathe and dress him, Ron had slapped Jacob's hand away and yelled at him. "Just dress me, get me in that God-forsaken chair, and leave me alone." Ron was in a foul mood. When he was finally ready, he dismissed Jacob with a wave of his hand. He pushed the button on his electric chair, wheeled himself to his study, and behind his mahogany desk. He looked at his Rolex again. It was only seven o'clock, but he didn't care. He needed answers, and he needed them now.

He grabbed the phone and called Raymond. He waited as it rang, tapping his fingers on the top of his desk. After a few more rings, a sleepy voice answered.

"Hello."

"Raymond, did you find out where Tom goes during the daytime yet?" Ron asked anxiously.

"Umm, Mr. Rian?" Raymond asked, still half asleep.

"Yes, yes. Are you deaf this morning? I asked if you knew where Tom was," He hated repeating himself, but did it anyway and then waited.

"Umm, he was at work the night before. Last night he had the evening off. He hasn't shown up at the boarding house during the day for the last two days," Raymond responded.

"Where does he sleep at night, and what does he do during the day?" Ron asked Raymond, irritated. He raked his fingers through his hair. He was used to having his questions answered quickly.

"I really don't know. I could take a few days off my part-time job, follow him around, and find out. But I would need more cash," Raymond replied quietly.

"Just find out what he does during the day and where he goes. How difficult can that be? Follow him. Do what you need to do. I'll send you cash by carrier. Is $1000 enough for the moment? Will that be sufficient for a few days?" Ron was annoyed that he couldn't get any results.

"Yes, sir. That'll be great. I'll call my boss and take a few vacation days." Raymond sounded excited.

"Get on it right away, and call me as soon as you find him, understood?" Ron said as he hung up the phone.

Where could the bastard be? He went to work so his parole officer didn't get on his back, but Tom didn't sleep at the boarding house. Where does he spend his time, then? He might be after his family! Ron wasn't being paranoid. He knew this man. He knew how he operated and how he thought. For ten long year, Ron had groomed Tom as his right-hand man.

Ron knew what Tom was capable of doing. He had felt it personally. He still had a piece of metal in his back from when Tom had tried to murder him. Because of that, Ron would be in this chair for the rest of his life. Tom had gone rogue and blown up Gabrielle's inn, trying to kill her to keep her away from Ron's son, Bernard. Ron sighed, rubbing his hands over his face. He was trying to erase those horrible memories, but they still haunted him whenever he thought about that man. He picked up the phone again and called Bernard's cell phone to warn him about Tom.

"Good morning, Father. How are you feeling?" Bernard said cheerfully. Ron knew he would have to be careful what he said to his son because he really didn't want to displease him.

"Very good. I was just checking to see how my favorite grandchild is doing." Ron tried to sound as casual as possible.

"He's having a ball. He goes to the beach with his friend Brian every day. By nightfall he's so tired he falls asleep on the couch," Bernard informed him.

"Bernard, the reason I am calling is to talk to you about Tom. No one knows where he is during the day and I'm—" Ron didn't have time to finish his sentence before his son cut him off.

"Father, I told you—this is nonsense! You have to move on. We are fine, and there is nothing unusual going on," Bernard said, exhaling loudly.

"Just hear me out, at least," Ron pleaded. "His whereabouts during the day are unknown. He works at night, but during the day, I want you to keep your eyes open. I hired someone to track him during the day to make sure that Tom doesn't come close to you or hurt you. I don't think I could bear it if he did," Ron tried to make Bernard understand the danger.

"You hired someone to trail him? I really don't think that is necessary." Ron heard the disapproval in Bernard's voice.

"Please, Bernard, for my peace of mind," Ron spoke softly to his son.

"Fine. I'll keep my eyes open. If I see anything out of the ordinary, I'll call the police. Does that make you happier?" Bernard answered him.

"Yes, yes! And tell Gabrielle about it, too," Ron said.

"I will not involve her and ruin her vacation when you have no evidence that Tom is around here. Don't say anything to her to upset her." Bernard tone changed again, and he sounded frustrated with his father.

"All right, I won't say a word—but please, please be careful," Ron insisted again.

"Very well. Have a good day, Father."

"Bye," Ron said, but Bernard had already hung up the phone. At least he was doing something, unlike his son, who had deluded himself into thinking that Tom wouldn't harm them. Ron would never forgive Tom for the hardship that he had precipitated on him and his family ten years ago. He would have to wait and see what Raymond had to report. Ron might end up being the one who protected his family. He just hoped it would not be too late. He glanced at the contracts in front of him, picked up one, and started to read it, but he couldn't concentrate. *I will kill you myself if you dare harm my family.*

***

Tom awoke at the boarding house in Worcester the following morning. He hadn't slept this well in ages. It was almost nine o'clock. He yawned and blinked a few times before he sat up in bed. He thought about the time he had spent with Chantal. He had mixed feelings about her. He needed to finish his mission, and he didn't want her near him. He still had time to get things together, and he couldn't do much while she was still in Newport.

His targets were easy to access because there were no security personnel around them in Newport. He had several options that would put the fear of God into them when he decided to go forward with his plan. Neil was living at the house in Ashburnham. Neil had acquired all the things Tom had asked him to get, but Tom still needed to pick up a few more things. These he had to get himself. He was the only one who had the connections to acquire these products since they were illegal. Tom didn't trust many people to do his dirty work; he'd rather do it himself. But he wouldn't do anything until Chantal left to go home.

Chantal's safety was his first concern, and Tom would make sure she was safe before he proceeded with his plan.

He closed his eyes and reminisced about the previous evening. He could still see Chantal's surprised expression when she had seen the yacht. The time he had spent with Chantal was worth every dollar he had spent to secure the boat from the captain. That night was worth all the money that he had tucked away in all of his banks around the world. It had been one of his best days of his life. The thing that would have made it perfect would have been spending the night making love to her.

He wanted to feel her naked skin against his and her small breasts rubbing against his chest. But if he had make love to her last night, he probably would not have been able to walk away. He could return to his memories of her whenever he wanted. But he had to stay away from her. He had no other choice. She was already interfering with his plan just by being with him, and he could not allow it again. Tom got up and headed to the shower. He absolutely needed to clear his mind of her. Today he had to report to his parole officer, and then he was free until he had to go to work tonight.

He felt better after he had gotten dressed. He was ravenous. He walked down the street to a diner that served delicious omelets. This place was a hole in the wall, but he liked it. He entered, found a seat at the counter where he could watch the cook, and ordered his breakfast. When the waitress brought his coffee, he thought he saw a man looking his way.

The man in question sat in one of the booths nearby. As Tom began to eat his eggs, he noticed that the man was watching him again. He looked like a cop, with his short haircut and straight posture. Even if he was trying to hide it, his demeanor screamed that he was a police officer. Why would a cop be following him? He wasn't sure yet, so Tom finished eating and left the cash for his breakfast on the counter. He then decided to see if the cop was going to follow him, so he took a stroll down the street.

He stopped at a convenience store, walked in, and headed to the back of the store near the coolers. He opened a door, grabbed a can of Red Bull, and brought it to the checkout counter, where he paid the guy and left. All the while, Tom kept his eyes opened. Once outside, Tom stopped in front of a store windows, bent down, and pretended to tie his boots. He scanned the area and noticed the same guy leaning against a building across the street. Who was watching him and why? Ron was the only person who would hire someone to tail him.

Tom walked back to his truck, got in, and looked in his rearview mirror to see if he could spot the cop. He stayed on the lookout as he drove to see his probation officer. On the way out of the building, he spotted him again. He would have to be very cautious about where he went now and what he did.

Tom drove back to the boarding house and went inside. He would stay there until he had to go to work later that evening. He sat on his bed and started thinking. He got up, stepped to the window, pushed the curtain aside, and looked to the avenue below. There was a blue sedan parked near the curb on the opposite side of the street. It was the man from the restaurant again. Why was he here? Who had sent him?

Tom lay back down on his single bed. Putting his hands behind his head, he stared at the ceiling and debated whether the cop was going to report to Ron. *I mustn't give Ron any reason to come after me*, he said to himself. For the time being, Tom would play along, walking a straight line; he'd resume his plan when Ron no longer suspected him..

He hoped that the cop would back off after a few days and tell Ron that everything was normal. Had he been hired to do more than watch and evaluate? Maybe Ron was planning his own revenge. A few years ago Tom had found out that he hadn't killed Ron when he had shot him—he had only paralyzed him from the waist down.

Tom didn't feel guilty about shooting Ron. He had only done what his boss—Ron himself!—had ordered him to do to eliminate the threat to Ron's empire. Later, Ron had changed his mind, but only after Tom had already begun to execute his orders. Tom had only been following his instructions. However, Ron had sent the cops after Tom as a result, so Tom had retaliated against him. He had served time in prison for the crimes that Ron had ordered him to do. Now Tom wanted retribution.

Tom reached into his pants pocket and pulled out the piece of paper with Chantal's number. He set it on the night stand. He rose and sat on the edge of his bed. He reached down next to him and retrieved his camera, which was in its case. He clicked one of the buttons, and images of Chantal appeared on the screen. He touched one of the pictures with his finger for a few seconds, as the memories of last night flooded his mind. He winced, closed his eyes, and then pressed the delete button to erase all of the reminders of her. He knew that the minute that he left his room for work tonight, the man from the street was going to come up to his room and search it. Tom didn't want him to find anything incriminating.

He picked up the paper and memorized the number written on it. Immediately after he did this, he wondered why he had taken it. He grabbed a lighter from his jacket pocket and lit the paper on fire. He needed to break ties with her before he hurt her or before Ron used her against him. He placed the remainder of the paper in the ashtray by his bed and watched as it burned away.

***

Chantal was having an iced tea while sitting in a rocking chair on the porch. It was late in the day, and she had hoped that John would call her, but he hadn't. She hadn't heard back from him in a few days, and she was starting to feel tormented about their relationship. She was daydreaming about him when Gabrielle came outside and sat next to her.

"Sorry I haven't had time to sit and talk with you before now, but Junior keeps me going like the Electric Bunny. Bernard took him out for an ice cream," Gabrielle told her.

The mention of ice cream reminded Chantal of the time she had spent with John a few days ago. She smiled to herself. She hadn't realized what she was doing until Gabrielle started to laugh at her. She turned her head away, embarrassed she had been caught reminiscing about John.

"So tell me about your mysterious date from the other night. I want details," Gabrielle said to her.

"I met him on the beach the other day. He's tall, dark, and handsome. He has dreamy blue eyes and—" Chantal stopped talking as she remembered his kisses. She ran her index finger across her upper lip.

"That's half of the population. What's his name? What does he do for work? Where is he from? Do I have to force everything out of you?" Gabrielle asked, laughing at her friend.

"His name is John Baker, he's an engineer, and he's from Boston," Chantal said.

"And the other day? Or should I say, night?" Gabrielle questioned.

"Well, I bumped into him at The Black Pearl. I had stopped there for lunch. He just happened to be at the same restaurant, so he came over and sat with me. We enjoyed a nice lunch and then we promenaded down Thames Street, and—" Chantal was interrupted by Gabrielle.

"A promenade? What the heck is that?" Gabrielle teased Chantal.

"Ha! Ha! We just window-shopped and shared an ice cream cone. I was about to call you, but he said he wanted to spend more time with me. So he chartered a yacht," Chantal said nonchalantly as she picked up her tea from the side table and took a sip.

"A yacht? Are you kidding?" All of Gabrielle's attention was on her.

"I swear, this ship had two levels, and John even hired a chef who cooked dinner for us. We sailed around the islands in the bay. He was so romantic and attentive. Afterwards John flagged a cab for me, and I came home." She was trying not to show her excitement. Her eyes were glued to the horizon.

"And did you kiss him?" Gabrielle asked, still watching Chantal.

"Yes, I did, and he is a great kisser." Chantal couldn't believe she had said that! She blushed just thinking about it.

"And are you going to see him again?" Gabrielle inquired.

"He asked for my number, and I really hope he calls. I really would like to see him again."

Chantal glanced at her phone, which was on the side table next to her. She didn't leave the phone out of her sight, wishing John would call.

"You know you're on vacation, and you'll be leaving in a week or so. Then what? Not much can come of this other than maybe a roll in the hay," Gabrielle giggled, and then gently punched Chantal's arm.

"We'll see. One day at a time, I suppose. I do like him, though. Plus, what else do I have to do at this minute beside enjoy myself?" Chantal answered. She bit her lower lip and thought, *I wished I had had a roll in the hay,* but it hadn't happened. She really was going crazy, waiting for a call from a man she barely knew. Would he call? Chantal didn't know for sure. But John had put her number in his jeans pocket.

"We'll see," Gabrielle said and then stood up.

"I need to start supper, so why don't you sit here and daydream about your prince." Gabrielle smiled at her, and then opened the door of the cottage and walked inside.

"Sure, walk away, when I need you most!" Chantal shouted jokingly at her best friend, but inside Chantal was desperate to hear from John. *Relax, it's only been a few days. You're being an idiot,* she thought.

He said he would call, but he hadn't said when. It could be today or never. Chantal figured John was a busy man and would call in time. She should have kept his number. She had deleted his number from her phone when he hadn't answered the other day. Now it was too late. She couldn't turn back time.

She just had to be patient and bide her time. She had to see him at least one more time—just one more time before she left town. Maybe they could have 'a roll in the hay,' as Gabrielle had put it. Chantal prayed silently John would get in touch with her, but she wouldn't utter a word to anyone about it. It would be her own little secret.

CHAPTER 8

Tom had had enough. He decided that he was going to confront the man today. For three days, the man—a former cop, by Tom's guess—had tailed Tom from his boarding house to work and back again. Tom had had his fill of it. To his right was an alley wedged next to a building that housed several stores. He moved into it, put his back flat against the brick wall behind the dumpster, and waited.

He could see the cop coming toward him. He braced himself for an assault. In his younger days, Tom had trained for Special Operations in the Army, and he still remembered all of the moves he had learned. They were engraved on his memory.

He heard footsteps approach. Tom jumped out and grabbed the man by the collar of his jacket. Tom twisted him around and slammed his back hard against the wall. As the man struggled, Tom punched him twice in the ribs. He pressed his forearm against the man's throat, keeping him in a choke hold as he pushed him to the wall with his other hand.

The former cop struggled to free himself, but Tom punched him in the jaw. The man grimaced after the blow, but Tom continued to hold him firmly against the wall. The man strained against Tom's arms, his own arms pulling against Tom's as he tried to get Tom to let go of his neck, but Tom was much stronger. Frowning, Tom brought his face close to the man's face and asked him in a hard voice, "Why are you following me?"

The cop didn't reply.

"Answer me." Tom yelled at him. He was trying to control his anger, but he quickly made a fist with his free arm and prepared to punch the man again.

"What makes you think I'm follow—" The former cop didn't have time to finish his sentence before Tom's fist slammed into his stomach. The man bent over a little and coughed loudly, trying to catch his breath.

"I don't have time to fuck around with you, so answer my questions the first time I ask them," Tom said to him between clenched teeth. Tom held up his fist, ready to strike again.

"All right! I was told just to keep track of you. That's all." The man was still struggling to breathe after the last blow.

"Who hired you?" Tom asked, although he figured he already knew the answer. "Was it Ron Rian?"

The tail just nodded. Tom let him go, and the cop crumbled to the ground, a defeated man, coughing and rubbing his neck.

"You're fucking crazy! Stay away from me." The man said.

"Tell your employer to stay away from me and to definitely hire better help!" Tom walked away with long strides, his head held high as he laughed out loud.

***

Raymond had followed Tom for three straight days now. He must have found out something about Tom by now, but Ron hadn't heard a word. They had agreed they would contact each other today, but Raymond still hadn't called yet. Ron was under a pergola in the garden behind his residence. He had been looking at his rose bushes. He could smell their fragrance from where he was sitting. If only he was still able to walk over to prune and pick them like he used to. His eyes watered at the thought. When his phone finally rang, Ron examined the caller ID it before he answered. It was Raymond.

"What do you have for me?" Ron demanded.

"This guy is insane. He tried to kill me—" Raymond started, but Ron didn't want to listen to him whine.

"I asked, what do you have for me?" Ron repeated in a louder voice, on the brink of losing his temper.

"He looks clean. He lives in a boarding house on Main Street in Worcester and works nights as a janitor cleaning an office building. He checks in with his parole officer regularly every week. I checked with the officer, who said Tom was squeaky clean so far. Nothing out of the ordinary," Raymond answered him.

"What did you find in his room?" Ron didn't like what he was hearing. It could not be that Tom was walking a straight line. Ron knew him too well to think that Tom wouldn't to seek his revenge for getting sent to prison.

"Nothing. Everything was in place. I did find a camera, but there were no pictures on it. There were some dirty clothes and money scattered around, but I didn't see anything to raise a red flag," Raymond answered. "I'm done with this guy. I don't want to be near him again."

"Continue to follow him and call me back in a few days," Ron ordered him.

"There's no reason to follow him. You're wrong. He's not up to anything, and I really don't want to be alone with him. He ambushed me and, I hate to say it, he beat me up. I need help," Raymond said, trying to make his case.

"Fine, find yourself a partner and keep watching him for a few more days. Call me Saturday. I want to make sure he's not planning anything. Understood? And don't get caught again, for Christ's sake. Don't you guys do undercover work? You should know better," Ron said.

"Yes, sir. I'm sorry, Mr. Rian," Raymond answered, but Ron had already hung up the phone.

***

Four days had gone by since her date on the yacht, and Chantal still hadn't heard from John. She was sad and disappointed that he hadn't called her. They were leaving for Boston in the afternoon and would stay there for the rest of the week before she flew home. Chantal was heartbroken. She really thought that she and John had a special connection, but she must have been wrong.

This relationship hadn't turned out the way she had planned, and her vacation was almost over. She would return to Canada within the week without ever hearing from him. She sat on her bed, folding her last shirts and placing them in her suitcase. She could hear Junior and Brian playing in the adjacent room. Gabrielle was telling Junior to pick up his toys and say his goodbye to his friend because they were ready to leave.

Unhappy, she zipped her suitcase and placed it next to her on the bed. She bent her head down and felt her eyes begin to water. A tear trickled down her cheek. She raised her hand and wiped it away. She was tougher than this. She came to the conclusion that John didn't want to be with her. It was another rejection—she'd just add him to her list, which had gotten long over the years. She had to move on. They had had only a few encounters. This was ridiculous. She got up and walked to the bathroom to wash her face. She splashed cold water against her face, trying to bring herself back to reality, and then dried it off. Chantal was determined to enjoy the rest of her vacation with Gabrielle and to not think about that man. A light knock at her bedroom door interrupted her thoughts.

"Chantal, are you almost ready?" she heard Gabrielle ask.

"Yes, I'm ready. Come in." She watched Gabrielle stroll in and smile at her. Gabrielle sat down on the end of her bed. Chantal came out of the bathroom after she had finishing wiping her face with a towel. Gabrielle patted the top of the bed and motioned for Chantal to come sit beside her. Chantal did so. Gabrielle wrapped her arm around Chantal's shoulders and began to talk to her as a good friend.

"Are you all right? I know you liked him, and I also know he didn't call. But guess what? We are going to remedy that. You and I are going out on the town tonight. I made reservations at a nice restaurant in downtown Boston called The Capital Grill. We'll have a few drinks, and we can have a few laughs. How does that sound?" Gabrielle gave Chantal another hug, and then she rubbed her back softly.

"That sounds like a plan. I'm sorry I been mopping around, but I really thought—" Chantal tried to explain how she felt, but her eyes began to water again. This time she controlled them, turning her head from Gabrielle as she blinked the tears away. None fell.

"You don't have to say anything. I understand. Now, let's put your suitcase in the truck and get going toward Boston," Gabrielle told her.

"You're the best!" Chantal picked her suitcase up and headed outside. She stood on the porch for a moment and inhaled the ocean air one last time. She resolved to have a good time with Gabrielle in Boston tonight and to try to forget the effect John had on her.

***

Tom hadn't seen anyone following him for the last two days. He had kept an eye out for his cop 'friend,' but the man must have gotten the message. Tom now knew that Ron was after him, so he would have to strike first, otherwise he might not get a second chance. He still had a lot of work to do, but he couldn't get Chantal out of his mind.

He desperately wanted to see her one more time before she departed for home. She consumed his every thought. He had to call her. He yearned to hear her voice again and—if he was lucky—to hold her in his arms, to feel her curls between his fingers, and to hear her laugh.

Tom fingered his phone and dialed the numbers that were engraved on his mind. He carefully punched the digits and waited. The phone rang and rang, but Chantal didn't answer. Why? He was sure he had the right numbers. Maybe she was upset with him because he hadn't called before now. He would try again in a half-hour. He took off his clothes and threw them onto the chair next to his bed. Naked, he walked to his bathroom, turned the knobs in the shower, and stepped under the flow. The hot water felt good on his body. As his sore muscles loosened, he wished Chantal were here with him. He would call her again. She would answer—but then what? What if she found out about him? How would she? No one who knew him had seen them together. It didn't matter. He just had to hear her voice and see her one more time.

***

Gabrielle and Chantal had reservations at The Capital Grill, a classy, upscale restaurant that was famed for its aged steaks. Steve, the chauffeur, dropped them at the front entrance. They were greeted at the front desk and then escorted to their table. Chantal sat and smiled at Gabrielle. The hostess gave them each a menu.

"This is a great place. I love the mahogany paneling on the walls and the red wallpaper," Chantal said as she examined the cocktail menu.

"Yep! And there's a lot of testosterone here, too," Gabrielle answered her, and then laughed. Chantal nodded. She pulled her leather chair closer to the table, which was covered with white linen tablecloth and red napkins. Chantal switched to the food menu, opened it, and started reading her options.

"It's a real steakhouse with a noisy atmosphere, but it's an interesting place," Chantal remarked to her friend. They ordered a nice bottle of Chardonnay wine and two filets, one for each of them, with potato and vegetable on the side. After they had finished their meal, they sat and chatted about all the beautiful men at the bar area.

"Shall we get another?" Gabrielle pointed to the empty Chardonnay bottle.

"What the heck? Sure," Chantal giggled. The wine had started to affect her, but in a good way.

Chantal pushed her chair back, put her napkin on the table and excused herself to go to the ladies' room. She walked to the back of the restaurant and was washing her hands when she heard her cell phone ring. She quickly dried her hands and unzipped her purse. She snatched her phone out of its side pocket. She didn't bother to check the caller ID before she brought the phone to her ear.

"Hello, gorgeous. Where have you been?" Her mind went blank. She was stunned. She opened her mouth to say something, but the only thing that came out was "Hi."

"I tried calling you earlier this evening, but I didn't get an answer," he said. Chantal moved toward a velvet couch that the restaurant had placed in the bathroom, barely making it before her legs folded under her. He was the last person she expected to hear from. It was John! She had waited, but now she was stupefied that he had actually called her. She had eliminated him from her mind, thinking that he didn't want her since he hadn't bothered to contact her for almost a week.

"I'm sorry. I'm having dinner at a restaurant in Boston, and it's a little loud. I didn't hear my phone ring." Chantal's heart was beating fast. She placed her hand on her chest, feeling the beat. She was excited.

"Are you alone?" he asked seductively.

"No, I'm with my girlfriend Gabrielle. Would you like to join us?" she asked without hesitation. She still wanted to see him. There was complete silence on his end of the line. She thought *How strange!* for a second, and then wondered if he had disconnected. Her heart sank.

"John, are you still there?" Chantal asked nervously.

"Yes, I am. How about we meet for a drink after you are done with dinner?" he finally asked her. "I, um, don't want to interrupt your time with your girlfriend."

"I don't know. I would have to ask Gabrielle if she wants to come," Chantal answered.

"I meant you alone," he said. Now it was Chantal's turn to be quiet. How was she going to leave Gabrielle here alone? Chantal hoped she would understand. Gabrielle knew how much this guy meant to her.

"All right, where?" Chantal finally answered, thrilled at the prospect of seeing him once more.

"Well, how about we meet at the Ritz Carlton on Avery Street. There's a small bar area near the entrance. Just have a seat, and I'll be there as soon as I can. Let's say one hour. Will that work?" he replied.

"That sounds great. An hour then. It will give me time to talk to Gabrielle," Chantal said.

"I'll be there. Bye, gorgeous." Tom said, and then Chantal heard a click. He was gone. She sat there for a few more minutes, waiting for her hands and legs to stop shaking. She was happy once again.

Five minutes later, she managed to walk back to the table and sit down. Gabrielle looked at her, concerned. "You look like you saw a ghost. Do you feel all right?" she asked Chantal.

"You won't believe who just called me when I was in the ladies' room. John! He asked me to meet him for a drink at the Ritz Carlton in the bar area in an hour. Would you mind if we cut our evening short, and I went to meet him for a while? I really want to see him one more time before I have to go home." Chantal was pleading her case. She had a spark in her eyes and the biggest smile.

"Even if I said no, I think you would go anyway. Are you sure you'll be okay by yourself?" Gabrielle asked her.

"I must be crazy, but yes. I trust him. I'm not worried. I'll be fine. I can take a cab home afterward," Chantal answered.

"Well, then. I'll call Steve to come pick us up. He can drop you on the way home, but promise to call me if you need me," Gabrielle said.

Chantal nodded. Gabrielle paid the bill and called her chauffeur. Chantal was thrilled at the prospect of seeing John again. She sipped on a new glass of wine, trying to calm her nerves.

The chauffeur picked them up in front of the restaurant and drove to Avery Street. He stopped at the main entrance of the Ritz Carlton and proceeded to open the back door of the sedan.

"How do I look? Do I seem high-strung?" Chantal asked Gabrielle, wanting her opinion.

"You look beautiful. Now, go and have fun—but be careful!" Gabrielle leaned toward Chantal and kissed her on the cheek. Chantal smiled, then stepped out of the car. She stood on the sidewalk and waved goodbye to her friend. She turned around and walked toward the entrance of the hotel. The doorman held the door open for her as she walked in.

***

Tom had driven to Avery Street immediately after he had gotten dressed. He wore a black sports jacket, a white shirt with two buttons open, a Louis Vuitton checkered black and gray belt around his black trousers, and black shoes. He had even gelled his hair back.

He felt confident.

He wanted to be there before she arrived. He found a spot to park his truck down the block from the entrance of the hotel. His truck was hidden in the shadows of another building across from the hotel. He sat in the truck as he watched Chantal get out of the car and wave to Gabrielle. He turned his back when the car approached him. He didn't want Gabrielle to see him accidentally.

Tom emerged from his vehicle and walked to the hotel. He kept straightening his jacket as he walked. He had never been one to be uneasy about anything, but for some reason he had butterflies in his stomach. He arrived at the front door and sighed. The doorman opened the door, and Tom stepped inside. He took a few paces forward, and he saw her sitting by herself at the counter of the bar, with a cocktail in front of her. Her back was to him. He took a few long strides toward her. As he neared her, he crept up, slipped his arms around her waist, and whispered in her ear. "Hi, gorgeous." She turned to face him, and he kissed her on the lips. He really wanted to continue kissing her, but there were too many people looking at them.

"Hi, how are you doing?" he asked, examining her from head to toe.

"I'm fine. How about you?" she answered. He was watching her every move. He looked at the empty seat next to her, then pulled the stool closer to her and sat down. He pressed his legs against hers and laid a hand on her knee.

He could smell her perfume; the floral scent of roses was intoxicating. He leaned closer.

"You smell delicious!" he said, and then smirked. He turned to the bartender and ordered a double vodka on the rocks. He then focused all his energy on Chantal. She wore a low-cut black dress that hugged her body perfectly. He could see the edges of her small breasts. They were perfect. He had to look away because he could feel an erection starting to grow.

"I missed you. I've been so busy that I didn't have time to call, but you were constantly on my mind." Tom had to lie to her once again. He couldn't tell her exactly what had been going on. What was she going to do once she learned the real truth? He wouldn't be able to bear her hurt. He had never liked someone as much as he liked Chantal. The only truth in what he had said was that he really had missed her. He noticed her shyness as she glanced down and turned her head away from him for an instant. She was a bit embarrassed, but she finally faced him.

"I missed you, too." Her eyes were locked on his. "I'm glad you called. I was hoping to see you one more time before I returned home," Chantal said. His heart bled as she spoke those last words. She was returning to Canada. He knew that he wouldn't be able to cross the border since he was still on parole. He didn't want to go back to prison for such a petty offense.

The bartender set his drink in front of him. Tom threw a $20 bill on the counter and waved for the bartender to keep the change. Tom's attention went back to Chantal. He lifted his tumbler, and they toasted each other.

"I wished you would stay a little longer. When are you planning on leaving?" he inquired.

"Really?" Chantal answered. "I plan to leave this Sunday—in two days." He stroked her leg lightly with his hand. Her skin felt so smooth under his fingers. He wanted to feel much more. He wanted to slide his hand way up her thigh, but he restrained himself.

"Why don't we go somewhere a little more private?" He looked around the bar area. "How about that couch over in that corner?"

She nodded and followed him. His hand lightly touched her back as they walked. They sat next to each other. His arm was around her shoulders as he pulled her slightly toward him. He liked the sensation of their skin touching together. "Come over here," he said.

"If I get any closer, I'm going to be sitting on your lap." She laughed at him.

"I don't mind," he responded, and then brought his face close to hers. He stared straight into her sapphire eyes and kissed her on the lips. He pulled back to whisper into her ear.

"I really missed you. You have to stay a few more days." He couldn't keep his eyes off her. He wished she'd stay for a while longer. Why? He didn't want to admit he wanted her like a child wanted candy.

"I can't. I have to return home and get my classroom ready for the start of the school year." He could tell she was torn and really wanted to stay, so he decided to try again.

"We could go to the beach at the Cape and spend the weekend together. I could take a few days off from work. We could get to know each other really well. Would you like that?" He grinned at her.

"I don't know." She smiled. "I really can't tell you right now. I'd have to change my plane ticket and then convince another teacher to help me with my preparations—" She continued talking but then trailed off as she looked at him.

He mouthed, "Please!"

Never in all his existence had he pleaded for a woman to come with him. He must be losing his marbles, but he didn't care. He desperately urged her to stay a little longer. He had never had feelings this complicated before in his lifetime. She stirred all his emotions upside down the minute he was near her. He couldn't deny her anything.

"All right, I'll see what I can do. That is the best I can promise right now. You can call me tomorrow and I'll give you my answer," she told him. He couldn't believe he might have a chance to spend more time with her.

He had lost control as he thought of keeping her here longer, but he didn't care. All that mattered was Chantal.

"I'll make reservations tomorrow—wait." He thought of something. "I have a friend of mine that has this small house by the beach at the Cape. I'll give him a call and ...." He didn't have time to finish. She poked him in the side, then wrapped her arm around his midsection and kissed him on the neck. Her lips were tickling him. She was driving him crazy with lust. He could feel it. He wouldn't take no for an answer. He could already feel her naked body under him rubbing against his in his mind.

"John, I still have to check everything out first." She chuckled at him.

"So, we are all set?" He kept on her. Chantal shook her head no. He loved to hear her laugh. They talked at the bar, had a few more drinks, then it was time to send her home. He really did not want to, but he knew she had to go. They walked outside, and he guided her by the hand to the side of the building, where few people could see them.

"Where are we going?" Chantal asked.

"Now, come here and kiss me like you're going to miss me," he said, and then pulled her to the side of the building. He pressed her back against the wall, wrapped his hands around her waist, and let his body press lightly against hers. He could feel her small breasts rub against his chest. He bent his head, and when his mouth touched hers, their tongues played. He felt the area between his legs begin to grow. Her arms were around his neck, and he slid his hands around her backside, bringing her closer. When they finally separated, they both were breathless.

He looked down at her and said, "See what you'll miss if you don't come?"

"Yes, I can feel it," Chantal replied, and then they both laughed. They walked to the corner to hail a taxi. He hugged her one more time and then let her go. He was left alone on the sidewalk as he watched her leave. He was pretty sure they'd see each other again—very soon.

CHAPTER 9

Chantal got home late. Gabrielle and the rest of her family were sleeping peacefully in their bedrooms. However, Chantal lay in bed, wide-awake, as her mind tried to process the last hours of her evening out with John. What was she going to do? She really wanted to spend more time with this man. She knew that if she went with him to Cape Cod she would definitely make love with him. She wanted to with all her heart, but would she be able to leave after being with him? What would happen if she got involved with him? Then what? Would her heart be torn apart? She had to realize that his life was here, and hers was not. She was so confused. She needed someone to help her make a decision.

Chantal decided that she would talk to Gabrielle in the morning. Gabrielle had gone through a similar situation when she and Bernard had first begun dating. Chantal hoped her circumstances would turn out as well as Gabrielle's had. Chantal turned on her side and closed her eyes. She would deal with it tomorrow morning. There was absolutely nothing she could do now, so she might as well get some rest.

Morning came sooner than she thought. She awoke at dawn and tried to fall asleep again but could not clear her mind. She decided to go ahead and get out of bed. She walked to the bathroom, showered quickly, and threw on the first things she saw—jeans shorts and a blue t-shirt. She then went looking for Gabrielle. Chantal needed her advice and someone to talk things over with, but she would make up her own mind at the end of the day. She already knew her answer.

Chantal entered the kitchen and let out a sigh of relief. Gabrielle was up and about, fixing breakfast as she liked to do for them every morning.

"Good morning. So, how was your big date last night?" Gabrielle asked, smiling Chantal's way while she scrambled eggs. The sun shone through the window behind Gabrielle. Humming birds dashed back and forth to drink sugar water out of the bird feeders. Chantal was glad she and Gabrielle were alone in the room. She sat down at the granite counter near Gabrielle. She noticed that coffee had been made, so she grabbed a mug from the cabinet and poured herself a cup.

"I had a absolutely great time. He's so handsome, considerate, and polite, and I have to say, I think he's a good man." She chuckled to herself as she added cream to her cup. She carried her cup back to the counter, pulled back a stool, and took a seat.

"I don't need that much info. Are you going to see him again before you return home?" Gabrielle asked, but when she didn't get a response, she looked up at Chantal. Chantal was sipping her coffee and staring at her.

"What? Spill it!" Gabrielle blurted out.

"He asked me to stay longer and go to Cape Cod with him for the weekend. There, I said it." Chantal just stared at Gabrielle, who had stopped scrambling the eggs. Gabrielle's eyes widened, and her mouth fell open. She was speechless for endless seconds. Then she placed both of her hands flat on the counter.

"Oh! My Dear Lord!" was all she could utter. Soon Gabrielle burst out laughing, and Chantal began laughing with her.

"It's not funny. What am I going to do?" Chantal didn't want to laugh, but she couldn't keep it in any longer. Both friends were laughing hysterically. Chantal wiped tears off her face and had doubled over with belly cramps from laughing so hard.

"Stop it! Please, this is serious!" Chantal kept trying to get Gabrielle's attention, but Gabrielle couldn't stop snickering. After a few more minutes, the laughter died down a bit, and they both looked at each other.

Chantal pointed her index finger at Gabrielle and said, "I need help. Advice." Gabrielle was still trying to catch her breath as she giggled.

"I think it's hilarious, because when I first met Bernard the same thing happened. I turned to Sophie for help. She told me not to go, but I did anyway, and guess what? I was right. So I'm going to tell you to go. Go and have a fabulous time. That's the only way you will ever know if this relationship has any chance of succeeding. Do what you need to do, but go. I'm not going to tell you otherwise. I'm happy for you." Gabrielle came over to where Chantal sat and wrapped her in a hug. Chantal felt a load lift off of her shoulders. There was no dilemma anymore. She knew what she had to do.

"Thanks, you're a true friend. I need to go make a few phone calls—I have to change my airline ticket and notify the school that I won't be there until next week. What the hell? I'm only going to live once, right?" Chantal was thrilled. All her concerns were gone. She couldn't wait to see John again and spend so much time with him.

"That's right, girl." Gabrielle deposited the eggs in the pan and continued making breakfast. Chantal walked away, overjoyed.

Later in the afternoon, Chantal's cell phone rang. Her heart skipped a beat because she knew it was John. She answered right away. "Hello?"

"Hi, gorgeous," Tom said in his naturally seductive voice.

"Will you stop saying that? Every time you say it, I blush. But at least this time you can't see me," Chantal replied.

"I wish I could see you. I love to tease you. So, are we on for this weekend?" he asked. "I got time off until next Tuesday," he continued.

"Then I suppose I'll have to go," she replied. "I called and changed my airline ticket so I won't have to leave for at least another week, and I'm all set at work," Chantal explained. She was looking forward to spending more time with this man. She was beginning to like him a lot, and she was getting sexually aroused just thinking of what was to come this weekend.

"My buddy said I could have his house for the weekend. It's in the Hyannis area. Oh! And please make sure to bring a bikini," he informed her, laughing.

"Anything else I should bring?" she joked.

"Just yourself," he replied. "I can't wait to see you again. But I have a small problem. Could you meet me in town? We could leave from there after I finish at work. I still have a few things to pick up, and then we can go."

Chantal was a bit disappointed that Gabrielle wasn't going to meet John, but maybe next time. "Sure, where do you want to meet?"

"How about I meet you at Faneuil Hall Marketplace. Do you know where it is?"

"Yes, I know it, but where do you want me to meet you?" Chantal was worried that John wouldn't be able to find her. The place was huge and had tons of people.

"I'll find you. Listen to me very carefully: there's only one Starbucks shop in the whole marketplace. It's in the beginning of The Quincy Market Building. Just go in there, order a coffee, and have a seat. I'll meet you there. I promise. I'll pick you up—let's say—around two tomorrow. How does that sound?" Tom asked Chantal.

"Hold on. I need to write this down." Chantal was nervous. She picked up a pen from her side table and found a piece of paper. She noticed that her hand was trembling slightly. She grabbed the phone again and placed it against her ear.

"Can you repeat it?" she asked, and he did. She wrote it all down.

"Are you all set now? I'll call you—just be there. I only have one more question for you. What will you be wearing, gorgeous?" He said the last sentence very slowly. It made her laugh and wish he was near her, but she would have to wait until tomorrow.

"You will have to wait and see. Ha! Ha!" she answered him.

"I can't wait. See you later," he said, and then hung up.

Chantal couldn't wait either. She started packing a small bag right away. It was going to be a long wait. She figured she might as well go see what Gabrielle was doing for the rest of the day.

***

Tom drove from Worcester to Boston in record time. He couldn't wait to see Chantal again. He parked his truck in a parking lot off North Street and walked as fast as he could without running to the entrance of Faneuil Hall. He kept his eyes opened, scanning the crowd assembled before he continued toward Starbucks. He wanted to be certain that his cop 'friend' wasn't tailing him again or, worse, that Gabrielle hadn't dropped off Chantal and would spot him. He wasn't prepared to face that challenge—

that was for sure. He didn't see anyone, so he put his hand up to shade his eyes against the glare of the sun and looked through the window of the coffee shop. He saw Chantal sitting by herself at a small table, waiting for him to arrive. Never had he thought that he would have such feelings for a woman in such a short amount of time. She could take all his tormented thoughts away with a touch, and the feeling of her skin against his soothed his worries.

He had had many women in his lifetime. He had loved them and then he had walked away without even thinking twice about it. This time, he knew it would be extremely difficult to leave, especially after he spend the weekend with Chantal. He knew that, as much as he wanted it to, this relationship couldn't go any further. Ten years ago, Chantal's best friend had hit him over the head with a vase to stop him from killing her future father-in-law, Ron Rian.

How could a relationship with Chantal ever work? Tom had to be realistic. When she found out who he really was, she would run in the opposite direction. The only consolation was that she had awakened something that had been buried deep within him. He had never thought that he would have feelings like this. He truly cared for her, and he knew he had to abandon her after this weekend for fear that she would find out who he was. But for now, he was going to make memories that would sustain him after she was gone.

He pulled the handle of the door and walked leisurely into the shop. He approached her quietly from behind, slid his arms around her shoulders, leaned down, and kissed her neck.

"Hi gorgeous," he murmured into her ear. She tilted her head so that he could kiss her on the lips. Tom moved a chair next to Chantal and sat down. He noticed how nice her exposed legs looked, one crossed over the other. She was wearing a pair of white shorts and a tight low-cut pink t-shirt. He brushed his fingers against her knee. She didn't protest. He glanced up at her and licked his upper lip as he thought of how much he desired her.

"You look—" He was speechless. "Wow!"

She looked away, flushing. Her cheeks were pink once more. "You're not bad yourself," she replied with a wide smile. She stroked his cheek with the outside of her hand. He cupped his hand over hers and brought it to his mouth, then let his lips lightly graze her palm. She gasped at his touch.

"Are you ready to go?" he asked as he reached for her small backpack. She stood up and walked toward the exit. Tom examined her hips and her butt as she exited the store. Just thinking about her naked aroused him. She was going to be his for the whole weekend. *How lucky could a man be?* Tom asked himself.

When they arrived at the parking building, he pushed the button for the elevator. After the door opened, they took the elevator to the top level where Tom had parked his truck. They were finally alone. He turned toward her, slipped his hand against the small of her back, and drew her against him. Her arms automatically went around his neck, and he could feel her small breasts against his chest again.

"Come here," he said, pressing his mouth against hers. She moaned as he kissed her passionately, reciprocating his advances. Chantal was so tiny, and he easily lifted her off the ground. Holding her drove him wild with desire. This woman knew exactly how to turn him on. He felt the elevator stop. As much as he hated to, Tom let go. He gently placed her on the ground, and they separated.

He took her hand in his and led the way to his vehicle, clicking his key to open the door. Once inside the truck, they just sat there. Tom wanted to tell her what was bothering him. Hands on the steering wheel, he stared straight ahead.

"Chantal." He turned his face toward her and locked eyes with her. He placed his hand on her leg. "I want you to know that I haven't been away with a woman for a very long time. It's not something I do on regular basis." He hadn't had a woman since he had been to jail ten long years earlier. Tom was a bit nervous, like it was his first time all over again.

She covered his hand with her. She held it for a few seconds, and then she spoke.

"I appreciate you telling me. I'm as nervous as you are. We'll take it one step at a time. How's that?" she replied, squeezing his hand.

"Thanks. I knew you were special." He leaned over to kiss her cheek. He felt like he could bare his soul to her, and she would understand. Everyone knew him as a big tough guy who could kill you in an instant. But deep down he wanted to be loved by a woman who understood him and who didn't judge him according to what people said. He wanted to show to her that he could be loving and affectionate like any other person. He turned the key and drove out of the parking building.

They drove out of the lot and headed south to Route 3. Depending on how bad traffic was on the Bourne Bridge, it would take at least an hour and a half to get to Hyannis. Tom didn't mind if it took longer, though. They talked about Chantal's job and her hobbies, but Tom didn't say too much about his own life. He didn't want to lie to her any more than he already had in the last week or so. Right now, he had good tunes and a woman he was falling for by his side. He was happier than he had been in years. He didn't have a care in the world. All he wanted to do right now was be with her, and Tom knew he had made the right decision when he had chosen to spend more time with Chantal.

They arrived in Hyannis late in the afternoon. They were both famished, so they agreed to stop at Baxter's Restaurant and Boathouse. It was one of the oldest eateries on Cape Cod, and the restaurant was built over the water. Tom walked up to the hostess.

"Hi, could we have a table outside, please?"

"Sure, just follow me, please." She brought them to their table.

"This has a great view of the local fishermen unloading their daily catch, and you can watch the other activities that are going on in the harbor," Tom informed Chantal.

"This is just perfect. I love it. What a great, relaxing place!" Chantal exclaimed as she perched herself on the edge of her seat. "Look over there at all the boats!" She was pointing at the fishing boats. "This is beautiful." Tom was watching her surprised expressions, her hair as it floated around her face in the wind, and her blue eyes as they sparkled like the ocean.

"You're the one that's beautiful," he said as he sat beside her. He then stretched out his hands, took both her hands in his, raised them to his mouth, and kissed them.

"I am glad you like it," he told her as he pressed his knee against hers under the table. She wrinkled her nose at the touch, then pouted her lips, her eyes dancing at him. Tom couldn't help but chuckle. She picked up the menu and quickly examined it before setting it to the side. "So, tell me about the house we're going to."

"Well, it's a shingled house. It isn't very big and only has two bedrooms, but it's cozy and has a fireplace and a wrap-around porch with rockers, I'm told. And it's close to the water. It's been a few years since I was there last, but I do remember it being nice," Tom answered.

They both ordered fish and chips, the specialty of the restaurant.

"What about dessert. Chocolate?" Tom remembered.

"Sure, anything—chocolate, but if you prefer, I can be dessert," she teased in a low voice. He inhaled and exhaled slowly. He curled his finger, beckoning her to come close. She leaned close to him. He could see the outline of her breasts, and that was not helping the situation.

"I would love for you to be my desert. I shall lick you all over and then eat you up," he whispered in her ear, teasing her.

"I'm finished. Let's get out of here," she replied and folded her napkin, placed it on the table, and pushed her chair back. Tom winked at her. He deposited cash on the table and escorted her out of the restaurant, back to his vehicle. They were on their way to the cottage. The thought of having her all to himself for a few days was driving him crazy. Just thinking of her naked body next to his was unbearable. He peeked her way, and she smiled.

She moved closer to him and placed her hand on his thigh. She began stroking his upper leg, running her fingers from his knee to his groin and then back down again. He turned his head toward her and grinned at her. They finally arrived, and he parked the truck in the driveway, stopped the engine, and hopped out to help her retrieve her bag. Even though the front door wasn't far, the walk from the truck to door felt endless. Tom took the key his friend had given him from his pocket and unlocked the door.

"Welcome. Come on in." He motioned, rather than telling her, to go forward because his mouth was a bit dry from all the fondling. He followed her inside and brought their bags to the larger bedroom. She was right behind him. She entered and walked to the bed, jumped on it, and then lay down, stretching her arms across the bed as she closed her eyes.

Tom watched her closely, as he stood at the entryway of the bedroom. He savored every inch of her body, dying to satiate his hunger for her.

"This bed is just—not too soft, not hard—just perfect." Chantal opened her eyes. She patted the top of the bed to call him over to her. He felt like he was moving in slow motion as he walked toward her. He wanted to immobilize this moment. He knelt on top of her, his knees on either side of her body, still watching her, not taking his eyes from hers. She rubbed her hands against his thighs.

"Did you want to try out the bed?" he asked her, smiling. She nodded to him. He leaned over her body and pressed his mouth against hers. He enfolded her in his arms and slid his hands up her shirt, feeling her soft skin. He could feel his rod growing as it rubbed against her body. He lifted his head away from her. He stopped and stared at her. He had to ask her.

"Are you sure that you want to—?" He never finished his sentence. She interrupted him and said the words he had been longing to hear.

"Never been so sure in my entire life," she answered him and pulled him back down to her. There was no turning back now. He yearned for the tenderness and affection this woman offered him.

CHAPTER 10

They were lying under sheets breathless, sweaty, and entangled in each other's arms. Chantal was still kissing John's chest. Her head rested under his chin. She could feel as his chest went up and down, and she heard his heart beating against her face. The house was quiet. There were no sounds except the ruffling of the bed linens and birds singing outside their window. She was content, and she could happily lie next to this man forever. One of her arms was stretched across his across his body. He stroked her bare back with his fingertips, lightly tickling her.

"So, tell me, where did you learn those moves?" she teased him.

"You haven't seen my best moves yet," he said, nudging her in the side. She burst out laughing. She had to tell him to stop. She loved the good humor he showed her at the most unexpected times. He was always so attentive to all her needs.

"Would you like a glass of wine? Maybe some cheese and crackers? I'm not sure what my buddy bought when I asked him to pick up a few groceries," he told her.

"Sure. Whatever you can find would be nice. I'll come and help," she answered him. She tried to move away, but he held onto her, his arm around her waist so she couldn't budge.

"Don't move even an inch from this bed, understood?" he said in a stern voice. She nodded her head.

"I'll find and serve whatever is available. I just want you to keep this bed warm because I am coming right back," he said, and then let his arm slip away. She felt a chill when his body moved away. She pulled the sheets over her mouth and hid her face.

"I won't move. I promise," she responded. She watched him as he threw the sheets off his body, stood up, and walked out of the room butt-naked toward the kitchen. *Nice derriere*, she thought. She couldn't wait for him to return.

She moved her head toward doorway of the bedroom and ogled at him until he was out of sight. She noticed a piece of his clothing that was lying on the baseboard of the bed. She reached over and dragged it toward her. It was his black t-shirt. She brought it to her nose and inhaled the scent of his cologne. It pervaded all of her senses. She pulled it over her head. It felt good to wear something that belonged to him. She pulled her buttocks up so she could sit up and rested her head against the headboard.

She could hear the noise of glasses clicking together and cabinets opening and closing. She really wanted to get up and spy on whatever he was doing in the kitchen.

"Are you sure you don't need any help?" She yelled in his direction. A few seconds passed by before she heard him yell back.

"Don't leave that bed."

She chuckled. She waited patiently in the bed and smoothed the sheets until she saw him walking back, still naked. Yeah! She really could get used to seeing this man walking around naked. He had the most toned physique she had seen in a long time. He wouldn't have to try hard to persuade her to jump his bones again.

He carried the tray toward her, not seeming to be disturbed by the fact that he was walking around naked. As John approached Chantal, he winked at her. He sat down next to her, pulling his legs into the bed while holding the platter. She covered his legs with the sheets. He turned his attention to her and frowned at her.

"Now, first, I did not tell you to get dressed. I do like the way you look naked. You have such beautiful body, but I'll have to overlook that you hid it from me." He leaned over, kissed her cheek, and then licked her earlobe. He offered her a wine glass.

"We only have red wine." He had already opened the bottle, so he poured some into her glass before filling his own.

"We have cheddar cheese, salami, and grapes and I found these crackers. His wife must have done the shopping because I know he wouldn't buy this stuff." He brought his glass up, and they touched their glasses.

"This is absolutely perfect. I couldn't have asked for anything more. Well, we could–never mind." She smirked at him. She took a cracker, placed a piece of cheese on it, then fed it to him. They ate the food and drank the whole bottle of wine within an hour.

"Since we no longer have wine, we've eaten all the food, and you don't like my attire, I guess there is nothing left for me to do but take it off." She grabbed the bottom of his t-shirt and pulled it over her head. She threw it on the floor. He tilted his head from right to left, snickered then rolled on top of her.

"Now you did it. I am going to have to take advantage of you," he whispered as he brushed his lips against one of her breast. She could feel his hard erection rubbing against her leg.

"That's fine by me." She raked her fingers through his hair then planted a lustful kiss on his mouth. She could feel the heat building between her thighs.

They made love again, but this time they moved slower, relishing every part of each other's bodies. By the time the moon was high in the sky, they were both exhausted. She rotated to her side, and he snuggled against her back in a protective way. His hand enveloped one of her breasts, and she could feel his breath on the nape of her neck. She closed her eyes and fell asleep within a few minutes.

The following morning, Chantal woke up first. She could hear John snoring lightly next to her. She decided to get up and make coffee–if there was any. She quietly slid out of the bed. Bending down, she picked up his shirt again and pulled it over her body. She closed the door of the bedroom as quietly as she could manage.

On the tips of her toes, she wandered toward the kitchen, unable to believe how happy this man made her and how comfortable she was with him. She didn't think it was just lust. She really would spend all her time with him if he asked her.

Come on, Chantal, you have only known him for ten days. You really don't know that much about him other than the fact that he is a great lover, he can make you laugh, and you love how silly he is. She sensed he liked her back. Otherwise why would he invite her here? He could have enticed anyone. She was sure he didn't have a problem with picking up women, but hadn't he said that he hadn't had sex in awhile? She wondered why. Maybe he hadn't found anyone who he liked. He had the looks, the body, and, apparently, the money to attract numerous women, but he had chosen her. Why?

She found both the coffee and the machine on the counter. She began preparing it and then waited while it brewed. She grabbed a cup from the cabinet and watched the coffee drip away. When it was finally ready, she poured a cup and decided to go sit on the porch and savor the morning. She was almost finished drinking her coffee when she heard the door behind her open. She looked up. John was coming out of the house holding a cup of coffee and wearing only his jeans.

"Morning." He sat beside her and kissed her. "I see you found the coffee. Thanks." He was looking out at the view of the ocean in front of them.

"You're welcome. You were still sleeping when I woke. Did you sleep well?" she asked. Her hand went to his knee, and she began to caress it.

"I haven't slept that soundly in a long time. How about you?"

"I was just fine next to you," she answered. "So, what are we going to do today?" she asked him, even though she wouldn't mind if he said they were going to stay in bed all day.

"Well, we could—let's see, go to the beach, go boating, go sightseeing, drive around, or we could go back to bed?" he said seductively.

"Okay, let me think." she tapped her index finger on her chin. She really liked the idea of going back to bed, but she had never been to Cape Cod and wanted to see a little bit of it.

"Let's go to the beach, and then maybe we could visit this market I looked up on the 'Net.' It is called Ocean Air Market. It looks interesting," she said. Maybe she should have let him decide what he wanted to do, but it was too late now. If he didn't want to go, he would say so, right?

"That sounds good. I'm flexible, and I have no plans. The only thing I want is to spent time with you. As long as you are having fun and are happy. I'm fine," he answered and kissed her on the neck, his tongue tracing up to the back of her earlobe. "Now that we have that settled, you think we could go back inside?" he asked.

"Whatever for? " she said then poked him in the ribs.

"Well," he suddenly grabbed her by the waist, lifted her up, and threw her over his shoulder. She was so surprised that she let out a cry, but she loved it. She was laughing and slapping him tenderly on his butt all the way to the bedroom.

"Now, you are in big trouble, missy," he told her as he dropped her softly on the bed, pinned her arms down over her head, and began kissing her neck.

***

A few hours later, Chantal exited the bathroom after showering. A towel was wrapped around her, covering her most important parts. Tom growled loudly at her. She opened her bag, and she found her bikini bottom. He watched as she slid it up her legs, shielded her butt, and then dropped her towel to put her top on.

"I'm suffering here. I think I need a cold shower," he joked as he pointed to his erection, now visible under the sheet.

"A cold shower might help," she responded and laughed as she strolled away from him. Tom got up and went to take a quick shower. Afterward he found his swimming trunks and shirt.

He found her in the living room, where she was reading a magazine. She looked up and smiled. "Ready?"

"Always," was his reply.

She chuckled then took his hand and guided him outside. He locked the door. They headed to the beach for a few hours of sunbathing.

The sun was warm, and the sand was hot. Chantal kept jumping up and down as they walked down the path to the ocean, the sand burning her feet. He was grinning at her, trying not to laugh. She stopped and said. "Sure, stay there and watch me suffer." How he loved to get her going! She stood still on the hot sand and pouted at him, her lower lip sticking out as she crossed her arms in front of her. He turned around and walked over to her. Lifting her off her feet, he carried her down the reminder of the pathway and then set her on a towel. She was so light that sometimes he was afraid she might break.

"Thanks, you are such a gentleman. I think I might keep you a while," she told him. What was he going to do when she left next week? He was beginning to really like her company. She made him laugh, and no one had ever been so gentle to him. He was going to miss her terribly. What if she ever found out who he really was? She would never accept him. He told himself not to obsess over it. If he was careful, then maybe once he was done with parole he might be able to go see her in Canada. *You're dreaming,* he told himself.

"Could you spread sunscreen on my back for me? I can't reach it." she said as she passed him the bottle.

"It would be my pleasure." There was nothing he wouldn't do to touch her. He rubbed sunscreen on her back then down her legs slowly. He heard her moan.

"I think I might have to go for a swim soon," she told him. The rest of the afternoon was delightful. They played in the water, splashing and running after each other. They took a pleasant walk down the beach. It was mid-day when she decided she wanted to leave and check out the market. That was fine with him.

They walked back to the house, changed quickly, and then headed to downtown Hyannis to the Market Place. It was being held at Aselton Memorial Park. They browsed one aisle at a time. There were so many things to see, ranging from contemporary artisan items to jewelry and specialty foods. They stopped at several tents to taste samples.

"This is so good," she said as she passed him a piece of homemade chocolate fudge. She placed it in his mouth, and he closed his lips around her finger and sucked on it. She smiled then slapped his shoulder affectionately. They stopped at another tent that featured hand-blown glass animals. Tom loved a set of humming birds that were suspended by a wire that was attached to a glass base. They were tiny and delicate, reminding him of Chantal. He decided to get them for her.

"I will take the humming birds. Could you wrap them up, please?" he told the sales lady. She took them and placed them in a colorful box. He paid the woman, and then she passed him his purchase.

Tom noticed a man with a camera nearby. He was snapping pictures, but Tom didn't know whether he was taking pictures of the market or them. Although he didn't look out of the ordinary, Tom was suspicious. He wondered if he was following them. There was nothing he could do now. He had Chantal with him, and he would never place her in any kind of danger. She must have noticed his unease, because she asked. "Is everything all right? You seem distant." He looked down at her and smiled.

"I was just admiring the scenery. How about we get out of here, stop to pick up something to eat, and then head back to the house?"

"That sounds perfect. I'm kind of tired anyway and wouldn't mind just relaxing with you at the cottage," she answered him.

"Great, let's go then." He led her to the entrance of the park where he had parked his truck. He kept an eye out for the guy with the camera, but he had disappeared. He probably was just a tourist taking pictures. No one knew where he was, and no one knew Chantal.

Stop being so paranoid and enjoy the time you have with her. They stopped, picked up sandwiches from a Subway shop, and drove home.

They had finished eating and were just talking when Tom got up and went to the kitchen. He picked up the box holding the humming birds from the bag he had purchased and placed it behind his back. He walked back to the living room and looked down at her.

"I'm really having an amazing time with you, so I bought this for you. When you look at it, I want you to remember our weekend together." He took the box from behind his back and placed it in her hands.

She unwrapped it and saw the hummingbirds." I—I don't know what to say. You shouldn't have, but thank you. They are beautiful, and I love them. You didn't have to buy me anything. Just being with you was enough."

"They remind me of you—tiny, delicate, and full of energy," he said shyly. Buying gifts for women had never been a habit of his. He raked his fingers through his hair, unsure of the present.

"Come here. Sit down," she told him, putting her birds back in the box. She reached over and placed both her hands on his cheeks and said to him. "That is the sweetest thing anyone has ever done for me. I will keep them forever." She then kissed him.

"I think it's time to go to bed," he told her. He stood up and offered her his hand.

CHAPTER 11

Tom unexpectedly woke up to the smell of something burning. He could barely see through smoke that was engulfing their bedroom. He started coughing and then placed a hand over his mouth. His eyes were burning. He rose quickly and closed the door of the bedroom, hoping that would stop the smoke from coming into the room as quickly. It would give him time to wake Chantal and escape. He grabbed his pants and jumped into them. When he had closed the door, he had seen a wall of flames consuming the kitchen. There was no way he could extinguish this fire by himself. It was too big, and he couldn't risk Chantal getting injured. *Don't panic,* he told himself. He had to find a way out of this house.

He yelled, "Chantal, wake up." He shook her. She opened her eyes, and then she started coughing. She was disoriented for a minute, and then she started to scream.

"What? Oh! God, the smoke, the house—on fire!" She coughed some more. He could see tears falling down her cheeks. She scrambled out of the bed. Moonlight shone through the window, illuminating the room. Tom ran to the bathroom and grabbed a towel from the rack. He ran water over the towel and then wrung out the excess out. He came back to the bedroom and gave it to her. She had managed to put on both his shirt and a pair of sweatpants.

"Put this over your mouth. It will help you breathe," He was still coughing. He had to get them out of there. He could see she was scared.

Her hands were trembling, and her eyes were wide. She looked up to him for guidance as she coughed sitting on the floor. While in the Army, Tom had learned how to escape from a burning building. He stayed calm and tried to remember what he had been taught, hoping that Chantal wouldn't panic while he thought it through as if he were on a Special Operation mission. His chest was starting to burn from inhaling smoke. He looked at Chantal and saw that she was now standing by the bed frozen from shock. He took her arm and guided her to the window. She crouched down near it. He tried to open the lock, but it was shut tight. He couldn't open it. They could hear sirens blaring. They were coming toward them, which meant that someone had called the fire department.

"It's stuck. Stay there," he yelled. He moved swiftly to the end table by the bed, took hold of one of its legs, and lifted it. Everything on top of the table fell to the ground. He could hear Chantal coughing even more. He held his breath. His lungs were burning, and the smoke was impairing his vision. He ran around the bed and back to the window in two steps.

"Turn away. I'm going to break the window," he yelled and then swung the small table with all his might. Shattered glass scattered all over the floor when the window broke, but at least there was fresh air coming in.

"Give me the towel," he told her. She reached out and gave it to him. He took it and wiped the broken glass from the sides of the windowsill. He stuck his head outside and looked outside. They were about six feet above the ground. Their landing would be cushioned by the grass. He then placed the towel on the floor to protect her from cutting her feet on the broken glass.

"Come. Give me your hand," he ordered. She reached over and placed her hand in his, still trying to catch her breath. He pulled her close and guided her to the opening.

"Go, it's ... not too far ... jump." He could barely speak. He held his breath he watched as her tiny body disappeared through the window. She was safe. Smoke had flooded the whole room. He was next. He lifted his legs out the window and pulled his body out, jumping to the ground. He landed flat on his back. He gasped, trying to get oxygen into his lungs. He could hear her coughing not far from him, but at least he knew she was alive.

The idea that she could have died terrified him. He felt dizzy. His head was spinning. He just needed more fresh air. He inhaled deeply and exhaled several times. It helped a lot. He stood up and stumbled toward Chantal. She embraced him, and they held on to each other, relieved they were safe.

She tried to yell above the sirens. "John, are you all right?" He saw tears running from her eyes. His heart tightened as he saw her cry. Her face was dirty from the black smoke. His heart melted, and he put his arms around her and pulled her closer. He kept kissing the top of her head. She was safe, she was in his arms. That was all that mattered. They staggered toward the sidewalk.

"I'm fine. Are you hurt?" He could feel her heartbeat against his chest. She was holding him tightly.

"No, I'm fine. I was so afraid," she managed to say before she started sobbing again against his chest. He stroked her back and held her. They walked further away from the house. He could see the fire trucks on the side of the road. The firemen were scrambling to get the hoses off the truck so they could hose down the house. People from the neighborhood were standing around on the opposite side of the street watching the firemen work as the fire roared. He saw an ambulance pull up next to the fire engine. EMT personnel ran toward them.

"Chantal, it's all over. Please stop crying. You're breaking my heart. We're fine." She raised her head up as he looked down at her. He gave her a slight smile. He could feel her body shaking. Her lips quivered—probably from shock and fear.

"Are you hurt? Is there anyone else in the house?" a fireman asked. An EMT stood next to him. Chantal didn't even have a scratch.

"No, we're all right. We were the only ones in the house," Tom answered him.

"What happened?" The fireman asked. Tom looked at him, shrugged, and shook his head.

"I don't know. I woke up and smelled something burning. All I can tell you is that I saw flames in the kitchen. I think that's where it must have started."

"Let me look at your arm. You might need a few stitches," the medical attendant said, carefully extending Tom's arm. Blood was running down his arm. He must have cut it on the glass coming out of the window. Tom hadn't even noticed he had cut his arm. They followed the EMT back to the ambulance. Chantal had her hand over her mouth, and she had started whimpering again. He squeezed her hand and said, "It's nothing that a few stitches can't fix. It doesn't even hurt much." The back doors of the ambulance were open, and Tom sat on the edge of the opening. He and Chantal watched as the medic cleaned off the cut. Tom grimaced as the disinfectant touched him. The medic then placed a bandage on the cut and wrapped it up with tape.

"You probably should go to the hospital and have a doctor look at it. I can take you if you'd like," he told them while putting away the rest of his medical supplies.

"I'll go later on. It can wait. Thanks a lot," Tom said. He had gotten worse cuts than the one he had tonight. He wondered what could have started the fire. Everything had been in order before they had shut the lights out last night. They hadn't left anything plugged in that could have ignited a fire. Maybe it had been an electrical fire. The house had been built in the seventies, and he knew it wasn't used that much in the winter months and only for a few months in the summer.

The fire chief had told them there would be an investigation later to determine the cause of the fire. Tom and Chantal just stood by the side of the street and watched in horror as the house had crumbled and then burned down to the ground. There was nothing they could do. The fire crew had tried desperately to save the house and keep the fire from spreading any further, but when the roof of the house had collapsed, Tom knew it was pointless. The cottage was gone.

It took the fire department a couple of hours to completely extinguish the fire. The morning sun had risen, and they were both sitting on the curb, bundled in a blanket and drinking a cup of coffee someone had brought over to them. There was nothing more they could do. He had called his friend and given him the bad news. Tom was really sorry, but his buddy had said not to worry. It was an old house, and it was insured. Tom felt relieved.

Chantal had called Gabrielle when the sun had risen, and she recounted the whole story to her, telling her how the house had burned down and that John had saved her life. She then assured her she wasn't hurt. Gabrielle had offered to come pick them up, but John had totally refused. He told her he would get her home and not to worry.

Something in the pocket of his denim jeans pocket was pinching his leg, Tom slipped his hand into his pocket and to his surprise, he felt his truck keys. He touched his back pocket. Thank God! His wallet was still in there.

"There's not much we can do here. I gave the fire chief all the information he needed. He said we're free to go." He took out his keys and dangled them in front of Chantal.

"Well, at least we have a way home," she said sadly. Her lips trembled, and she tried to give him a smile but didn't manage to do it. He hated to see her this unhappy. They still had one more day at the Cape. He wouldn't let the fire ruin their vacation time.

"I have a better idea. We still have one more day together, and I'm not going to sit here and weep about something we can't change. It's done now. Let's move on. You aren't going to believe this, but my wallet was still in my back pocket." He laughed. He pulled out his wallet and showed it to her.

"I love plastic. What do you think? We aren't going to let this ruin our weekend," he told her enthusiastically. He patted her knee and offered her his hand to help her from the side of the curb they were sitting on.

"Let's get out of here, get ourselves some clothes to start, and then maybe get breakfast," he told her. He held her by the waist and escorted her to his trunk. He turned the key, and they were on their way to the nearest clothing store.

***

"Did you figure out where you would like to spend our last night?" he asked her while putting another bite of his omelet in his mouth. They were sitting in a booth in a quaint country restaurant off Main Street in Hyannis. The tables had checkered red and white tablecloths, and there was a long red counter where other patrons were eating breakfast quietly.

The food was good. John forked it into his mouth. She watched him. He acted as if nothing had happened, and it was just another day. He was unbelievable, but that was what she liked about him. Not much bothered him. He seemed to live one day at a time and made the best of whatever was happening that day. She pushed her pancakes around in her plate with her fork, not really hungry.

"You know, I can never repay you for what you did for me last night. You saved my life," she stated. He just looked up from his plate.

"That was nothing. Forget it. I would have gone through fire for you," he replied. She could see he meant it, and it warmed her heart to think maybe he had feelings for her.

"That was the sweetest thing anyone has ever said," she answered him.

"I can think of a few things you could do to me to repay me," he whispered. He leaned forward, the corners of his mouth upturned. Chantal just bent her head down and smirked. She was probably turning pink after what he implied. She turned her face toward the window so other people wouldn't see her. She heard him laugh quietly. She couldn't help but smile. She then slapped him lightly on the hand.

"I won't do it again, but we still have to find a room for tonight. That is what we are going to do the minute we leave this establishment," he told her. He stuffed a piece of toast in his mouth.

"Yes, sir," Chantal said and started to laugh. This weekend hadn't turned out the way she had thought it would, but at the moment, she was still sitting with the only man who she cared about and wanted to be with. Her feelings for him kept growing the longer she was with him. She didn't want to leave. Her heart was already starting to melt at the prospect that within forty-eight hours she would be on a flight bound for Canada. She was going to try and be like him—not thinking about it, taking it as it came.

***

They were relaxing with a cup of coffee when Tom got up from the table and said to her, "I want you to stay here for a few minutes. Have another cup of coffee and I'll be right back." She opened her mouth to protest and ask him where he was going, but he brought his index finger to her mouth and said, "Shhh! Trust me, I will be right back." He was gone in seconds, and she was left sitting at the table by herself.

He walked to the hostess at the entrance and quickly told her what happened the night before. He asked her where the most romantic bed-and-breakfast in the area was. She called over her boss, and they went to his office. Tom called the inn and booked a room while the hostess wrote down the address for him. He thanked her and left.

Twenty minutes had passed since he had left her at the table. When he resurfaced her first question was, "Where did you go?" He didn't answer her. "Why all the secrecy?" He reached out and took her hand.

"Just follow me." They drove around for about ten minutes before they came upon what looked like a Victorian home from the 1800s. It was painted green with beige shutters. They could see stained glass windows from the driveway, and it had rocking chairs on the front porch. The sign read: Beachwood Bed and Breakfast.

"Do you like it? It is supposed to have the most charming rooms in the area," Tom said.

"Yes, I do like it." She leaned across the seat, grabbed his collar, pulled him toward her, and kissed him.

"Let's go. I am dying to see the inside. It reminds me of back home, you know." She was bouncing in her seat like a child. It made Tom laugh. They walked up to the front door with their new purchases in hand. He had even bought her a new phone. They entered the foyer area of the house. To their right was a grand room that was furnished with an antique living room set, card tables, and a piano. To the left was a quaint dining room with tablecloths made of lace.

"Good evening, how may I help you?" the owner asked them.

"Hi, the name is Baker. I spoke to you earlier about a reservation," Tom said to him.

"Oh, yes. You're very fortunate—we just had a cancellation today. If you'll fill this out, I'll bring you to your room." He gave Tom a form, which he quickly completed and passed back to the owner.

"Very good. If you'll follow me," he said. Tom and Chantal trailed behind him as he led them up the stairs to their room.

The owner opened the door to their accommodations and then handed the key to Tom.

"I hope you have a nice stay. If you need anything, I'll be downstairs. Breakfast is from eight to ten o'clock."

"Thank you," Tom said, and then closed the door and turned the lock. He stood against the door, watching Chantal investigate her surroundings. She touched the wooden canopy bed and then turned and faced him. The room had two antique chairs and a small bathroom. It also had a queen-size bed with a quilted blanket. Two small windows next to the bed were made of stained glass that gleamed coral and blue as the sunlight shone through them.

He took two steps toward her and whisked her into his arms. He cradled her against him for a minute, but he had trouble resisting her when she was so close to him. He pulled her toward the bed, all the while undressing her as he moved.

CHAPTER 12

Ron was sitting in his study waiting for Raymond to arrive and report his findings. He was trying to concentrate on a business contract, but for some reason he couldn't keep his attention on it. His mind was on Tom. He wondered where he was and what the hell he was doing during the daylight hours. Frustrated, he threw the document on his desk and wheeled his chair to the small bar area at the other end of the room.

He snatched up a bottle and poured himself a neat Scotch in a crystal tumbler. He swallowed it in a single mouthful. His face twisted into a grimace, and he could feel the liquor as it burned down his esophagus to his stomach, but that didn't deter him from pouring himself a second one. He looked at his tumbler and decided to bring it back to his desk. He rolled his chair back to its original spot. He looked at his watch. Raymond was fifteen minutes late.

"Why can't people be on time?" Ron grumbled. "Christ, I pay them well enough. I'm in a damn wheelchair, and I'm never late." He turned his chair around to face the windows and the gardens behind his house. He sipped his drink while admiring the rose bushes. A knock on the library's mahogany door echoed through the room. Ron did not turn or move from his spot.

"Come in," he called out. He heard the door open and listened as footsteps approached his desk and then stopped.

"You're late," Ron scolded. Raymond was silent for a instant. Ron wanted to make sure Raymond understood who Ron was and that no one made him wait. Raymond began walking again, his feet shuffling against the wooden floor.

"I'm sorry, Mr. Rian, but there was a lot of traffic and I got caught up with—" Raymond tried to explain but was cut short.

"Failure with an excuse is still failure." Ron turned his chair; his face wore a stern expression, his eyebrows furrowed into a frown. He set his glass on the edge of the desk.

"Tell me you have news for me." Ron entwined his fingers and placed them on top of the desk. Ron never took his eyes from his face. Ron could tell that Raymond was uncomfortable. Raymond's eyes kept darting around his surroundings, but that wasn't all that was wrong with him. Ron noticed that his cheeks and neck were black and blue, as though he had been in a fight.

"What the hell happened to you?" Ron inquired, but Raymond was still quiet. "What? Speak up," Ron ordered him. Raymond was fidgeting and seemed nervous.

"He found out I was following him. He ambushed me. I wasn't expecting it and I was unprepared, so he—" Raymond's touched his throat with his hand.

"You mean he beat the crap out of you, and now he knows about you and me? You idiot." Raymond nodded. Ron had to close his eyes to think. His temples were banging like a drum, and he could feel the beginning of a migraine coming on.

"A colleague of mine, Lee, has been helping me. Tom doesn't know who he is. He said he tracked Tom to Faneuil Hall, where he picked up a woman. Lee followed him to Hyannis. He's been there since last Thursday," Raymond told him.

"Who is this woman?" Ron asked him. He picked up his drink and gulped it down. Ron winced as it went down.

"We don't know who she is, but Lee took a few pictures of her," Raymond answered.

"Hell, you are absolutely no help at all. What else? Show me the pictures." Ron extended his hand for them. Raymond glanced to the side and cast his eyes downward. He didn't make a move. Ron knew he didn't have the photographs. Ron pulled his hand back.

"Lee has them on his camera. He's still in Hyannis, and he hasn't developed them yet. He told me he was on his way home when I talked to him earlier today. I'll bring them to you as soon as I receive them. Should we continue to watch him?" Raymond asked Ron.

"Did Tom notice this guy—Lee?"

"No, I don't think. Lee's Asian and blends in well with other tourists. From what Lee told me, Tom hasn't made him yet." Raymond said and looked up at Ron.

"Keep track of him, but tell him to stay far enough from Tom so he doesn't get suspicious. Tom is a very clever man. I want him to think that we've stopped observing him. That's when he will make his biggest mistake, and I'll be there to catch him. And bring me those pictures. I want to see them. Or better yet, overnight them to me. Understood? That's all," Ron waved his hand to dismiss Raymond.

He turned his chair to face the garden once more. Ron listened as the footsteps became fainter and faded away. He pondered on who this woman was and how he was going to find out what connection she had to him. He would find a way, but right now he needed another drink.

***

Gabrielle passed a man on her way to Ron's study. She was carrying a small tray that held Ron's lunch, which consisted of a roast beef and tomato sandwich on wheat bread, a Greek salad, and tea.

"Who was that man, Ron? I've never seen him at the house before. Is he a friend of yours?" she asked him. Ron gazed up and smiled at her. She noticed the tumbler in his hand. He had been drinking, but she ignored it.

"Thank you so much, Gabrielle. You didn't have to bring me lunch. We have servants who are paid nicely to do that." He watched her as she placed the tray in front of him.

"You know I don't mind. Plus the servants have enough to do. So, who was he? He looks familiar," she said as she pulled a chair next to his desk and sat down. She crossed her legs. She tried to keep him company as often as she could while he ate. She felt somewhat sorry that he was confined to his chair. She felt partially responsible for what had happened to him.

"Well, if you must know, I hired him to keep an eye on Tom since he is now out on parole. I want to know his whereabouts at all times. I'm afraid he might decide to come after you. I don't want any of you to get hurt in any way," Ron responded. He reached over to the tray, took the napkin. and laid it on his lap. He lifted the sandwich and took a bite. "Not bad," he said as he chewed and then took another bite.

"Ron, do you truly believe he would? I don't think he would come near us. He just got out of jail, for God's sake." Gabrielle didn't want to tell him she thought he had served his time and that he probably had moved on.

"Raymond told me he has been spending a lot time with a lady friend at the Cape. Raymond is going to deliver pictures to me today," he told her. He took a sip of his drink.

"That doesn't mean anything. It might be his girlfriend, or, I don't know. Has he been seen near us?" she asked, a little concerned.

"No, but—" He tried to explain to her, but she cut him off.

"No buts. Now leave him alone. I have forgiven him. What happened was a long time ago. I'm sure he has moved on to better things than us. You shouldn't drink so much." She extended her hand and took the drink from his desk as she chastised him.

"I will never forgive him for what he has done to me," he replied as he tossed his napkin on the tray over his sandwich. "I am the one who suffers here every day." She could tell he was getting upset. His face was becoming red, and Ron was staring straight at her with hooded eyes.

"Ron, you have to calm down before you become ill. I understand your position, but you have to forgive him or at least accept what you cannot change. Maybe then will you have peace of mind and be able to live your life like you should. Don't worry. We are safe. Now, finish your lunch. I'll be back. I have to check on Junior. I love you." She stood up, leaned over, and kissed him on the cheek, and then walked out of the room without another word.

What Ron could not admit was that what had happened to him was mostly his own fault. He had been the one who had ordered Tom to get rid of Gabrielle ten years ago. Ron had thought she wasn't good enough for his only son. It wasn't until she became pregnant that he had finally accepted her. She had given him an heir to his fortune. After that he had tried to stop his initial plan but it had been too late. It had backfired. Tom had attacked him, and Ron was the one who had paid the ultimate price. He would spend the rest of his life in a wheelchair.

Gabrielle had survived when Tom had bombed her inn ten years ago, and she had survived when Tom had attacked Ron's house. Time and Bernard's love had healed her, and she had moved on with her life. She was not going to trouble herself with whomever Tom spent his time with as long as he didn't interfere with her family.

***

Chantal was awake and lost in thought. She didn't want to budge a muscle for fear of waking John. She was nuzzled against his chest. She had never been so happy in her life. When this weekend had begun ,she had only thought of it as blissful fun, but now she was contemplating her future. She didn't want to be separated from him. *This is insane,* she thought. How could she be—she didn't want to say the word, but she knew deep down in her heart that it was true. She had fallen in love with him. What was she going to do? What did she know about love?

"Hey! What are you thinking about? You look so serious," Tom said as he wrapped his arm around her waist and pulled her closer to him.

"Oh! Just that today is our last day together, and I was wondering what we were going to do," she lied. Her heart was aching just at the idea of being alone again.

"I have a confession to make. When I booked this room, there was a clause attached," he told her, and then smirked at her. She lifted herself on her elbows to face him and waited, but he didn't continue.

"Tell me what are you talking about!" she demanded, looking straight into his dark eyes.

"I couldn't get the room for one night. I had to reserve it for a minimum of two nights."

"What?" She couldn't believe that she still had more night with him.

"We don't have to leave today, just tomorrow. Is that all right with you?" he asked her.

"All right, that's the best news I've heard in a long time." She kissed him with ardor. Their tongues played together. Chantal could feel him growing and twitching against her. One of his hands massaged her breast while the other held her close. They had one extra day, and she was pleased. He must care if he wanted to keep her one more night.

It was noon, and they still hadn't left the room. They were in bed, their bodies entangled as they looked blissfully at each other.

"Are we ever going to leave this bed today?" Chantal asked him as she sat up in bed.

"I kind of like it here," Tom said. She stuck out her tongue at him and laughed.

"I like it too, but I think we should take advantage of the nice day and at least go for a short walk downtown. Yes, get up. That's what we'll do. I'm going to take a shower," she pushed the sheet off of her and stood by the bed naked. She bent down to clutch her bag, and then she turned and slowly walked to the bathroom. She left the door wide open on purpose, knowing he would be watching her.

"Hey, gorgeous! Would you like company?" he called softly. She didn't answer, even though Chantal had heard him. So he got out of bed and walked over to join her in the bathroom. She started giggling as he pulled the curtain of the shower.

***

An hour later they were walking hand in hand down a row of shops. Chantal dragged him into every store she saw, and he complied with whatever she wanted. At one of the store, Chantal was trying on a bathing suit when Tom saw a jewelry store called Cape Cod Jewelers and Artisans across the street. He wanted to get Chantal a memento of their time at the Cape. He knew that tonight was going to be their last night together.

"Chantal, I'll be right back. I'm going next door to check something out," Tom told her.

"Sure. I'll be right here. Go ahead," she answered her. Tom crossed the street in a hurry and entered the store. He was looking in the showcases when a salesperson approached him.

"Can I show you anything?" she asked.

"Yes, I would like to see this bracelet." He pointed at one that was near the top of the case.

"That's a very popular one. It's called a Cape Cod bracelet. It's made of silver, but the two balls on top are made of gold." The salesperson took it out and placed it on a square velvet cloth. Tom held it in his hand for a moment and examined it closely.

"I'll take it. Could you gift wrap it?" He took one of his credit cards out and gave it to her.

"I'll be right back with your receipt and your purchase," the salesgirl told him and walked away with the card to the desk.

He liked the bracelet. It was dainty and small. It wouldn't weigh her wrist down. He wanted her to have it, especially since the humming birds he had given her had perished in the fire. He needed to give her something else that would remind her of him so that she didn't forget him and what they had had over this weekend.

Dear God! He was too sentimental. This wasn't him at all, but he couldn't help himself. He was a soldier. He was supposed to be tough and not get emotionally attached to anybody. He didn't want her to go. Maybe if he told her the whole truth about himself—that he had really met her while spying on the Rians and that his name was not John. They could stay together.

The fact that he was an ex-convict on parole would not fly with her. He had better keep his mouth shut and let her believe what she thought she knew. The truth would break her heart, and she would hate everything about him, as well as the week that they had spent together. He couldn't destroy her by telling her the truth of it all. There was absolutely no way they could work this out and have a future together.

"There you are, sir. Everything is all set." The salesperson gave him his credit card and a small box wrapped with silver paper.

"Thank you." Tom told her. He placed the box in the pocket of his cargo short and crossed the street to see Chantal. "I'm back," he told her as he waited for her outside the door of the dressing room.

"I'll be right out. Where did you go?" she asked him. "I went to see where the nearest beach was so you can wear your new suit." He laughed a bit.

"And did you find one?" she inquired.

"Yes, not far down the road," he lied, but he wasn't concerned. There were beaches everywhere. Chantal came out in a skimpy bikini that barely covered her breasts.

"Do you like it?" She walked out then turned in front of him.

He pulled her to him and whispered, "If you keep this up, we won't be going to the beach." He slapped her lightly on her derriere.

A few minutes later she told the salesgirl, "I'll take it, but I'm going to keep it on." Tom paid for the bikini and then they were off to find a beach.

Tom and Chantal didn't notice the tourist parked down the block in his Toyota. He followed them and took pictures of them.

CHAPTER 13

"What do you say we go dancing tonight?" Chantal asked him. She was lying on her belly, propped up by her elbows, as she watched the sunset over the ocean.

"Dancing? I don't dance," Tom replied then shook his head.

"We are going dancing," she told him. "I'll show you how to dance."

"I have two left feet. I—" Tom began, but Chantal got on her knees and pleaded.

"Please, let's find a place where we can have dinner and dance. That way you can think about it." She was trying to make him agree, so she gave him her puppy eyes and dipped her face down. She knew he would give in. He hadn't refused her anything so far on this trip.

"All right, all right, I'll go." He gave in. Chantal hugged him.

"Let's go," She said. She jumped up, quickly picked up her towel, and threw her cotton dress over her head. She was ready. "Great. I'll ask the bed-and-breakfast owner. I'm sure he knows a nice place." Chantal looked down at him. He hadn't moved an inch and was still sitting on the sand.

"You know it's a good thing I like you, because I really don't dance." He rose and placed his arm around her shoulder.

"Thanks. I like you, too," Chantal told him, but what she really wanted to tell him was that she loved him. She was afraid she would scare him away. She had never said those three small words to any man.

An hour later, they were at standing at the reception area of their B&B.

"Good evening, how may I help you?" the owner said. Chantal took a step forward and asked, "Do you know of a place in town where we could have dinner and then do some dancing afterward?"

"As a matter of fact, there's a restaurant called Embargo on Main Street. It's a tapas and martini bar, and they also have live entertainment on weekends," he answered.

"What kind of food do they have?" Chantal asked. The owner opened a drawer in the desk, took out a menu, and passed it to Chantal.

"Here's the menu. You can take a look. I highly recommend it. The food is great, and it has great martinis." The owner replaced the menu in the drawer. She thanked him, and they were on their way.

***

"Wow! This place is booming. I hope we can get a table," Tom said to Chantal when they arrived at Embargo. But in less than half an hour, they were sitting in a corner booth; they had ordered and were waiting for another rounds of drinks.

"I love this place. It's so vibrant, and the people here have a lot of energy," she said to him. She observed the people on the dance floor as they moved to the music.

"I have a gift for you. I wanted you to have something that would remind you of me when you returned home." Tom pulled her the box from his pocket and placed it in front of her.

"You shouldn't have. Now I feel bad because I didn't get you anything," Chantal said, all choked up. She bowed her head and looked at her hands.

"I don't need a gift. I'll never forget our time together," he told her.

He pushed the box toward her again. She took it in her hands and unwrapped it slowly. She removed the top and saw the Cape Cod bracelet.

"It's beautiful! Thank you so much! You are too kind," she placed it on her wrist and touched it lightly with her fingers.

"It's perfect—just like you." Her eyes watered. She blinked several time, trying not to cry, but a single tear rolled down on her cheek. Tom reached over and wiped it away with his finger.

"Guess what? It's time to dance," He took her arm and led her to the dance floor. She started to laugh because he was an awful dancer. His arms were all over the place, and he couldn't coordinate them with his feet. The next song was a slow one. She extended her arms and reached out for him. He placed his hands around her waist. She didn't care that he was a bad dancer, only that he was holding her. She laid her head on his shoulder and enjoyed her last night with him.

Tomorrow was going to be a painful day. They would head home, and then she would packed to return to Canada in a few days. What was she going to do? She wished she could live here, but it was impossible.

Chantal and Tom never realized that a man who was sitting not too far had taken several pictures on his iPhone while they were dancing. He looked no different than any of the other people having a drink at the bar.

***

The next morning, they slept late. Tom could hear Chantal breathing next to him. He opened his eyes and stared at her. Her curls were all over her face, and her skin as smooth as silk. She looked so peaceful sleeping next to him. Her face was less that a foot from his.

"I love you, Chantal," he whispered so low he could barely hear the words.

He had to tell her, even though she could not hear or respond to him. He had never told anyone those three words, but for some reason he felt as though a load had been lifted from his shoulders. He had told her. Chantal stirred and rolled over. He watched her until she woke up.

"Hi there, gorgeous!" Tom said to her, as he had every morning since they had been together.

"I might have to record that sentence so I can play it when I go home. I'm going to miss hearing it." She leaned forward and kissed him on the mouth.

"When will you be coming back to Boston?" Tom asked her. He couldn't believe he had asked her that question, because after today he had to let her go. He had plans that couldn't involve her, His mission—that was all he had thought about when he had been in prison. Revenge had given him strength and hope for the future, but now it didn't seem as important. He had to finish his mission though.

"I really don't know. I start teaching next week, and the next break I'll get will be Christmas. Why?" she asked.

"I was thinking. I just thought I'd ask," he answered. He couldn't give her hope because he didn't know if he would survive the next few weeks.

"Oh! I think we should get going back to Boston. I still have lots to do," she said, then smiled at him. He could tell that his answer had surprised her and that she was hurt, but she would get over it. She was better off without him—but was he better off without her? She would be the only woman he would ever miss and long for.

"Sure, let's get going. We can stop for breakfast along the way. Is that okay with you?" he asked, but turned his face away so she wouldn't see how sad he was.

"That will be perfect." She gripped the covers and pushed them off of herself, got up, and walked to the bathroom, but this time she shut and locked the door. He could hear the sound of shower water running. He grabbed the remote control, pressed the on button of the television, and looked for a sports channel to muffle the sounds he knew were coming and he definitely didn't want to hear.

***

Tears, mixed with the water, were flowing down Chantal's cheeks. She had to gain control before she went back out to the bedroom. What had shocked her the most was what he had said when he had thought she was sleeping—"I love you." He had asked her when she would be coming back but then hadn't tried to make plans. After that, he had kind of pushed her away. Why?

Maybe he was afraid of commitment, or she came on too strong. She didn't know. He had given her a bracelet to remember him by, so what was his problem? Maybe he feared that she might not love him and feel the same as him. She would have to tell him how she felt about him before she left to go back to Canada. She finished dressing, and then—only when she was ready—did she exit the bathroom.

They were back on the road, driving toward the Boston. Neither one talked much. There was a bit of tension in the air. Chantal was determined to let him know how she felt, but when was the right time? Why had he told her he loved her?

"There's a restaurant up here. Are you hungry yet?" Tom asked, but his eyes were glued to the road. He wouldn't look at her. It broke her heart to even think he was going to leave her, but there was no other way.

"Sure, that sounds great. I could use some food and a cup of joe," Chantal said with as much enthusiasm as she could. She turned her head toward him and glanced at him. She placed her hand on his knee. He moved his head toward her, so she gave him a small smile.

"Good, because I'm starving," he replied, covering her hand with his own then squeezed it lightly. It made her feel much better. They entered the restaurant and were seated quickly. The waitress came, gave them coffee, and then took their order. Chantal was playing with her bracelet, turning it on her wrist.

"I wanted to tell you something this morning, but never got a chance to tell you. I just wanted to let you know that if you want to come to visit me in Canada, you are more that welcome." Her eyes were on him, waiting for a response.

"Thank you. I might just do that one day," he said, and then raised his cup and took a sip of coffee.

"I mean it. I would love to have you," Chantal said when she didn't get the answer she was expecting from him. She yearned to tell him the truth: that she not only wished for him to come visit, but that she loved him, that she already missed his touch, his kisses, and most of all how he made her feel when she was with him. Her happiness was slowly being extinguished just by thinking that she might never see him again.

"There is nothing I would love to do more, but right now with work it's going to be a very difficult period. But maybe in a few months," he lied. That was what she wanted to hear. The waitress interrupted their conversation as she placed two plates of food in front of them. They ate in silence until they finished their meal, then continued on their way back home.

***

Gabrielle was in the solarium. She was sitting in a wicker chair that enveloped her with the feathered cushions. The sun was shining through the glass panels that surrounded her. This was her favorite place on the whole estate. It was her quiet place when she needed to escape and be alone. She was reading the local newspaper, but she was haunted by what Ron had told her. Tom was at the Cape with an unidentified woman.

Her best friend Chantal was also at the Cape. As matter of fact, now that she thought about it, why had she never met or seen him? Chantal had described him as dark and handsome, but that could describe half of the men in Boston. Chantal had told her his name was John Baker and that he was an engineer. Gabrielle pondered what else she knew about this man. Nothing.

Not much, she thought. *But wait? Why hadn't he picked her up from the house when they were heading to the Cape? He had told her to meet him at a public place, Faneuil Hall Market Place. Why?*

Think! The answer was so he could evade meeting them. Tom knew who Chantal was and he knew if he came near any of them, they would never let her go. He would be exposed, his identity discovered. He hadn't wanted her to pick up Chantal after the fire either. Strange. All the facts seemed to indicate that Tom was the man that Chantal was with. A chill passed over her. Gabrielle was desperate for information. She tried to remember what Chantal had told her. Chantal had met this man in Newport. If it was Tom, he might have been at their home and might be planning to hurt them again.

Oh! God help us.

She brought her hand up to cover her mouth. What was she going to do? She needed to make sure she was right before she did anything. Maybe Ron was right to think that he wanted revenge and was going to try something. But what? What if he hurt Chantal to get to her? She had to stay calm about this until she had proof it was Tom. But how could she prove it? She stood up. Her legs trembled, beads of sweat formed on her brow, and her newspaper fell to the floor, but she didn't care. She had to grab the side of the chair to steady herself as a wave of nausea passed over her. She closed her eyes and tried to concentrate. She had to get Chantal out of harm's way. She waited until the nausea had passed and her legs were steadier. She took several exaggerated breaths.

Finally she remembered Ron saying something about having a guy follow Tom and take pictures. Those pictures would either verify or alleviate her fears. She had to go find the photographs. Ron must have them by now, but where would he keep them? The only place she could think of was his desk. At least that was a starting point. She would have a look at them before she told anyone else her theory. She had to be certain. She straightened up and headed to Ron's study.

CHAPTER 14

Tom was driving down I-93, heading back toward Boston with Chantal beside him. As usual, the traffic was heavy. Everyone was coming back from the Cape for work the next day. Chantal was telling him stories about her teaching job back home. She told him how she loved to be with her young students and how rewarding it was. Tom listened, but his mind was elsewhere. He was trying to figure out how he was going to get her back to Gabrielle's house without having to drive her up the driveway of the Rians' estate. This had been a thorn in his side ever since he had woken up this morning. He was really dreading the thought of having to lie to her again and then make another excuse about why he couldn't meet her best friend.

There was no way he could bring her to the house. He had to find an excuse, but what? He only had about half an hour left before he arrived at city limit of Newton. Maybe he could get her a cab when he was in Newton and tell her he had to return to work immediately—that it was an emergency. As he was thinking about this, he realized that he needed to move into the slow lane so he could exit the interstate. He flipped on his turn signal, waiting for his chance. What was he going to tell her? He couldn't even tell her about the headache it was giving him. The back of his head was throbbing. It was starting to distract him. He rubbed the back his head with his free hand, but it didn't seem to help.

A few cars drove by him, and then he saw his chance to merge into the other lane. He turned the wheel to his right, but suddenly a blue

Honda was speeding through the same lane he was trying to get into. Tom wrenched the steering wheel to the left to avoid a crash, but the front end of the other driver's car hit the back right side of Tom's truck. The vehicle swerved into the path of the other car. Tom lost control of his vehicle.

"Shit!" He tried to regain control and redirect the truck away from the other car. His foot was on the brake, but they were being pushed so fast that he knew they were going to hit the guardrail. He braced himself and gripped the wheel tighter until his knuckles were white.

Tom heard Chantal's fearful screams echo through the cabin of his truck. He glanced over and saw Chantal clinging to the dashboard as the truck made a pirouette. The truck crashed into the front of the other automobile. The impact of the collision pushed them forward. He felt the adrenaline rush through his body as his heart beat against his chest. His only worry was that Chantal would be harmed. He reached to her to try to protect her but was thrown to the right as they smashed into the guardrail. The force of the collision against the railing caused Tom's truck to flip over it. Tom was shoved against the door again as the vehicle rolled twice then slid down into the ditch. He saw Chantal jerk back and forth against her door, trying to hold on to the door handle.

Finally, the vehicle stopped moving. Tom was in extreme pain. He grimaced and moaned as he turned his head toward Chantal. She was crying, her tears mixing with her blood, her hands were shaking as she tried to unbuckle her seatbelt.

"John!" she yelled as he unbuckled and reached for her hand. He could see she had a deep cut above her eyebrow that would need stitches. Blood was gushing down her face. She was pale, her eyes were wide, and she had an expression of pure terror on her face. Her eyes darted around.

"Chantal, are you all right?" Tom asked her, reaching out for her. A sharp pain shot through his left shoulder and arm. He winced and had to close his eyes as the pain pulsed through him. The pain was so intense that he knew he must have broken his shoulder. He had heard a loud crack when he hit the door. He was having a hard time speaking and breathing. It hurt so much.

"I'm okay. What about you?" She asked. As she was examined him then her hand went to her mouth.

"Oh! My God. Your arm. You're injured." Tom could hear people shouting.

"I called 911 already. He's hurt."

"Don't touch him."

"Are you guys OK?"

Tom felt Chantal gently touch him and heard her say, "Hold on, John. It's going to be fine. I'm not going to leave you. Help is coming. Don't you die on me. Do you hear me!" Those were the last words Tom heard before the pain overwhelmed him, and everything went black.

***

It was now late afternoon. Gabrielle knew that Ron usually did physical therapy with his nurse at this time of the day, and then he took a nap to refresh himself for the evening dinner. She needed answers. She had felt an awful feeling in her gut. She hoped that her intuition was wrong. She navigated the hallway with long strides, heading toward Ron's study. She scanned the area, making sure she was alone. She passed several pictures of her and Bernard on her way.

She arrived at the mahogany door of Ron's office. She sighed and thought she had better knock just in case Ron was still inside. She lifted her hand and tapped lightly. She listened for an answer, but it never came. She gripped the door handle, turned it slowly, pushed the heavy door with her shoulder, and popped her head inside. She quickly swept her eyes over the surroundings. The coast was clear. No one was inside. She entered the room, closing the door behind her. She stood with her back against the door, calculating her next move.

Her heart beat faster. She felt like a thief even though it was her home. She walked on tiptoe to his desk, occasionally turning her head to be sure that no one was at the door. She examined Ron's bureau and sorted through the papers on his desk, making sure that she put them exactly as they were. She then opened the drawers on the right side of the desk. Gabrielle only saw filing sleeves, so she moved to the drawer in front of her.

She gently pulled on the handle. *Damn it. It's locked.* Ron must keep the key close, because he didn't go far from this room for any kind of business transactions. She searched the top of his desk again. Where would he hide a key? She started lifting his phone and ornaments on the desk surface. It was not there. Maybe it was under his desk pad. She slid her hand along the border of the pad. She felt something. *Yes, a key.* She inserted the key into the lock and turned. She heard a click. She pulled out the drawer. Sitting on top of other papers was a yellow envelope. She grabbed it and unclipped the back of it.

Her hands started to shake a bit. She knew this was what she had searched for. She hoped and prayed she was wrong for Chantal's sake. Gabrielle held her breath. She didn't want to have to tell her friend that the man she was dating was an assassin, who had been trained by the Army and who tried to kill her father-in-law, as well. She took out the pictures and gasped.

"This is not possible," she said. The photographs she was holding began to tremble in her hands as she replaced them in the envelope then laid it in the compartment of the desk. She turned the key again and locked the drawer. She replaced the key back where she had found it. She scurried out of the room as fast as her feet would take her.

Her footsteps were heavy as she walked back to the solarium. Her whole body quivered with every step. Her mind was unable to process what she had found in the drawer. When she arrived at her destination, she dropped into the wicker chair, stunned and shocked. She looked down at her hands. They shook uncontrollably. Should she say something or keep quiet? How was she going to deal with this? She would have to say something, or someone might get hurt. She thought of her family's safety. What was she going to do? She had to think this through. She decided to keep it to herself until she could find a solution to this problem. *Lord, help me find the right answer*, she prayed. It was a shock. Gabrielle closed her eyes tried to absorb and analyze what she had seen and tried to think of a way to deal with the information she now had.

***

Chantal was frantic. She was still in the truck next to John. People around her were trying to keep her calm until the paramedics and the ambulance arrived. Someone had given her a cloth to press on her forehead so she could try to slow the bleeding from her cut. She held John's hand.

He had regained consciousness but kept moaning from pain. She could hear sirens coming closer to her. Someone was talking to her, but she was unable to process whatever they were saying. She looked out the broken window and saw a state trooper standing next to her.

"Ma'am, are you hurt? My name is Officer Black," he said as he peered into the cabin of the truck.

"I'm fine, but my boyfriend isn't. He's badly hurt. He blacked out a few minutes ago, and I don't know what to do. You have to help him," she cried, tears dripping down her cheeks.

"Help is on the way. Could you tell me what happened?" he questioned her.

"I really don't know. John was driving, and all of a sudden someone hit us, then the car spun around, and I think we hit the railing and flipped over. How long do you think it will take for the ambulance to arrive?" She was so worried about John. She rubbed his hand in hers and sobbed.

"I'll be fine. Please—stop crying," John murmured to her.

Her tears were flowing like a river. She had to stop weeping, she told herself. *You have to be strong for him; he needs you. It's going to be fine.*

"Here they are, ma'am. Would you mind stepping outside of the vehicle so they can assess the situation and care for your boyfriend?" the trooper asked and then offered his hand to her. She took it and stepped out, but stayed next to the truck. Her eyes were glued on Tom. She watched the men unload their equipment and run toward them. Someone touched her arm. She turned her head to see who it was. It was the paramedic.

"Let me bandage your head until you can get to the hospital for the doctors to examine you," the EMT said, and then he pulled a large piece of gauze from one of his bags, applied it to her wound, and taped it so it wouldn't move. "You should go to the hospital and let a doctor check you out in case you have a concussion," he said to her.

"I will, thank you."

"Ma'am, I need information about the driver and this vehicle," the state trooper said courteously.

"His name is John Baker and that is his vehicle, I think," Chantal answered.

"You don't know if it's his or not?" he asked her.

"Well, I'm not sure. You will have to ask him, I suppose," Chantal was being polite.

"Could you take a look in the compartment to see if the vehicle registration is in there?" Officer Black asked her.

"Sure." She sat down into the cab, opened the glove compartment, and took out a bunch of papers. She found the registration and shoved the other papers back in.

"Here you go." She passed it to Black. He examined it.

"It says here the truck belongs to a Tom Smith. Do you know who this person is?" he asked her.

"No, I don't know who that is," she replied and turned her focus back to John.

"Is that all? If you'll excuse me, I just want to make sure he is well taken care of." She tried to smile, but she had been crying for the fifteen minutes, so she couldn't. She was trying to think straight, but she was so worried for John.

"OK, I'll follow up later. I'll see you at the hospital. Thank you."

Another fire engine had arrived. She took another peek at John and heard him moan. *At least he was alive*, Chantal thought. She watched as more firemen ran toward the vehicle. *Thank God! They're finally here.* A fireman took a metal instrument and jammed it in John's door. It opened right away, and a paramedic yelled, "Bring a board!" Another EMT spoke to John.

"Sir, we know you're in pain. We're here to help you. Don't move. I'm going to check a few things first," the paramedic said as he checked John's neck. When he touched John's shoulder, John winced in pain.

"Chantal, are you hurt?" she heard John say.

"John, I'm fine. I'm right here. Don't move," Chantal answered him. She saw a slight nod of his head as he closed his eyes.

She watched as the paramedic put a neck brace on him. He groaned once again as he bit his lower lip from the pain. "My shoulder and arm—" John told the paramedic.

"I know you're experiencing a lot of discomfort, sir. We'll be as careful as we can," he answered him. "I need to move you onto this wooden board, sir, so we can transport you to the hospital," he said to John. Another man was standing next to him to lend a hand.

"It would be better if you didn't try to help us. Let us do our work, and it might be less painful. Do you understand, sir?" he asked John.

"Yes, I understand," he whispered.

"Now, I would like you to not move your arm and your shoulder. Understood?" The paramedic took Tom's arm and placed it in a sling. Tom nodded slightly.

The paramedics pulled him out slowly and laid him on the wood board. Chantal's heart sank as she saw the pain John was enduring. They laid him on the ground and strapped him to the board, and then a paramedic started an IV in his uninjured arm. The EMTs carried him up the hill to the side of the highway, where they laid the board on a stretcher. John then was wheeled into the ambulance.

"I want to go with him in the ambulance," Chantal told him as she pointed to John. One of the state troopers interrupted their conversation.

"Ma'am, you can call the Department of Highway Patrol tomorrow, and they'll tell you where you can find your vehicle," he told her and gave her papers.

"Thank you." She watched as he walked back toward his squad car.

Chantal hurried to the back of the ambulance and jumped in. She sat down next to John. The ambulance moved slowly at first but picked up speed as the highway opened for them. She could hear the sound of sirens as they went along.

"Where are you taking us?" she asked the EMT who was taking care of John.

"We're going to the trauma center at Massachusetts General Hospital in Boston. They're the best equipped to deal with car-accident victims. They'll take good care of him," he answered as he checked John's pulse.

"Thank you for all your help. It's greatly appreciated," Chantal said.

"Just doing my job. Just doing what I love to do. You're very welcome." He smiled at her, took John's blood pressure once more, and checked his IV. Chantal rested her head against her seat and closed her eyes.

CHAPTER 15

Tom lay on a stretcher in the trauma unit of Mass General. He heard doctors giving orders and people moving around him. Nurses and physicians were all over the place. He could hear cries coming from other rooms. The room he was in was open, the beds separated by only a curtain. They rolled machines in and out of the room as they poked him, pricked him, and examined his entire body. They had finally taken his neck brace off, and a physician in blue scrubs examined every limb while a nurse checked his vital signs again. To his right, Tom could see doctors discussing x-rays. He figured they were his but couldn't hear the conversation. He was in a lot of pain and was trying to understand what was going on. One person had cut off most of his clothes when he had arrived at the hospital. He was wearing only his boxer shorts. Another nurse had given him a shot for the pain, but the pain from his shoulder still shot down his arm.

Finally, a doctor came over and bent over his face to speak to him.

"Mr. Baker, I'm Dr. Rousseau. You were in a car accident and brought here. We took x-rays of your shoulder and arm when you first arrived. Your clavicle, that would be your collarbone, was shattered by the blow you received in the accident. Your humerus, the bone in your upper arm, is also broken. Do you understand?" Dr. Rousseau asked. Tom nodded slightly to him.

"You also have a concussion. The problem is that your clavicle bone needs to be repaired. That means surgery. We have to insert a plate and screw both bones to it. There's no other way. I've called in an orthopedic surgeon to look over your x-rays. He'll be the one to perform the surgery, which he will begin as soon as possible. Do you have any questions?" Dr. Rousseau asked.

"Just one. The woman who was in the car with me—how is she? I'd like to see her," Tom said. He wanted to make sure Chantal wasn't hurt or in need of anything.

"I'll check, but I believe she only had a cut on her forehead, which was stitched, and a headache. I'll send someone to find her and bring her to you. What's her name?" he asked Tom.

"Chantal Arsenault. Thank you," Tom said. His head was pounding really badly, so he closed his eyes to waited for the painkiller to take effect and ease his body's pain. He knew that the worst pain was yet to come. He knew that his secret was going to be revealed and that he would be alone once more. Maybe it was for the best, because now he would be able to complete what he had started. Once his shoulder healed, there would be no more distractions.

Tom had the strange feeling that someone was watching him. He opened his eyes and not far from his bed stood Chantal. He gave her a small smile, trying to tell her he was going to be all right. She had a bandage on her forehead, and her eye was swollen and turning blue. She looked so freighted and lost. Her shirt was covered in dried blood, and her beautiful hair was a mess. Her curls had been pushed away from her face and were wet. It looked like she had tried to wash blood out of them. Even so, Tom still thought she was the most stunning woman he had ever seen in his life. He was so grateful that she had suffered only a cut on her head. God knows what he would have done if she had been seriously hurt. Better him than his Chantal.

Chantal tentatively approached him. He could tell she was nervous. She kept looking at all the instruments around him, and she rubbed her hands on her shirt.

"Hi, John. How are you doing? I was so scared that—" Her eyes watered. A single tear rolled down her face, followed by another.

"Shoot! I promised myself I wouldn't cry, but here I am doing it again." She wiped away the tears with her hand. She reached the bed and walked to his right side. She touched his cheek with the back of her hand and then stroked it. Her touch was more effective than the painkillers they had given him. She was trying to soothe him. She bent forward and kissed his cheek. Tears dripped onto his face.

"Tell me, how are you doing? I see the doctors took care of your cut. How many stitches did they put in?" He winced as he felt a sharp pain. He was hoping that she hadn't had to get too many stitches. He didn't want her to have a scar on her beautiful face.

"Only five. It's not bad. The doctor said that the scar probably will disappear after it has completely healed. But I'm more concerned about you. How are you?" Chantal waited anxiously for him to speak.

"I'm going to be just fine. Don't worry your little head. I'm tough." He didn't want her to worry or cry anymore.

"So, what did they say?" she asked.

"Well, if you promise not to cry—" she nodded and held his hand in hers.

"My collarbone and my arm are broken. I must have slammed into the door when the truck flipped," he told her. Her hands flew to her face. Tom could see her eyes tearing up again.

"You promised," he said to her.

"Okay, what else did they say?" she questioned. Tom hesitated for a moment, but she was going to find out anyway. Better from him than the nurse.

"I have a concussion, and they are going to take me to surgery to put a plate and screws on my collarbone because it's shattered. After that I'll be good as new." He was trying to be upbeat, but when he looked up, it seemed as if Chantal had been struck by a train. She was sobbing quietly again. She mopped the tears away with the tissues she was holding.

"When—?" she asked, sniffling.

"As soon as the orthopedic surgeon gets here, I suppose," he answered. "Chantal, please, stop crying. It hurts me to see you like this. Now stop. I'm not going to die—not yet anyway." He was trying to make her laugh, but he could see that it wasn't working.

She stood next to him and rubbed his arm up and down. "I'll try. Is there anyone you'd like me to call?" she asked.

"No, no one," Tom answered her.

"I want you to go home and not fret over me. I'll be fine." He wanted her to leave, but at the same time he wanted to keep her near. He knew she would call Gabrielle eventually, and everything would blow up in his face. He felt sad, and he wanted to protect her from any more pain, but he knew that he couldn't stop the wheels from turning if Gabrielle showed up here.

"I'm going to stay with you until you're out of surgery and able to function again, " she said, determined not to go anywhere. She retrieved a nearby chair and pulled it to his bed. She sat down and crossed her arms in front of her. She looked around, examining her surroundings.

"Very well. Stay if you must, but I would rather you went home," Tom tried once more. She just shook her head at him.

An hour had gone by, when an orderly came to take him to surgery. Chantal stood and watched as the orderly unlocked the wheels of Tom's bed, hooked his IV to the pole, and started pushing the gurney. He wheeled Tom past the nurses' station and down the hallway. Chantal followed close behind. The orderly turned to face her.

"You can come with us to the doors of the operating room, but after that, you'll have to go to the waiting room," he told her.

"Very good," Chantal said. A minute or two later, they stopped in front of a set of double doors. "Here we are," the orderly said. Tom raised his right hand and looked for Chantal. In seconds, she was holding his hand and leaning over him.

"I'll be right here when you come out. It's going to be just fine," she said and kissed him on the cheek.

"I'll be fine. Thanks," Tom said.

"I'll be back in a few minutes to take you to the waiting room," the orderly told Chantal. She nodded.

The hospital attendant started to move the gurney forward again when suddenly Tom heard Chantal's voice.

"Wait!" The bed stopped rolling. She was beside him once more. She leaned close to his ear and spoke in a low voice.

"John, I want you to know something—I love you," she told him and then kissed him on the mouth. Tom was so stunned he couldn't reply. He just closed his eyes tightly and nodded. The bed rolled through the doors of the operating room. She didn't see the tear that fell from Tom's eye.

What was he going to do? The last thing he wanted to do was to cause her sorrow, but what had he expected? It was supposed to have been only a fling, that afterwards they were both to go their merry ways. *What am I going to do?*

He was still thinking of her and searching for answers when the anesthesiologist placed a mask over his mouth and nose. Within seconds, everything went black.

***

Chantal sat by herself in the small waiting room. Minutes passed like hours. She fiddled with her hands, tried to read a magazine, and looked at the television, but nothing kept her mind off the one she loved: John. Four hours later, she couldn't take it anymore. Tom should have been out of surgery by now. She stood, looked down the hallway at the nurse's desk, and decided to walk over. Her legs ached with every step she took.

"Excuse me." One of the nurses behind the desk looked up.

"Yes, can I help you?" the nurse asked while writing another note.

"Could tell me how John Baker's surgery is going? Has he come out yet?" Chantal inquired. The nurse turned and examined the board behind her. Chantal looked at it, too. John's name was written on it, but she didn't understand what the symbols written next to it meant. She hoped the nurse would give her some news. The nurse picked up a chart and read the notes for a moment.

"He's out of surgery, and everything went very well," she answered and turned back to her work.

"Excuse me again," Chantal said politely.

"Yes?"

"Could you show me where I can find him, please?" Chantal asked. The nurse glanced at her and didn't say anything for a brief moment.

"I am truly sorry, but I have instructions from Mr. Baker not to tell you or anyone else where he can be found. Sorry," the nurse said, and then went back to her work.

"What do you mean you cannot tell me where he is? I'm his girlfriend," Chantal said. Suddenly Chantal wasn't feeling well. She felt a chill rush down her back, her hands became clammy, and she could feel her heart-beat ring in her ears. She reached for the desk.

"I'm so sorry, he specifically said, 'No one, not even my girlfriend.' Those were his exact words, and the file is confidential, so I can't help you. Are you feeling all right? You look a pale. Would you like to sit down or have some water?" the nurse said as she stood up.

Why would he do such a thing? I told him that I loved him. I must have scared him away, but I heard him say he loved me this morning. The nurse was talking to her, but she couldn't comprehend what she was saying to her. Her head was spinning, and she felt weak. Her knees gave way, and she fell to the ground, passing out in front of the desk.

***

Gabrielle hadn't eaten or gone to the dining room since her discovery in the afternoon. She sat in the solarium by herself as she tried to grasp the situation that her friend was in and how she was going to help her out of it. Junior was sleeping at a buddy's house, and Bernard was working late as usual. Thank the stars, because she couldn't function properly. The sun had gone down, and darkness had overcome the grounds without her noticing. One of the servants stood next to her and spoke, but Gabrielle paid her no mind.

"Mrs. Rian, Mrs. Rian," the servant kept saying until she touched Gabrielle's shoulder. It brought Gabrielle back to reality. She hadn't even heard her walk in.

"Yes, Susan?" Gabrielle flinched and finally answered her.

"You have an urgent call from Miss Chantal. She wants to talk to you. What should I tell her?" Gabrielle inhaled, extended her hand to take the phone, and then exhaled.

"Thank you, Susan. I will take it." The housemaid turned and walked away. Gabrielle glanced quickly at her Rolex watch. It was almost nine o'clock in the evening. Chantal was supposed to have been back four hours ago. Something must have happened.

"Chantal, where are you? It's late, and I've been so worried," Gabrielle said, very upset about her friend. Gabrielle raked her trembling hand through her hair.

"I'm fine. I don't want to alarm you or anything, but I was in a car accident," Chantal told her.

"Oh my God! Are you hurt? What happened?" Gabrielle asked, jumping from her chair. She started pacing the floor, afraid for Chantal.

"I'm not hurt. John was though—Anyway, I'll explain everything later. Could you come pick me up? I'm at the Boston Mass General Hospital," Chantal asked.

"Of course. I'll be right there. Are you sure you're OK?" Gabrielle needed to be reassured.

"Yes, yes. I'll be at the front entrance. I'll explain everything later," Chantal said and hung up the phone. Gabrielle heard the phone click, and Chantal was gone. Gabrielle threw the phone on the chair and left the solarium.

Gabrielle walked as fast as she could without running. She grabbed her pocketbook off the counter and headed toward the garage. She opened the door of her Mercedes and touched the button to start the automobile. Her mind was in a whirlwind. She had a lot of questions for Chantal, but right now she needed to go pick her up and keep her away from that madman. She had to make sure that she never saw him again. He was a danger not only to Chantal but also to Gabrielle and all of her family. Her whole body shook at the thought of what could have happened. Hopefully, Chantal would be reasonable about all this. Gabrielle would make her understand the situation. Chantal was leaving to go home in two days, and she would be safe. Gabrielle would find out what her friend knew about Tom.

CHAPTER 16

Tom had made it through surgery. He woke up in the recovery unit, drowsy and in pain. He opened his hooded eyes and then closed them. The nurse came over to him. "Mr. Baker can you hear me? My name is Mary. I'm your nurse. How are you feeling?" He blinked his eyes several times, trying to concentrate and wake up. He watched her as she brought the blood pressure machine closer to the bed and laid his chart on the rolling table.

"I'm just going to check your blood pressure and your temperature," she told to him as she lifted his good arm, wrapped the cuff around it, and read his pressure. She put the thermometer in his mouth, looked at it, and noted the reading.

"I brought you some apple juice to sip on." She brought it close to his mouth, and he took a sip through the straw.

Tom felt so sleepy and groggy that he didn't want to move. He noticed that his shoulder and left arm were in a tight sling that rested on his chest.

"Just lay down and sleep a while. The surgery went very well. Is there anyone you would like me to get for you?" Mary asked him.

"No, I don't want to see anyone—not even my girlfriend. Absolutely no one, understood?" Tom told to her and then frowned at her.

"Very well, I'll write it in your chart. No visitors," Mary said.

"Please make sure, no visitors." Tom saw her nod. "Thanks." He was severing all ties to Chantal. That is how it had to be. He couldn't afford to have any more distractions, so he would end the relationship now. This way he didn't have to say any long goodbyes, and she would get over him faster. She had dropped a bombshell when she had told him that she loved him right before he had been wheeled into the operating room. He hadn't expected to hear her say that. Her words were now engraved on his memory. He hadn't been prepared for that statement. He couldn't even reply to her, he was so shocked. He had left her standing at the doors, but that was how it had to be. No one had ever told him that they loved him. Not ever.

It was the most painful thing that he had ever had to do—to leave her hanging without a response. Even all the killings he had done in the military as a sniper operative hadn't bothered him as much as her words today. It would get better with time. That was all he could do. There might be room for her down the road, but he doubted it would work because he was targeting her friends. He drifted to sleep again, still thinking about Chantal.

A few hours later, he woke up again. This time he felt much more alert. He reached over and pushed the red button attached to the railing of the bed. A sharp pain struck him—as hard as a bat might hit a baseball. He flinched and then moaned, but he was determined not to let it deter him from getting out of here. He decided that he had to start moving, so he sat at the edge of the bed. He looked up and saw that Mary was coming into the room.

"Well, I see you are feeling much better, but please stay where you are for a moment until I can help you. First, how is your pain level? Do you need something for the discomfort?" She asked him and then came closer and stood next to him.

"I could use something," Tom answered her, not looking at her.

"I want you to drink this and eat a few crackers. I'm going to go get you medication. Don't move," she told him.

"How long do I have to stay here? When can I go home?" Tom asked as she was walking away. He wanted to leave and go back to the boarding house. At least he knew that Chantal wouldn't be able to find him there. He had almost expected her to come barging in through the door. He didn't trust the medical staff. They might have told her where he was. He didn't feel like explaining why he didn't want to see her.

"You'll be able to go in a few more hours if everything is satisfactory," she answered him. She turned on her heels and was gone. He hated hospitals. He looked at the clock on the wall. It was already ten o'clock. He might as well rest until she came back with medication. He drank the juice and slid back into the bed as he waited for Mary. Five minutes later, she was back with a bunch of papers, two pills, and a glass of water, which she handed him with the painkillers. He took and swallowed them.

"I'll give you a little more time before I release you. Do you have anyone who can help you get home?" she asked. Tom had no one anymore. He had banished the only person he had ever cared for. Hopefully he had made the right decision, at least for her sake.

"No, there is no one. I'll be fine, but I'd appreciate it if you could call me a taxi," he told her. He closed his eyes trying to deal with both the pain in his shoulder and the pain of sending Chantal away.

***

Gabrielle picked up Chantal at the entrance of Mass General. She took one look at her friend and knew she wasn't the same woman who had left her house a few days ago. Chantal seemed lost in her own world, and pain was written on her face. Her eyes had tears in them, and she had dark circles under her eyes. She walked hunched over, and her lips pointed downwards. She had a bandage on her forehead, a black eye, and dried blood all over her clothes. What the hell had happened to her friend?

"My God! Chantal, are you all right? What happened to you over the last few days?" Gabrielle asked Chantal, very troubled to see her in such a state.

"I'll be fine. I'll tell you all about it after I've had a good night's sleep. I promise. Please, don't question me now," Chantal answered as she turned to face the window.

Gabrielle kept her eyes on the road, her knuckles turning white from gripping the wheel so tightly. She would honor her friend's wishes for now. Not another word was spoken on the drive home. Gabrielle was sad to see Chantal so distraught over a man who had once tried to kill Gabrielle and hurt her family.

How could Chantal feel anything for him? He had tricked her into believing he was an ordinary man, but he was not. He was the most ruthless, merciless man on this planet, as far as Gabrielle was concerned. She now hated him more than ever. She thought she had put all the misery he had caused her behind her, but now he had returned into her life to torture someone else: her Chantal. Gabrielle would make sure he never saw or touched Chantal again, even if she had to beat him with her bare hands. How could he hurt her that much?

They pulled into the Rians' driveway, and Gabrielle parked her Mercedes at the front entrance. She shut off the car but didn't get out right away. She reached to Chantal and touched her arm gently.

"If you need someone to talk with, my door will always be open. I love you. You know that?" She didn't get a response from Chantal; she didn't even glance Gabrielle's way. Chantal's face was expressionless. Gabrielle opened her door and stepped around the car to let Chantal out. Gabrielle extended her hand to Chantal, who cast her eyes upward. She took Gabrielle's hand in hers and got out of the sedan.

"John and I broke up. I'll probably never see him again," Chantal murmured.

"Let's get you into a hot bath and then bed. You'll feel better tomorrow," Gabrielle told Chantal as she continued to cry. Chantal nodded and followed her inside the house without another word. Gabrielle wrapped her arm around her shoulder and directed her to her bedroom in silence.

A few hours later Chantal was sound asleep in her guest room, but Gabrielle wasn't sleeping yet. She was sitting in her sleigh bed waiting for Bernard to arrive home. She had been staring at the chandelier for at least an hour. Her mind was racing with all kinds questions that she wanted to ask Chantal, but she hadn't dared ask any because of Chantal's condition. Gabrielle figured she'd drill her tomorrow.

Gabrielle didn't want to upset Chantal more than she was by inquiring about her accident or Tom. Chantal hadn't said anything specific concerning Tom or their long weekend together. She hoped that Chantal felt better tomorrow and would explain everything. Gabrielle's thoughts were interrupted as Bernard walked into the master bedroom. He came forward and kissed Gabrielle on the neck.

"Sorry I'm late. The meeting went longer that I anticipated. So how was your day?" Bernard asked her, unaware of all the drama that had taken place. She watched him as he took off his clothes and placed them on the chair near the window that faced the gardens. Gabrielle hadn't responded, so he stopped and saw she was in deep thought. He took two steps toward her and sat down beside her on the edge of the bed. He took her hand in his and looked at her, a serious expression on his face.

"Did something happen today with Junior or with my father? I know my father can sometimes be a pain in the butt," he said, still staring at her. She debated whether she should tell Bernard about the pictures she had found in Ron's office and the whole story about Chantal. It would come out eventually, so she might as well tell him now. Maybe he would have some ideas concerning Chantal's situation.

"Junior is fine. It has nothing to do with him or your father. Everything was fine until I found something. Something that I didn't expect to find." She was still tentative about telling him.

"Now you have all my attention. Dish it out," Bernard told her, still looking at her and waiting patiently.

"I don't want you to judge or get mad, OK?" He nodded. He was always a very good listener, but she hoped he would not blow up.

"I'll start from the beginning, then. The other day as I brought lunch to your father, I passed a guy coming out of his office, so I asked Ron about him. Ron told me he had hired him to keep track of Tom since he was out on parole and Ron was afraid he might be up to something." She paused and looked at Bernard, toying with the bed sheets.

"Go on," was all Bernard said, so she inhaled deeply and then continued her story.

"Well, Ron had told this guy to get pictures of Tom, and I was curious. So yesterday I sneaked into his office, opened his desk drawer, and found them. They were pictures of Tom and Chantal together." She felt relieved that she didn't have to keep a secret any longer, but now she had to explain a lot more now that she had mentioned that Tom and Chantal had been together.

"What are you talking about? You mean to tell me that Chantal is spending time with Tom? How did this happen? Are you sure?" Bernard asked her in disbelief. He kept his eyes on her. He didn't move an inch from where he was sitting next to her.

"Yes, I'm sure. He's the guy she has been dating since she arrived. Remember I told you she had met someone? Well it was him," Gabrielle told Bernard. She could tell he was a bit confused and angry. He frowned at her.

"You mean the one she met while we were in Newport?" he asked her. Gabrielle nodded.

"What was he doing in Newport? And what does she have to say about all of this? Doesn't she know this man's history?" he asked her.

"He was probably watching us!" Bernard's voice got louder. He stood and walked to the window. He didn't say anything for a minute, and then he turned toward her again.

"My father was right all along, I thought maybe he had moved on, but now—" Gabrielle could see that Bernard was upset by all of this. He clenched his jaw and closed his fists tightly. "Go on," he said.

"She doesn't know he is Tom. If I recall, he told her his name was John. He tricked her. It's not her fault. She's completely innocent. Last Thursday he invited her to go away with him. She accepted, and they went to the Cape together. She came home tonight very agitated. They were in a car accident on their way home. I don't know what happened yet, but when I picked her up from the hospital earlier, she was shaken up and wouldn't speak to me. I didn't want to ask her too many questions because she was so distraught. She had been crying, so I didn't ask her too much about him. I figured I'd talk with her about him tomorrow after she has calmed down. The only thing I thought I heard her say was that she and John, meaning Tom, were no longer a couple." Gabrielle summarized the story as best she could. She could tell that Bernard was preoccupied with questions. She didn't know the answers.

"Well, that's a good thing. Did you mention this to my father?" Bernard asked.

"God, no! That I couldn't deal with. He would have a heart attack if he knew. He didn't recognize Chantal in the pictures. I'm sure of that, because he told me he didn't know who she was. What are we going to do about this?" Gabrielle asked Bernard. She didn't know what to do. She was torn between protecting her friend and protecting her family. She knew the answer: her family came first.

"All we can do is wait until Chantal wakes up tomorrow and question her then," Bernard answered.

"Let's keep this between us for now and try to keep Chantal away from Ron, because I don't know what he's going to do when he finds out. I wonder why Tom was in Newport in the first place. I don't trust him. Make sure to keep an eye on Junior, and I'll tell security to keep an eye out for anything suspicious. There's nothing else we can do at the moment," Bernard told her. She watched as he walked out of the room to talk to head of security.

CHAPTER 17

Chantal was still in her bed, lying under the covers. The only thing she could think about was last night's events. Her eyes opened when the morning light burned through the window. She must have finally dozed off at some point while crying and trying to understand how this relationship had gone so wrong in so little time. She kept reliving her time with John. She had never anticipated that their relationship would end so horribly. She was heartbroken, and she was extremely worried about John. All she had been told was that he had made it through surgery and that he had requested no visitors, not even her. He had told her he loved her. Why had he pushed her away so quickly after all the time they had spent together? *Maybe ... too many maybes*, she told herself. She needed answers. She pushed the covers off of her body and sat on the edge of the bed. Standing up, she slowly walked to the bathroom.

She flinched when she saw her face in the mirror. Her eyes were puffy, red, and underlined with dark circles from all the sobbing she had done. She reached up to remove the bandage from her forehead so that she could examine her cut. Five small black stitches closed the cut. The area around it was tinged with black, blue, and yellow. *I'm a mess.*

She needed to call him. If he didn't answer, she would go to the hospital to find out if she could get any information on John's recuperation. But first she turned on the faucet, cupped her hands, and splashed her face with cold water. She wiped her face with the towel, looked at herself again, and cringed. She walked back to the bedroom, grabbed a turquoise sweater and a pair of Wrangler jeans, and dressed. She then bent down and searched for her shoes.

She put on lipstick and concealer to trying to hide how wretched she looked. She had a lot to do today. She was leaving tomorrow, and she knew Gabrielle was going to bombard her with questions. Chantal wanted answers too, but she wouldn't be able to get them just yet. It was seven in the morning, too early to contact anyone. Instead she went in search of some Tylenol and possibly a cup of coffee. Her head was pounding.

She could smell the coffee brewing as she was stepped down the staircase. Someone was up. She just hoped it wasn't Gabrielle. She wasn't ready to talk to her just yet. She walked the archway that opened to the kitchen area and saw Gabrielle. She winced, but kept going forward. Her friend turned toward her with a pot of brew and two cups of coffee on a tray. Judging by her stern expression, Chantal could tell she wasn't going to be sympathetic. Chantal tried to smile, but it was only a half-smile that Gabrielle didn't even acknowledge.

Gabrielle walked toward her. *What's the matter with her this morning? I'm the one whose heart was broken, not hers,* Chantal thought. Gabrielle stopped abruptly in front of her. Expressionless, she spoke without emotion.

"Follow me to the solarium. We need to talk." She didn't wait for Chantal to answer. She moved past her and headed toward the solarium, not even looking to see if Chantal was following. *Now what?* Chantal thought, turning on her heels and followed. Why was Gabrielle mad at her? Neither said a word until they arrived at the solarium. Gabrielle put down the tray on the low table in front of the sofa and chairs, which were decorated with sunflowers. Gabrielle sat in one of the chairs and indicated that Chantal should sit across from her, on the couch. Chantal sat. Chantal watched as Gabrielle poured them each a cup of coffee in silence. Chantal was getting a bit nervous due to Gabrielle's behavior, so she decided to say something when Gabrielle passed a cup to her.

"Thanks. And thank you for picking me up last night. I'm really grateful, and I'm sorry you had to see me that way." Chantal spoke softly, then raised her cup to her mouth and took a sip of coffee.

"You're welcome, but I need to explain to you something of crucial importance. Please don't say a word until I'm finished. OK?" Chantal nodded. What the hell was going on with her? Gabrielle raised her cup and drank. She was fidgeting, and it made Chantal tense.

"All right. What's up?" They just sat there and stared at each other for a minute.

"I'm not sure how to tell you this, but I know for a fact that the man you have been dating isn't who he says he is. His name isn't John Baker, it's Tom, Tom Smith. He's the one who tried to kill me about ten years ago. You didn't know me then, but he was responsible for blowing up my business. He also tried to murder my father-in-law. He got out of prison about a month ago, and he's on parole." Gabrielle cast a glance at Chantal.

"What are you talking about? That's not John. You're telling me that John tried to kill you ten years ago and that his name is really Tom Smith?" Chantal said, her mouth open. The cup she was holding started to shake. She tried to steady her hands but couldn't, so she placed the cup back on the tray.

"I know this is hard for you, Chantal, but you have to believe me. I know this man."

"How do you know who he is? You've never met him!" Chantal could feel heat rising in her face.

"I saw pictures of you and him at the Cape," Gabrielle said to her.

"What pictures? You had someone follow me?" Chantal was upset. She didn't understand where all this was coming from. She didn't want to believe Gabrielle. "Show me the pictures!" Chantal demanded, now agitated with Gabrielle. She was holding the side of the sofa so tightly it hurt her hand. She had rubbed her hands together, doing her best not to say something to Gabrielle that she would regret later.

"Chantal, please calm down. You know I would never want to hurt you. I love you, but you need to understand. My father-in-law is a powerful man. Ron had Tom followed when he found out Tom was given parole a few weeks ago. He was afraid he might come and hurt us again. He has pictures of you and him. I saw them. You were dancing together in a lounge," Gabrielle told her as she got up to sit beside her.

"I— You're telling me John—Tom—is an ex-convict? The one who tried to murder you? He told me he was an engineer and that he worked in downtown Boston. Are you for real? I don't believe you. He'd never do that. I know him. I love him!" Chantal was extremely distressed, but she also was uncertain about what she was hearing. It felt like a nightmare that she couldn't wake up from. She could feel her eyes stinging with tears.

"Let me ask you something: why didn't he ever come to the house pick you up or drop you off? It was because he knows who we are! He met you in Newport when we were on vacation. Why? Why do you think he was there? He had to have been watching us. He's a dangerous man, Chantal. You have to stay away from him before he attacks us or hurts you. He isn't a stable man." Gabrielle's words stabbed Chantal in the heart. Why was she doing this? There was no way John was the same man as Tom Smith. She thought of the man who had kissed her so passionately and touched her so tenderly. He had awakened something in her that she hadn't known existed: love. He had saved her from a burning house and had bought her gifts. *NO! NO! NO!* her mind screamed.

"He's in the hospital with a broken arm, a broken collarbone, and a concussion. How could he attack me? He loves me. He told me. I don't believe you. He's not like that. Show me the pictures and prove to me he's not who he says he is. Gabrielle, why do you want to hurt me?" Chantal asked and then stared at Gabrielle, waiting for her response.

"Chantal, please. I never wanted to cause you any pain, but it's the truth. I'll show you the pictures, and you'll believe me. I'm so sorry, I really am." Gabrielle went to touch Chantal's arm, but Chantal pulled away.

Chantal couldn't keep the tears from falling down her cheeks. She stood, looked down at her friend, and said, "I'll be in my room when you're ready to show me the pictures and prove to me John is not who says he is. Until then, we are finished talking."

"Chantal, please," Gabrielle said, but Chantal continued down the corridor and up the stairs to her room. She felt like her every step was in slow motion, and it took all of her strength to get to her bedroom without breaking down. Finally, she opened the door and dropped herself onto the bed. Tears flowed quietly down both of her cheeks. She was numb, but she wasn't convinced that Gabrielle had told her the truth.

He wouldn't shame her or cause her such agony. Why would he play her like this? He was the one who had approached her, and now he was the one who was cutting her heart to pieces. She still had faith in him. He would never hurt her. He could have told her who he really was, but would she have wanted to go out on a date with ex-con? Probably not. She touched the bracelet he had bought for her and placed it on her wrist. He had said he wanted her to have a memento to remember him by when they were apart. She slipped the bracelet off her wrist and threw it onto the side table beside her bed. She truly hoped that Gabrielle was mistaken, wrong about all of it. Chantal closed her eyes and tried to unscramble everything that had happened during the last week with John and to comprehend what Gabrielle had just told her.

***

Gabrielle was stunned that Chantal didn't grasp the severity of the situation. She had to protect Chantal and her own family from this man. What if he came after them? Chantal had said he was in the hospital, so he probably wouldn't be able to do much now. That was the first good news she had heard today.

She had to get a hold of the pictures again without Ron finding out they were missing. Maybe if she just took one, he wouldn't miss it. He had quite a few, and Chantal might believe her if she saw a photo. Better yet, she was going to get on the Internet and print pictures from the tabloids and articles about the trial that had happened nearly ten years ago. The court case had been published in every newspaper all over the world because of the family's wealth and position.

Chantal would have to listen to her then when she gave her the proof of whom this man really was. Gabrielle stood and headed toward Bernard's office so she could print evidence that John was really the ex-con she had said he was. She would save her friend from him. She just hoped it wasn't too late to save their friendship.

Gabrielle marched out of the room, her head held high, convinced she was doing the right thing. She had her own mission: to destroy Tom. She walked down the corridor and entered Bernard's office. It was so much smaller than Ron's. She could always smell her husband's cologne in this room. Maybe that was why she loved this part of the house. Brown velvety drapes hung on the large windows behind his desk, and a gold Persian rug covered the hardwood floor. A few chairs stood in front of his desk.

She strolled to his desk and sat in his leather chair. She always had to stop and admire the awards that hung on the walls and the pictures of their son, Junior. Bernard kept those precious pictures on the top of his bureau, but today Gabrielle didn't even glance at them.

She typed in the password on his computer and went to Google to search for the trial. Page after page popped up on the screen. She scrolled down until she came to the articles and pictures from the trial. She clicked Print and heard the printer next to her spit out the pages that she would use to convince Chantal. She picked them up, straightened them, and placed them in a yellow envelope. She then left the room and walked up the spiral stairs to Chantal's room.

CHAPTER 18

Tom had taken a cab to his boarding house around midnight. It had been a very bad night. His shoulder and arm caused him constant pain. He had taken his painkillers but still hadn't slept much. The medication made him very drowsy and upset his stomach. He would have to spend a few days resting in his room. He couldn't move around much, plus he no longer had a truck. The owner of the boarding house had brought him food and had told him to call her if he needed anything.

The only thing he wanted was Chantal, but he had to be realistic. There was no chance she would want to date him when she found out he was an ex-con. He had called his parole officer. Tom told him what had happened and that he would be out of work for at least six weeks, maybe longer, depending on his physical therapy. Tom didn't care if he worked or not. He was financially secure because of his hidden bank accounts.

The only problem was that his plan of revenge was on hold. He couldn't risk getting injured any more than he was now, and he wouldn't be able to defend himself while his shoulder was like this. He felt like an invalid. He laid on his back watching television while he healed, but his mind was on Chantal. He couldn't concentrate on anything else but her. His memories of her comforted him when he was in pain. Tom wondered how she was coping after he refused to see her. *She's better off without you*, he told himself. He didn't even know if she had left Boston yet. He tried to convince himself that it was for the best, but his heart told him otherwise.

He loved her. He was stuck in bed, full of drugs, and had nowhere to go. All he could think of was Chantal's touch. She was a respectable woman who would never want to be seen with an ex-con. He couldn't conceive of her loving him. But he very clearly had heard her say, "I love you." She was in love with the man she thought he was, not who he actually was. At least he still had his memories of her. No one would be able to take them from him. One day, when everything was quiet, and he was no longer on parole, he could consider going to Canada to see her. No one would be able to stop him. He could become an engineer and—what was he thinking? He had to forget her. She was gone, and there was nothing he could do. But he felt empty without her by his side. He had to erase his memories of her.

Days passed, and still he was at the boarding house, recuperating from his bad luck. His room was becoming depressing, with its beige curtains and beige walls. It didn't have any personal touch, but at least he had his own bathroom, and the bed was comfortable with its feathered pillows and thick comforter. He was going to go crazy if he didn't leave this room for a few hours—or even an hour. He couldn't look at these four walls anymore.

Tom had too much time on his hands and too little to do. All he did was think, think, think all day about the person who had stolen his heart. As hard as he tried, he couldn't escape the torture—not the torture from his arm and shoulder, but the torture he felt in his heart. He decided he should go for a walk to change his surroundings.

He managed to put on sweatpants and a sweatshirt. It had been a difficult and agonizing task, but he was determined to leave this room. He locked his door and was walking down the sidewalk when he noticed a man on a bench across the street, reading the daily newspaper. He looked familiar. Where had he seen him? Tom pretended like everything was normal. He kept an eye on the man and noticed that the man was looking at him. Tom crossed the street, watching him from a distance.

He would have to reverse his role from the hunted to the hunter. But how would he do that with a broken shoulder? Not having both of his arms could be catastrophic, but at least he still had both his feet. He walked into the convenience store on the corner block. He walked down the aisle toward the back. He passed the chips and chocolate, biding his time while he evaluated his prey through the window. He grabbed a bag of chips, a power bar, and a Red Bull and slowly walked back to the counter. He pulled a ten-dollar bill from his pocket and handed it to the cashier. "Would you like a bag?" the cashier asked Tom. He just nodded.

His eyes were on the man. Tom knew he couldn't fight him without injuring himself. Not yet at least. He would have to wait and find out who this man was and take care of this problem. He took the bag in his free hand and left the store. He managed to make it back to the boarding house without incident. He knew he had seen the man before, but where?

After he arrived, he stepped to the window. He pushed the beige curtain to the side just enough to be able to see the man if he was outside. Suddenly, it came to him. *Son of a bitch!* He recalled where he had seen him. He had been the Market Place and then at Embargo on the Cape. This type of thing rarely happened to him, but he had been distracted by Chantal. He hadn't been on his A game because he was captivated by the woman's every word and every move. He had been careless, and now he realized this guy must been taking pictures of him and Chantal. He had seen him with his iPhone, but he had thought he was a tourist taking snapshots of the venue. He would find a way to maneuver around this injury and retrieve those photos. He was sure Ron had to be behind this surveillance, because he was the only one who could have him followed. Tom thought he had taken care of the problem earlier with the other guy, but apparently not. Tomorrow he would go after this fellow, despite his injury. Chantal might be in danger. Ron might think she was collaborating with him. He had to set things straight before Chantal got pulled into his world of violence and was harmed. He would protect her at all costs.

***

Gabrielle stood in front of Chantal's bedroom door. She inhaled slowly and exhaled. In her right hand, she held a large yellow envelope that contained evidence to prove what Gabrielle had tried so hard to explain to Chantal earlier. Gabrielle just prayed that her friendship with Chantal wouldn't be lost because of this man. She closed her eyes for a second and then raised her hand to knock lightly on the door.

"Come in," Chantal answered from the other side.

Gabrielle opened the door, hoping that this wouldn't be her last conversation with her friend. Chantal was folding sweaters and placing them in her suitcase, but when she lifted her head, Gabrielle could tell she had been crying again. Chantal's eyes narrowed as she looked toward the envelope. Gabrielle felt like the envelope was a grenade about to explode and destroy their close relationship. Gabrielle wanted to get rid of it as fast as she could, so she placed it on the high dresser that was next to her.

"Let me help you pack," Gabrielle said, sitting on the edge of the bed, but Chantal didn't acknowledge her presence or stop what she was doing. She went to the closet and retrieved a pair of pants hanging there. She laid them on the top of the bed and continued folding and packing things away. Gabrielle extended her hand to help her but was rebuffed instantly.

"That's not necessary. I need something to keep my mind occupied right now." Chantal spoke with no emotion. She never lifted her head or looked Gabrielle in the eye.

"Chantal, can we talk? I know you don't believe what I said to you about John, but it's the truth. I don't want you to leave like this. I brought you some proof of what I was telling you. I'm so sorry. I never meant to hurt you. I just hope we can still be friends. I love you." Gabrielle told her in a soft motherly tone, but Chantal never said a word. She just went about her task.

A few minutes went by. The air seemed to have been sucked out of the room. Gabrielle felt very tense. She rubbed her hands on her legs. It was so quiet that she could have heard a pin drop on the hardwood floor. The silence was suffocating. Gabrielle rose and started walking toward the exit, her head bowed low, and her shoulders slumped forward. She heard Chantal say her name. She turned and faced her friend. Chantal never glanced at her. She gathered her toiletries and placed them in a purple pouch.

"Gabrielle, I love you too, but right now I need to return home. I changed my flight, and I'm departing for the airport within the next hour. I'll read the articles and call you later," she told her without emotion.

"All right, that's all I can ask. Please call me later." Gabrielle was devastated that she was losing her girlfriend of so many years, but she had her family to think about and that was her priority. She walked out and closed the door behind her. She leaned against the door, sad that the situation had deteriorated so quickly. She wanted this ordeal to end happily, but Gabrielle knew that wasn't going to happen today. Gabrielle pulled her head up, her shoulders back and left the situation behind her. She walked down the hallway toward the kitchen. She had to be strong if she was going to face what might come her way.

***

Chantal saw the package that Gabrielle had left on the dresser. She took the envelope in her hands and turned it over, but she couldn't look at its contents right now. Without opening it, she slipped it into her carry-on. She couldn't read it now. It was too painful, and she wasn't ready or strong enough to face the reality that she knew was going to hit her. It would destroy her hopes and dreams of having a relationship with someone she longed for. She called a taxi to take her to the airport. She stood outside of the entrance to Gabrielle's house, waiting patiently, when she heard a voice.

"It's you! You're the one in the pictures! Who are you, and what are you doing here?" the voice demanded. Chantal turned to face whomever was talking to her. The man was well-groomed, dressed in a navy-blue pinstripe suit with a red tie. He was in an electric wheelchair, and his eyes were narrowed and staring right at her. His lips were pressed together tightly.

"I'm sorry?" Chantal said, surprised by the outburst. She didn't know what to make of this man. He was looking at her with utter distaste.

"Who are you, and what are you doing here?" he demanded once more. His hand tapped the handle of his chair. Chantal got the impression he would wrap his hands around her throat if he were able to stand.

"I'm Gabrielle's friend. Who are you?" she asked politely, even though she wanted to tell him off for being so rude and then run away.

"I'm Ron Rian, Bernard's father. I own this estate. What exactly are you doing here? If you think you can come to my home and try to hurt my family or me, you are mistaken! SECURITY!" he shouted on the top of his lungs. "SECURITY!" Chantal was shocked and frightened at the same time. She took a step backward from the man. Her mouth fell open, and her eyes darted everywhere. She didn't know what to expect.

"What are you doing?" Chantal asked, petrified—especially when she saw two armed men running toward them. Chantal stood her ground. She hadn't done anything wrong, so she shouldn't be afraid. She saw revulsion on the man's face.

"Are you all right, sir?" one guard asked. They stood next to him, their hands on their hips. They waited for instructions from Mr. Rian, wondering why he had screamed for them.

"This woman is trespassing. Take her in custody and call the police. I want her off this property at once." The younger guard took a step toward her and stretched out his hand to grab her arm. Chantal stepped back and slapped his hand.

"I beg your pardon! Don't touch me. I am Gabrielle's friend from Canada. I'm here visiting her," Chantal told Ron and crossed her arms in front of her chest. The older security guard bent down, cupped his hand, and whispered into Ron's ear.

"Are you sure?" Ron asked the guard, and he nodded. Ron then dismissed them with a wave of his hand. She watched as they walked twenty feet away and stood there, observing the situation.

"If you are Gabrielle's friend, why are you hanging around with this madman Tom? I have pictures of you and him getting all cozy. That man put me in this fucking chair! You shouldn't be near him," Ron told her with an air of superiority, his chin pointed upward, and his eyes never leaving hers for a second.

"Oh my God! Gabrielle was telling the truth! I didn't know who he really was until this morning. I swear that if I had known I wouldn't—" Chantal couldn't speak. As the truth hit her, she could barely breathe. She felt a cold sweat come over her. Her hands shook, and she hoped her knees wouldn't give out.

"Where are you going? I see you have a suitcase," Ron said to her and pointed at her bag.

"I'm waiting for a cab. I'm returning home," she answered, unable to believe what she had just found out. She had trusted the word of a total stranger, and she had been unable to accept what her longtime friend had told her.

"Do you need to sit down? You look pale," Ron told her. "Get her a chair," he ordered. One of the guards ran into a room and brought her a chair just in time. She collapsed into it, unable to stand any longer.

"I didn't know," she told Ron, who still was watching her closely. His expression had softened, and he now had a small smile on his face. He touched her arm lightly and rubbed it. Chantal would have sworn he was trying to comfort her.

"It's not your fault. That's the kind of man Tom is. He's ruthless. I should know—he worked for me for over ten years. Listen, I'm sorry I frightened you, but I need to know. Did he ever talk about our family while you were with him?" Ron questioned her.

"No. Never. He didn't even come close to the house. I think maybe you are mistaken about him. I don't think he wants to harm you or anyone else," she said and then realized she was defending the man who had lied to her and used her. How could he do that? He had deceived her the entire time they had been together. Nothing was real anymore. She sighed and looked out the door toward the driveway. She saw a yellow cab coming toward them.

"I hope you never see that man again. He's evil. And I am sorry I scared you earlier," Ron said as he navigated his chair away, disappearing behind an archway. Chantal was still in shock, but she got up and walked outside in a trance. Everyone hated the man she loved. She climbed into the taxi and told the cabbie to take her to Logan Airport. She sat silently and felt numb throughout the entire ride into the city.

CHAPTER 19

The next week flew by. Tom finally decided it was time for him to do something about that man who still lurked around the boarding house. Tom went out the side door of the establishment and walked directly to the man's automobile, approaching it from behind. The man was sitting in his car reading while he waited for Tom to walk out the front door. He never saw Tom approach. Tom knocked on the driver's side window. The man jumped and dropped his magazine, clearly startled.

Tom motioned for him to roll down his window. Tom knew he couldn't fight this guy. He'd probably hurt himself even more if he tried, but he'd be damned if he didn't try to scare the shit out of the guy. Tom's eyes followed his every move. He watched as the man rolled the window halfway down. The man never said a word; he just stared, unable to believe that he had gotten caught. Tom noticed that the man was trembling.

"Why are you following me? Do you know what happened to Raymond when he shadowed me?" Tom was leaning into his face. The poor guy just nodded, his eyes bulging.

"Listen up, you should leave while you still can and not come back, because if I see you hanging around me again, I'm going to fucking blow your brains out. Do you understand?"

"Yes," the man answered, turning pale. Tom saw his lower lip quiver, so he decided to scare him a little more. He pressed his face closer to the man's.

"I have one more question. Where are the pictures that you took of my friend and me at the Cape? I want them. NOW!!" Tom shouted and waited for an answer.

"They're on my phone," the man told him, pointing at his phone. He picked up the phone, reluctant to relinquish it.

"I only have one phone and—" the man began, but Tom interrupted him.

"Give it to me or—" Tom said in a harsh voice. Without further hesitation, the man handed his phone over. He'd just get another as soon as he could.

"Now get the fuck out of here. I might be injured, but I still can shoot straight with my other hand. You hear me? Just remember that. Now go." Tom watched as the man fumbled to turn the key of his car and put the gear in drive. The man had given up his phone and left without another word. Hopefully that would end the surveillance.

Tom walked back to his room and sat in the chair by the window. He opened the man's phone, grateful that it wasn't password-protected. He scrolled down to Pictures. He clicked on the icon, and an image of him and Chantal showed up. They were dancing together on the Cape.

All kinds of emotions assaulted him all at once. He felt joy, but also sadness. He missed her terribly. Never had he missed anyone as much as he missed her. His thumb passed over the image of her face, and he could somehow still feel her tenderness and hear her laughter. What had he done? He should of have fought for her. Maybe, just maybe—no, it never would have worked out. They were from two different worlds. He put the man's phone on the dresser, lay down on his bed to rest, and closed his eyes. He still had a couple more weeks to heal before he'd be able to move around town well enough to execute his plot.

Days went by, but Tom still couldn't forget Chantal. He looked at the pictures on the man's cellphone. It brought him joy, but sadness crawled in soon after. He spent another lonely weekend sitting by himself in his room at the boarding house. He missed Chantal terribly. She was the one who made him laugh, and he left all his troubles behind when she touched him. He longed to hear her voice and to see her again. All that mattered was her happiness and pleasure. When he was with her, he had no problems, and it was as though time had stopped.

He thought about how her curls fell into her eyes and how he loved the feel of them in his fingers. He desperately needed to hear her voice. He put his hand in his pocket and pulled out his phone. For some unknown reason, he hadn't erased her phone number. Tom pondered whether she had deleted his number after all this time. Surely she wouldn't have kept it. What reason would she have to keep it? He mulled it over before he decided to find out for sure. He pushed speed-dial and waited anxiously.

His heart steadily beat faster at the thought of hearing her voice. What would he say to her if she answered? There was really nothing he could say. He had left her standing alone in the hallway of the hospital. She had told him she loved him. How could he have dismissed her so easily? He loved her, too, but he also was petrified. Of what, though? *What are you afraid of?* he wondered. The phone rang and rang, and then she answered. He was unable to speak. He wasn't able to articulate a simple greeting. He felt as if someone had sucked all the air out of him.

Incapable of speech, all he could do was sit there paralyzed as he listened to her voice.

***

Chantal had been home for weeks. School had begun, and she was teaching again. The leaves of the trees were starting to turned orange, yellow, and red. Usually autumn was her favorite season, but this year her mind was preoccupied with other matters. She never made it through one day without thinking of Tom. She never spoke his name out loud, but he was alive in her thoughts. She was embarrassed that she had been duped by the man she had fallen in love with. She now knew his real name, but other than that, she knew nothing. The envelope that Gabrielle had given her was still in the drawer of her night table, where she had placed it upon arriving back at her apartment. She hadn't had the strength to open it and read it. She was afraid of its contents. She truly loved this man. She probably could forgive him anything, but she was terrified of the truth.

The day she had left Gabrielle's house, she hadn't quite believed what Gabrielle had told her. But reality had quickly hit her in the face. Ron had made it real. She saw the hate he had for Tom. Her loving man was hated.

How could that be? Tom had put him in that chair for the rest of his life. She believed Ron. She wasn't sure why, but she did.

It was the weekend again, the days that Chantal loathed and thought would never end. At least during the week, she was busy and the days were tolerable, but the long days by herself on the weekends made her miserable. Alone in her empty apartment, she reminisced about the time she had spent with Tom on Cape Cod.

It was Saturday morning, and she decided that today was the day she let Tom's past history into her world. Maybe then her heart would mend. Perhaps she could return to her normal life after learning the truth about him. She sat on her bed and pulled open the drawer of her night table. She reached inside, picked up the envelope, and tugged the papers out.

The headlines read, "Tom Smith, found guilty of attempted murder." There was a picture of Tom standing at the defense table. He was wearing a brown suit and a beige shirt, and his hands were in cuffs. It almost seemed like he was looking at her from the courtroom. Reality hit her instantly. Her hands trembled, but she read all the reports carefully. Then she read them again. Her tears saturated the articles as she read.

Now she knew the whole truth of what had happened ten years previously. She wondered what had made him go rogue. The newspapers said that his defense attorneys had argued that Post Traumatic Stress Disorder attributed for his behavior and stated that he had been under the care of a psychiatrist for years. His lawyers said that Tom was innocent and that he was mentally ill, but he had been found competent to stand trial. He had been judged guilty of attempted murder.

The reporter writing the story also implied that the jury felt sorry for him because he was a war veteran. He had given up a lot to protect his country and had served several tours in Iraq, which was why after days of deliberation, the jury had given him manslaughter instead of attempted murder. No one had been able to prove that the jury had been sympathetic and had sided with him. It did say, though, that the judge had ordered Tom to take specialized psychotherapy sessions in prison to help him cope with his PTSD. He'd also had to take medications until he was eligible for parole.

Maybe he was cured or at least he had the PTSD under control, because he hadn't shown any symptoms of it while she was with him. He had been a sick man. Why hold it against him. He had served his time. What was she thinking? *Be rational. He's an ex-con. You can't get involved with him. It would be crazy.* Chantal thought. She replaced the papers in the envelope and stored it in the drawer again.

Nighttime came. She had debated Tom's faith and situation all day. It weighed heavily on her mind. Chantal was bundled under a knitted afghan on the only sofa in her one-bedroom apartment. It was a quaint place. She had a tiny kitchen painted in white and yellow, with a wood table that seated two. The bedroom was just big enough to fit a queen-size bed with a teal crocheted bedspread and a bureau. She didn't need much space. She was alone.

The television was on, but she wasn't listening to it. She was day-dreaming about Tom again. Tears were a regular occurrence these days. She couldn't forget him. Her heart was totally broken. Just the thought of him caused a waterfall to pour from her eyes. She was surprised to hear her phone ring. It spooked her. She wasn't expecting anyone to call this late at night. It was almost eleven o'clock. She grabbed it off the coffee table and looked at the caller ID. It said unknown. Her eyebrows came together. She wondered who was calling her so late on the weekend. She swiped the bar to answer. "Allo, this is Chantal." She listened, but no one answered.

"Allo, can I help you?" No sound came from the other end. She hung up. She was still staring at her phone when it rang again—she almost dropped the damn phone. It still read unknown ID. She knew she shouldn't answer but she had to do it anyway. "Allo." Still no response. A chill went down her back. She rubbed her arm with her free hand, trying to shake the cold feeling that had overcome her.

"Who is this? Say something, whoever this is." Nothing. She waited a few seconds, then she hung up. She couldn't think of anyone who would call her with an unknown ID. Unless—what if it had been Tom? She wished it had been, but she knew she had to be realistic. It wasn't. Why would he call her and not speak to her? She untangled herself from the blanket and then stood, folded her wrap, and hid the afghan in the chest in the corner. It was time to go to bed, but Tom still haunted her even after all this time. Tomorrow was another day. For once, she would not cry.

CHAPTER 20

Ron was curious why Gabrielle hadn't told him that a friend of hers was visiting and that she was dating Tom. *How in the hell had that happened?* he asked himself. He decided to investigate, but first he wanted to talk to Lee. He had never mentioned that he had followed this woman to their home. He picked up the receiver of the phone and dialed Lee's number. It rang three times but no answer. Ron tapped his fingers against his chin, impatient as usual. He would have to wait for his answer. It drove him crazy when people in his employment didn't answer his calls right away. They should be grateful they had a job, but no, they made him wait.

"Hello, this is Lee. How may I help you?"

"You can help me by first answering your phone faster. Now, what do you have for me?" Ron hated having to contact him. He should call in his reports to him. He was damn well paying him enough money.

"Oh! Well, Tom has been confined to his boarding house for the last few weeks. He was in a car accident about a month ago and broke a shoulder. He hasn't been to work nor does he have a truck. It was totaled in the mishap." Lee didn't tell Ron he hadn't returned to the boarding house for fear of his life.

"The blonde girl he was with at the Cape—has he ever accompanied her to my house?" Ron asked without saying why he wanted to know.

"Umm, no. He never went near your place, sir. I would have told you."
Lee answered. "If I may say, sir, I feel like this man you are making us follow
has changed his ways, because for the last month he has been a straight
arrow. If he was planning something, we would've seen him talking to
other people from his circle of friends, but that isn't the case. He's still dangerous, but he reports to his parole officer weekly. Now that he's injured,
it'll take him months to get his arm and shoulder back to where they were
before the accident. I don't think he'll be a threat to you or your family,"
Lee told him directly.

"Don't underestimate him. Are you sure about your assessment of the
situation? What does Raymond say?" Ron asked Lee, because he wanted
both of their professional opinions before he could feel free of his threat.
Regardless, he would keep his security personnel around the property at
all times.

"Raymond doesn't like him much after the beating he received, but he
doesn't think he'll be coming around you too soon, with his shoulder and
all. We would've detected something," Lee answered.

"Very good. Stay on him for a while more to see if he moves around or
talks to anyone out of the ordinary," Ron told him.

"Sir, I'm no longer trailing him. Ray took over again, and he's watching him but from far away," Lee didn't want Ron to know about the incident between him and Tom.

"Fine, keep me posted." Ron clicked his phone off. He truly didn't
trust Tom, but maybe this woman—what's her name—Chantal—had
changed him, but it would be a while before Ron let his guard down.
Maybe Gabrielle knew more.

He pushed the button of his chair and headed down the corridor to
find Gabrielle. He rolled into the living room area and spotted her playing
Monopoly with Junior. They were sitting by the window where there was a
small carved wood table and two chairs. It was the perfect place to indulge
in a game. Ron stopped his chair about a foot from them. He gave them a
broad smile, not wanting to alert Junior that anything was wrong.

"Don't tell me he is cheating again!" Ron said to Gabrielle, teasing his
grandson.

"Grandfather, I don't cheat. Mama tell him." Junior threw the dice down on the board. He grabbed his game piece and started moving it down the boardwalk.

"I am sure Grandfather is only teasing you. Is there something I can help you with, Ron?" Gabrielle asked casually. She watched Junior move his piece to his next spot on the board.

"Yes, I wanted to ask you a few questions concerning your friend Chantal. Junior, could you run into the kitchen and fetch some juice for your mother and me? I'm so thirsty," Ron asked him. Junior placed his cards down and left the table, heading for the kitchen.

"Sure. I'll be right back."

"Thank you," his grandfather said and then watched him until he was out of sight. Gabrielle sat with her back against her chair, her hands folded in front of her. Ron smiled at her. He didn't want to upset her, but he needed answers.

"Has Tom ever come to this house with your friend Chantal?"

"Absolutely not. He never came close to the house. I would have known," Gabrielle answered.

"Where did they meet? Do you know?" Ron asked her with curious attention. He never took his eyes off her. Gabrielle fidgeted in her seat. She shifted her weight and sat straighter.

"They met at a restaurant. She dated him for most of the time she was here. She fell hard for him. Apparently Tom told her he loved her. I think he might have changed his ways, from what she told me. It's been a long time since he attacked us. I think you should leave it be and try to move on—" Gabrielle stopped because she noticed Ron hands ball into fists.

"How would she know if he had changed or not? He lied to her, didn't he? I understand your point of view, but I will never forgive him. You of all people should know that. Do you know if she is still in contact with him?" Ron inquired, not believing that Tom could be innocent.

"I really don't know. Do you want me to find out?" Gabrielle said, turning her head as she heard footsteps approach. She saw her son heading back to his spot. He handed his grandfather a bottle of juice.

"Thank you, my child. I would appreciate if you could find out about him." Ron directed his words to Gabrielle. She picked up the dice and resumed the game.

"Sure, no problem," Gabrielle said as Ron rolled back to his study.

***

A few hours later Gabrielle decided it was time to call Chantal. They hadn't talked since Chantal had left the house a few weeks ago, and Gabrielle felt guilty. She should of have settled this issue long before now. She decided that she would be the first one to reach out. She missed their special talks. She looked at her watch and noted that Chantal should be home from school by now. She was probably preparing her supper. She dialed the number and waited. Chantal picked up on the first ring. "Allo, this is Chantal," she heard from the other end.

"Hi, Chantal. How are you doing? This is Gabrielle. I thought I'd give you a call to see how things were going with you." Gabrielle hoped Chantal would still talk to her despite their fight before Chantal left for home.

"I'm fine. School started, and I've been a busy bee since it opened. How are you doing?" Chantal answered casually, as if nothing had ever come between them.

"Everyone is good. I— I really wanted to call you to find out how you were coping with the information I gave you the day you went home. I'm so sorry that we parted in such a bad way. " Gabrielle needed to get it off her chest. She had been thinking about it for a long time. She missed her longtime friend and the special bond they shared. She hoped they could resolve this mess and move past it.

"Oh! Gabrielle, I'm sorry too. I should have known you only wanted to protect me. I've wanted to call you too, but I was afraid you wouldn't talk to me. It's been terrible. I read all the documents you gave me, but I—I miss him. I truly love him, and I don't know how to get in touch with him. I understand your situation, and I am so sorry but—" Chantal's voice broke. Gabrielle knew her friend was crying on the other end of the line. She wanted to console her friend.

"Chantal, I might not agree with what you are doing, but I just want you to know I forgave him a long time ago. I don't ever wish to reconnect with him. He hurt me badly, but if you love him, I can't stop you from going after him. You know what is best for you." Gabrielle said to Chantal.

"Thank you so much. Tom has always been kind to me, and I trust him. He loves me. The problem is that even if I wanted to be with him, I don't know where he is, and I don't have his phone number anymore. He broke off our relationship the night we were in the hospital. I now know why he did it. He didn't want me to find out who he really was. It's tearing me apart not knowing how he is doing. He was badly hurt in the car accident. He broke his left shoulder and arm when we crashed. I don't believe he would hurt you," Chantal tried to explain to Gabrielle.

"I'm so sorry, Chantal. Do you want me to help you find him? Let me see if I can find out where he is living?" Gabrielle said, against her better judgment. She hoped to God she didn't regret this down the road. She had mellowed in the years after the incident with Tom and the family. She truly believed there was good in every person—you just had to bring it out. She wasn't saying she would be friends with Tom, but if it brought happiness to Chantal, Gabrielle would see what she could find out. She was willing to try for the sake of their friendship. Gabrielle knew that Ron knew exactly where Tom was. He had had him under surveillance for months.

"What can you do?" Chantal asked. Gabrielle was silent for a moment.

"Let me worry about that. I'll let you know what I find. I just pray for your sake that you are making the right decision. I'll get back to you soon. Love you."

"Thanks. I love you, too," Chantal said as her voice cracked. Gabrielle hung up the phone. She knew that the only way she would find where Tom lived was to ask Ron directly, so that was what she was going to do. Bernard wouldn't be home for a few more hours, and Ron was probably having a drink in the library.

She walked past the grand room that boasted crystal chandeliers, Italian silk drapes, marble floors, and priceless art, but she never looked twice. She kept on a straight line until she reached the library. She arrived at the mahogany door, opened it without breaking stride, and walked to Ron. He was having a cocktail, and she decided to join him. She needed a stiff drink, maybe two, to carry out her plan.

"Good evening, Ron. I see you already have a drink. I think I'll join you." She was about to walk to the bar, when Ron stopped her, saying

"Please sit. I'll get it. What would you like?" he asked her pleasantly and even smiled her way.

"I'll have a Grand Marnier. Neat, please." she replied. She watched as he maneuvered his way to the bar. She always let him do certain things for her, finding it made him feel happy and satisfied that he could still function by himself. She stood by the bar and watched him as he poured the drink. He held her drink in one hand and guided his electric chair with his other hand.

He handed the drink to her. "Thank you, Ron." She took it from him and then sat in front of the fireplace in the only available chair. One of the chairs had been removed so Ron had a place where he could slip his chair. One of the servants had made a fire to keep the chill out of the room. The shadows of the flames danced on the walls. Gabrielle took a sip and then raised her glass to Ron. She inhaled the orange aroma of her cognac. She decided that she would have to be blunt with Ron when she asked him about Tom, otherwise she might not dare ask again.

"Ron, I have a very delicate matter I need to talk to you about. I don't want you to be upset so—" He brought his glass down from his lips, and his eyes burned on her. "Do you know where I can find Tom? Where he lives?" She had said it. Now she waited for the answer or the battle that she might have to fight to get the information.

"What would you want that for? Why on earth would you want to know that?" He was drumming his fingers on the armchair. His eyebrows came together, and his eyes opened wide.

"It's not for me. Please, Ron. If you know the answer, give it to me," she begged him. His eyes never left hers.

"Why? I do not want you to get hurt. He's a madman. You know that. What if he harmed you? Bernard would never forgive me." Ron was not budging. Gabrielle sensed his disapproval.

"I want it for my friend Chantal. She wants to find him—she loves him," Gabrielle answered Ron and then took a sip of her drink without looking at him.

"He doesn't deserve to be loved. Look at what he did. He should be thrown to the pigs as far as I'm concerned." Ron was upset. His face grew red, and his voice got louder.

"Please, Ron. I know you can help me. I saw the pictures in your desk. I know you have had him under surveillance since he was paroled," she said softly, trying to convince him. He turned his head away, but she knew he would give her what she asked. He rarely said no to her. He loved her too much. She waited quietly, listening to the fire crackle and pop. He chugged his drink. After several minutes of silence, he turned to face her.

"Very well, but promise me you will stay away from him. I couldn't bear it if he hurt you or killed you," he said, reluctant to give her the information she wanted.

"Thank you, Ron." She stood, kissed him on the cheek, and followed him to his desk. He opened a drawer, took a pen and a piece of paper, and wrote down the address where Tom could be found. He passed it to her. She nodded and exited the room, as Ron sat alone behind his desk.

CHAPTER 21

Tom felt much better. He was rarely in severe pain. He had gone back to the orthopedic doctor the day before, and the doctor had removed his stitches. His injuries were healing perfectly, but it would take time for him to recuperate from such a bad break. He would have to spend several more months in physical therapy before his arm and shoulder completely healed. He had stopped taking the pain medication because they messed with his mind and impaired his ability to concentrate. When took the drugs, all he wanted to do was sleep during the day, when he should have been trying to get stronger.

Today, he was determined to move forward. The first thing he wanted to do was buy a new means of transportation. He had received the check from the insurance company and although it wouldn't be enough to cover full cost of a new car, he had sufficient funds. He stood outside the boarding house waiting for a taxi to pick him up when his mind wandered back to Chantal.

Every step, every hour of the day was hard for him. His memories wouldn't let him forget her. He was becoming obsessed with her. How could he be so preoccupied with one woman? He knew the answer to his question: he loved her. The worst part had been the other evening when the longing had overcome him, and he had called her. Hearing her voice so far away from him had been torture.

Digging into his jeans pocket, he retrieved the only thing he had left of her: a picture on a cellphone. He replayed her words over and over again in his mind while he caressed her picture. It was the only piece of her he had, and he couldn't give it up. He should have said something to her the other night on the phone, but what? He couldn't. Never in his life had he ever been afraid of anything, but Chantal's love could bring him to his knees.

He had misled her from the beginning by lying to her. Why had he done that to her? He knew the answer to that question, too. He had never thought he would fall in love with her, and he truly hadn't thought she would affect him as she had. He had thought he was stronger, but love did funny things to your mind. He had to forget her. She would find someone else to love. He wasn't the man for her. He would have to suffer in silence.

The cabbie finally arrived. Tom put the phone away, got in, and told the taxi driver to drop him at the Toyota dealership near his house. He browsed for an hour at the dealership, looking at multiple vehicles. He came out driving a 2014 Tundra. He knew he needed something sturdy and reliable. He left his new truck in a parking garage a few blocks from the boarding house. He didn't want people to talk or ask him questions about his vehicle, so he hid it away until he needed it and then walked back to his room.

As he came closer to the boarding house, he noticed a black sedan with tinted windows parked at the curb near the boarding house. He slowed down so he could determine whether or nor it was a threat. He was about twenty feet from the sedan when Tom saw the driver open the door and step out. It was a chauffeur.

The man was dressed in a black suit, tie, and white shirt. He stood straight beside the car, his hands in front of him. Tom noticed right away he was watching his every move. He didn't move a muscle until Tom was almost on top of him. He had been waiting for him to come closer. Tom knew he probably couldn't win a fight in his condition, but he would give him a run for his money if it came to that.

"Mr. Tom Smith?" the man asked. No one had ever called Tom "mister." The only person who he knew could afford a chauffeur and sedan like this was Ron Rian. Today might be the day he had spent so many years waiting for.

"Who's asking?" Tom asked him, staring him down as he approached. He stopped three feet away. He still could kick and had one free hand. Tom stood his ground and stared at the man.

"Are you Mr. Tom Smith?" he asked again politely.

"Yes, I'm Tom Smith. What do you want?"

"I was asked to find you and bring you with me. Someone wants to talk to you."

"I bet. And who would that someone be?" Tom replied.

"I'm not at liberty to divulge that to you, but if you would, please have a seat. I shall bring you to the person in question," he answered respectfully. He leaned over, opened the back door of the sedan, and stood there waiting.

"Would I please have a fucking seat?" Tom said, but the chauffeur just nodded and ignored him. He didn't seem intimidated by Tom. He just waited by the door.

"What the hell?" Tom muttered and peered his head inside the backseat. There was no one there. The sedan was empty. He really didn't have much else to do at the moment, so he got into the back seat and sat down. The chauffeur closed the door, sat in the front seat, and proceeded to drive away. Tom noticed that the glass partition between the back and front seats was up. Oh well, maybe he'd have a chance to execute his plan sooner than he'd thought. Or maybe he'd die before he got the chance. Looking at the seats, he noticed a capital R stitched in the leather. The car belonged to the Rian family.

***

Gabrielle sat nervously in a booth by a window at the back of a pizzeria. People were coming and going from the establishment. It was the busiest time of the day: lunchtime. Families talked with their children while eating their pizza. She drummed her fingers on a cup of coffee, patiently waiting. She ordered a cheese pizza and tried to look as normal as possible. The waiter placed it in the middle of the table, but she hadn't touched it. She wasn't hungry at all. Her stomach was in knots. She didn't dare take a bite. She didn't think she could keep it down.

She kept an eye on the window, peering through the blinds as she waited for the black sedan to arrive. She was second-guessing her idea. Maybe she shouldn't have risked this meeting. She knew it was dangerous to meet with Tom. Maybe Ron was correct in thinking that Tom was evil, but for some unknown reason, she had to give this man the benefit of the doubt. He had served his time, and she had forgiven him. She had moved on with her life; she hoped he had too. She was going to see what information she could glean from Tom during this short meeting. That was, if he ever showed up.

She jumped in her seat when her cellphone rang. She picked it up and looked at the ID. It was Steve, her chauffeur. She had told him to call to let her know whether Tom was coming or not.

"Hello," Gabrielle said quietly. She held the phone tightly to her ear, trying to stop her hand from shaking.

"Mrs. Rian, I have your package, and we're on our way. We'll arrive in a few minutes," he informed her.

"Thank you, and please don't forget to come in with him," she reminded him. She didn't want to be alone with Tom.

"Yes, ma'am," he answered, and the phone went dead. She had briefed Steve on her situation with this man. Steve was a good man who doubled as her personal bodyguard. He had been in the family's employment for many years. Because of the wealth that the Rian family had acquired over the years, they faced potential threats daily, so they all had bodyguards. Tom had served one of those positions for Ron for over ten years. Steve was trained in self-defense, plus he always carried a concealed firearm. He had always been very discreet about her comings and goings. She trusted him and knew he would do whatever was necessary to protect her if this meeting didn't go as anticipated.

Minutes seemed like hours as she waited for the man who, many years ago, had tried to ruin her relationship with Bernard and then to kill her. She raised her arm and looked at her Chopard watch. It was almost one-thirty. She hoped she was doing the right thing and wouldn't regret this later on. Gabrielle had trusted Chantal when she had told her that Tom was a changed man and that he wouldn't harm her.

She finally spotted the car coming toward the restaurant. She watched as the black sedan parked. She could hear her heart pounding in her chest.

She wiped her sweaty hands on her jeans and tried to pretend she wasn't scared. Then she folded her hands in her lap to stop them from trembling.

"You can do this. Its going to be okay. It's for Chantal," she whispered, inhaling deeply then exhaling. She wouldn't let Tom see that she was still afraid of him after all these years. She would face him head-on and tell him exactly what she needed to, and then she would be on her way. Oh God! Her eyes were glued to the window. She couldn't hear any of the noise around her. She was in her own world as she focused on Steve and watched him open the back door of the sedan. She saw Tom get out. "There he is," Gabrielle murmured.

It's going to be just fine. Don't let him know you are scared, she kept telling herself. She could feel her pulse quicken, but she wouldn't let him have the satisfaction of seeing her fear. Tom had a sling wrapped around his left arm. As usual, he was dressed in black jeans, a black t-shirt, and black boots. He still walked as if he owned the world. He held his head high and narrowed his eyes as they approached the front door. Steve was beside him, scrutinizing his every move closely.

Be positive. You just want to talk to him about Chantal. She wondered if she should have brought some kind of weapon. She dismissed the thought and decided she was being paranoid. She had Steve. He was her weapon. She looked across the restaurant and saw Tom open the door and walk in. Steve moved in front of Tom so he could follow him. He led the way to Gabrielle with Tom close on his heels. Gabrielle closed her eyes for a second and prayed, *God help me!*

***

Tom was mentally preparing for the fight of his life. He knew how ruthless his ex-employer was. He had sat quietly on the ride over, but to his surprise, they hadn't gone to the main house, but to a pizza joint. Tom had seen the driver make a phone call, but he hadn't been able to hear the conversation. He assumed it had been with whomever he was supposed to meet.

He now followed the chauffeur to a table in the back of the room. He had tried to pass him so that he could gain an advantage over his opponent, but he hadn't been able to succeed. He had braced himself for an attack, but suddenly the man in front of him moved to the left and stood next to a booth. Tom face must have registered his shock. He hadn't anticipated this. His jaw dropped, and he stared in disbelief. It was Gabrielle. She sat by herself, poised and in complete control. She lifted her head and looked up at him, her eyes giving away nothing. *Why was she here?* All he could do was stand in front of her and grin. He tilted his head to the right and said, "Nice to see you again, Gabrielle."

CHAPTER 22

Ron sat outside in the garden admiring the rose bushes, but in the back of his mind, he was worried. He kept coming back to the conversation he had had with Gabrielle the day before. A cold sweat came over him as he thought of something. What if Gabrielle went to meet Tom instead of giving the information to Chantal as she had said she would? He hadn't seen her all day. He wheeled himself back into the house and asked one of the security personnel.

"Do you know where Gabrielle is?" They always knew where each person of this family was at all times.

"No, sir. I saw her earlier today at breakfast, then she left the house," he answered.

"Do you know where she went?" Ron asked, now tapping his fingers on the arm of his chair. His forehead was damp with perspiration.

"No, sir. She left with Steve about an hour ago, but I might be able to find out where she went," the guard answered. He radioed the other security personnel.

"Does anyone know Mrs. Rian's whereabouts?" He brought his finger to his earpiece to listen and then told Ron, "I'm sorry, sir. She didn't say where she was going."

"Thank you." Ron turned his chair and headed for his office. He needed to warn Steve to not take Gabrielle near Tom. Ron didn't trust her. He had a feeling she had gone to meet Tom to reassure herself that he would not harm her friend. She was very protective of her girlfriend. He punched in Steve's cellphone number. It rang once, then twice. There was no answer. That told him he was in guard mode. He rarely picked up his phone when he was watching Gabrielle. That was his protocol.

What was Ron to do? He sat still, his mind spinning as he tried to find an answer to his dilemma. He wiped the sweat off his forehead and tried to refocus his energy on the solution. He couldn't help her. What good was he in a wheelchair if she really had gone to meet Tom? How could he find out? Raymond was the answer.

He decided to call Raymond. He would know if Gabrielle was with Tom. Raymond was supposed to be trailing him. He punched speed-dial and waited impatiently for Raymond to answer.

"Hello," Ron heard Raymond say.

"Raymond, do you know Tom's whereabouts?" he asked quickly.

"Yes, sir. He just walked into a pizzeria restaurant about five minutes ago."

"Good, good. Was he alone?" Ron needed more information.

"As a matter of fact, he wasn't. A black sedan picked him up at the boarding house and brought him here. There was another man with him. Why?" Raymond questioned.

"Dear God! Get in there right away and find out if he is meeting my daughter-in-law. Go now and help her! She might be in danger," Ron screamed at him. "Call me back." Ron's punched his fist on his desk. A picture on his desk fell to the ground. His nostrils were flaring, he was so mad. He should have known better than to give Gabrielle that information. He wouldn't forgive himself if something happened to her. There was nothing he could do but wait and pray that she would be all right.

***

"Have a seat. We need to talk." Gabrielle said with as much confidence as she could muster. She was grateful her voice wasn't quivering. Despite the fact that his arm was in a sling, Tom slid effortlessly into the booth. Seeing him sent a chill down Gabrielle's back. She had her hands under the table and thanked the stars he couldn't see them. They were shaking so much. She rubbed them together, trying to make them stop. She kept her eyes on the prize and refused to flinch from it.

"What can I do for you?" he asked her. She had a feeling that he meant it sexually and was trying to intimidate her. She wasn't going to let him distract her from saying what she wanted to say. Steve cleared his throat. She knew it was meant for Tom, telling him to be polite. She appreciated the gesture.

"I came to talk to you about Chantal," she told him. She saw the surprise in his eyes, but otherwise he didn't react. He didn't say anything. He placed his right hand on the table and waited for her to continue. He lifted his chin up after a few seconds, indicating that she should continue. She had a feeling this conversation was going to be one-sided.

"I know you were dating her while she was vacationing here. I also know you tricked her into believing you were someone you were not," Gabrielle said. Her heart pounded in her chest, but her voice was steady. Tom still didn't say a word, and his face didn't gave away any emotions, so she continued. While she waited for him to arrive, she had mentally rehearsed what she wanted to say. She had been expecting a response, but he wasn't saying anything. He quietly absorbed her every word.

"I found out she was seeing you the day before she came home. I saw pictures of you and her at the Cape." Still he didn't respond. He just sat there, staring into her eyes. Fear was slowly creeping into her. She expected him to lunge at her throat at any minute, but she dismissed the thought.

"I told her the whole story about me and you—how everything unfolded—but she didn't want to accept what I was telling her. So I gave her the trial transcripts so she could read them when she returned to Canada. She needed proof. She did not want to believe that you could do such terrible things." Tom clenched his lips together and stared at her with intensity. She noticed that he had made a fist and was clenching it so tightly that his knuckles turned white. But still he listened without a word.

"She also told me that she loves you and that you broke up with her. But guess what? She still wants to see you despite everything I told her." Gabrielle sighed and waited. "Could you say something?" He didn't utter a syllable.

"I don't want you to hurt her again," she said. He opened his mouth and spoke.

"I would never hurt her." His tone was hard and direct. She watched as he turned his head toward the window and looked outside. His voice and demeanor had changed after she had mentioned Chantal. He was protective of her. His shoulders slouched a bit, and his features seemed to soften. He closed his eyes, and she could see he was thinking.

"She also told me you said you loved her. Is that true?"

He turned toward her. "She told you that?" he whispered. He seemed shocked for some reason.

"She wants to see you, and I have the address of your boarding house. Do you want to see her? I can give it to her, or you could call her and talk to her." He didn't answer. He just sat there motionless. Gabrielle wondered what he was thinking. She could tell that there was some sort of battle going on inside him, but she wasn't going to push her luck. It had gone far enough. He wasn't going to give her anything.

"Very well, then. Just for the record, I want to let you know that I've forgiven you for what you did years ago, and I truly hope Chantal is right about you. Please don't hurt her anymore!" She looked at him, but he didn't respond right away.

After a moment, he said "Is that all?"

"Yes, that's all," Gabrielle told him. He slid out of the booth and stood beside the table. Gabrielle saw Steve take a step forward toward him, but Tom just gave her a deadly grin and walked away without another word. She watched him stride toward the front door. He stopped momentarily to say something to the man sitting on a bar stool at the bar and then kept walking. Her eyes followed him outside until he disappeared down the street. In a blink of an eye, he was gone.

***

It had taken all of Tom's strength to get out of that booth and leave the restaurant without giving away his feelings and shock at what Gabrielle had told him about Chantal. All he could think about was Chantal. She had reached out to him through Gabrielle. Now what? The desire he had felt for her was still strong. He remembered the way her hips had moved, her soft moans, and her touch, which still sent shivers through his body. She could bring him to his knees anytime.

Every fiber of his being lusted for Chantal. He wanted her to come and rescue him from this evil world, but he had to be realistic. It wasn't going to happen. Gabrielle told him that Chantal still had feelings for him. Even if she took him back, she eventually would realize that he wasn't the person she thought he was, and she would hate him because of it. He couldn't have both worlds. He had to choose between being with her and getting his revenge. The two didn't mix, and he wouldn't risk Chantal's safety.

Could he trust that Gabrielle had told him the truth? She had stunned him when she had said she had forgiven him. But could he trust her? Was she telling him the truth?

As he walked, he mumbled, "She loves me and wants to see me again." Even after she had found out everything about him and what he had done, she still loved him. Gabrielle had given her proof of what he had done. Chantal had read the articles about the trial. Despite what Gabrielle told him, he still doubted that Chantal would want anything to do with him.

The woman loved him. That was the last thing she had told him before he had been wheeled into the operating room. He was at a crossroads, and he had to decide whether or not to cut all ties with her. He knew it was the right thing to do, and he'd rather die than have her get involved in his plans and get hurt. He had to let her go.

He really wanted to see her again, but he had waited ten years for his revenge. He had dreamed about this day. It had kept him sane while time had ticked away in prison. The injuries from the truck wreck had set him back again. He wouldn't be physically ready for another month or so. Maybe if he saw Chantal again, he might not have the same feelings as before. Maybe it was all in his head. How could you love someone that didn't know who you were? How could she forgive him so easily after he had tricked her?

Gabrielle had thrown him a curve ball by telling him she had forgiven him for all the wrong he had tried to do to her. He thought back how he had threatened her with bodily harm and then had blown up her inn in Canada as he tried to get rid of her. She had suffered a brain injury, and worst of all, she had been pregnant at the time of the attack. She could have lost her child, but thankfully the doctors had been able to save the baby. She had barely made it through, but Bernard's love had never wavered—it had grown stronger.

It was all Ron's fault. Tom should never have tried to kill Gabrielle, but at the time, he had been following orders and he had attempted to protect his employer's reputation. How could she forgive him? She was making him feel guilty. Until he had met Chantal, he had never felt guilt nor encountered forgiveness. The woman was changing him even though she wasn't near him. Maybe it was because he knew that if Gabrielle suffered, Chantal would too, and he didn't want her to cause her any more pain. He had been wrong—Ron was the wicked one, not Gabrielle. It was clear now what he had to do.

He was mentally exhausted; he needed to try and sort this mess out. The only way was to talk to Chantal and evaluate the situation. But if he dared to do that, she might try to alter his intentions. He had to stay away from her. He could not afford any distractions or diversions.

He had walked for hours, looking at everything and nothing before he realized that the sun had set and that darkness was on him. He walked back to the boarding house. He had lost track of time, but it had been worth every minute. He needed answers, and he had debated a lot, but he had made his decision. He could never see Chantal again. He headed to his room and collapsed on his bed.

***

Gabrielle walked into the house, where Ron was waiting for her. Raymond had called and told him that she had met with Tom without incident. Raymond didn't know what they had talked about, but she was safe, and Tom hadn't harmed her. Before she had time to reach and open the door, Ron was on her like a bee on honey.

"How could you think of meeting with that man? Don't you know how diabolical he is? He could have—" He didn't have time to finish before she raised her hand.

"Stop. I was perfectly safe. Steve was with me, and I had to face him to know if he truly cared for Chantal or not. I had to know. Now, if you will excuse me, I have an important phone call to make," she responded, as if she had just had tea with the girls and nothing significant had happened. She walked past Ron and headed up the stairs to her quarters.

"Gabrielle, we have to talk about this," Ron shouted after her, but all he could do was watch her take step after step until she disappeared around the bend. She never even turned to look at him.

CHAPTER 23

The next day, Chantal had had enough. Now that she knew Gabrielle knew where Tom was, she would face him and find her answers. She was going to follow her heart, something she rarely did. She was going full steam. If she hit a wall, she would deal with it when the time came. She called her travel agent and booked the next flight to Boston. It might be the worst or the best thing she had ever done on the spur of the moment, but she needed closure.

If he didn't want her, then so be it. At least then she would be able to move on with her life. She wanted see him face-to-face and hear him say whether or not he loved her. If he didn't, then she would leave him, but she wouldn't believe it.

The pain was already unbearable, so what was the worst that could happen? She loved him. Maybe they still had a chance to have a life together and be happy. Her whole world was upside down. She needed answers, and she was determined to get them, even if it meant being rejected by the man she loved. She would make him change his mind, but would that be the solution, or would it cause more problems in the long run? So many uncertainties. She hoped that she was strong enough to bear it if things didn't work the way she wanted them to.

She sat on the plane, numb from all the heartache that this relationship had caused. She returned to reality when the pilot came on the intercom.

He told the passengers that they would land in Boston in a few minutes and to buckle up and prepare for landing. She braced herself against the armrests—not for the landing, but for what was ahead of her.

She finally walked out the front doors of the airport with her carry-on in hand. She raised her hand to flag a taxi. When one stopped, she sat in the back and told the cabbie where she wanted to go. She hadn't told Gabrielle that she was coming nor had waited for her to call back. She was on a mission, and nothing was going to stop her. She just needed Tom's address so that she could confront him and tell him she loved him. Her phone rang. She looked down and answered it.

"Hi! I was waiting for your call," she said, a little uncertain of how Gabrielle would react when she told her she was in Boston. She was prepared for whatever Gabrielle threw at her.

"Hi, do you have a minute? I have something I want to talk to you about," Gabrielle said cheerfully.

"What about?" Now would be a good time for Chantal to tell her where she was.

"I met with Tom yesterday," Gabrielle answered. Chantal was silent for a moment, then spoke.

"Well, you might not understand this, but after I talked to you yesterday and you told me you could find out where John—or should I say Tom—was, I took the next flight out. I'm on my way to your house this minute." Chantal held her breath as she waited for Gabrielle's response. Chantal hoped she would understand why she was doing this.

"Wow! I knew you were bold, but I never expected you to be impulsive. Okay then, I'll tell you about it when you arrive." Gabrielle laughed.

"Great, I should be there in about fifteen minutes. We can discuss my strategy to get Tom back in my life." She was elated and relieved that her friend understood her need to finish this once and for all. Chantal clicked her phone off and settled in for the rest of the ride. A broad smile appeared on her face. She was confident that she would get her man back. This would work. She didn't want to think otherwise.

***

Tom sat in his new truck a block from the Rian residence. He was parked on a hillside under a large oak tree. He had decided that he might as well do some reconnaissance to assess the security that they had on the grounds. He knew the estate pretty well since he had been the head of security for ten years before everything had gone wrong. He needed to determine when the guards rotated and how many new cameras had been installed. After that, he would move to execute his plan. He placed his binoculars on his lap as his mind wandered back to yesterday. When he had left the restaurant after meeting Gabrielle, he had noticed that Raymond was still tracking him. Unable to stop himself, he had confronted Raymond.

"If I see you following me again, I'll shoot you between the eyes. Understood?" he had told him in a whisper, giving him a sly smile. He had seen the fright in Raymond's eyes. Raymond hadn't spoken a word. Tom had nodded and continued walking down the road. He chuckled at the memory.

This morning when he had left the house and walked to his truck, he had not seen Raymond or anyone else on his tail. He had driven around for half an hour and had kept an eye on his rearview mirror to make sure that no one was following him. Raymond must have understood.

Tom sat in his vehicle, checking the estate from time to time through his Steiner military binoculars. They allowed him to see the grounds perfectly. He had been surveying the estate for about an hour when a taxicab turned into the driveway. Tom brought his binoculars back to his eyes.

He couldn't see whomever was sitting in the back seat. He zoomed in to get a better look. The cab driver went to the back of the vehicle to pull a suitcase from the truck. Tom had just focused on the passenger when she turned. Suddenly he was looking right at her. He sucked in his breath and held it. *Chantal, what are you doing here?* he whispered to himself.

He froze for a split second. He could feel his blood pumping through his veins. He felt alive again. His feelings for her hit full force, and he could feel an erection growing. Just looking at her made him light-headed. What was she doing here? What was he going to do now?

He wanted her, but he had thought he would never see her again. Now she was back in the States. Tom felt confused. Why was she here? He focused on her every gesture until she walked to the entrance of the house and embraced Gabrielle. His heart sank as the door closed. He laid his binocular down and sat motionless, trying to sort out what he felt for this woman and how her presence would affect his game plan.

***

After Chantal was settled in the guest bedroom again, she and Gabrielle had a cup of tea in the solarium and a Caesar salad with chicken that the chef had prepared for lunch. Chantal decided to begin the conversation about Tom.

"So, tell me what happened when you met Tom?" She knew that Gabrielle didn't like him, and she truly appreciated Gabrielle's meeting him instead of just talking on the phone.

"I met him at a pizzeria. I'm sorry, but I needed to be in a public place. I still don't want to be alone with him. I'm not sure if I trust him yet. I told him you knew about his past and that you still wanted to see him again," Gabrielle said, summarizing her meeting.

"You shouldn't worry about him. He's just a big teddy bear, really. So, what did he say to you? Does he want to see me?" Chantal bit her lower lip as she waited, uncertain about the answer. She still hadn't touched her food, even though her stomach was growling.

"He didn't say anything. Nothing. He responded loudly when I told him I didn't want him to hurt you. He said he would never harm you, so that was good, right?" Gabrielle took a bite of her salad, raising a finger for Chantal to wait until she swallowed. "He was very surprised when I told him that you knew he had said he loved you. He wasn't expecting that one, but otherwise his expression didn't change much. He never said that he would call or that he wanted to see you, so I don't know. What do you think?" Gabrielle said.

"I came here to get answers, so I'll be damned if I don't. Tomorrow I'm going to go find him, and we're going to have a heart-to-heart talk. If it doesn't work out, then so be it. I'll have to accept it and move on." Chantal was committed to resolve it one way or another.

***

Tom couldn't get Chantal out of his mind. His every thought was consumed by her. He couldn't concentrate anymore. He had to go back to his boarding house and think about Chantal's unexpected arrival. He hadn't thought in a million years that he would ever see her again this soon. The remote possibility that he might be able to touch her again made his blood boil with pleasure. He lay motionless on the bed and wondered if she really had forgiven him for deceiving her.

I'm so sorry for hurting you, Chantal. I didn't mean to, he thought. If only she could hear him. What was he to do now? He needed time to figure things out. If it was meant to be, then they would be together. It would happen. Otherwise there was nothing else he could do or say. He was in love with her, but he wouldn't go after her. He still had to finish what he had started. It was pulling him toward disaster, but he had to do it anyway. The last thing he wanted to do was hurt her, and his feelings for her were beginning to grow stronger than his need for revenge. Tom didn't know what to think anymore.

CHAPTER 24

Chantal was up early. She showered, letting the water run down her body. It invigorated her and made her even more determined to gain her love back. She dressed in jeans, a white sweater, and a pink scarf. The weather was cloudy and windy. She could see the branches of the trees moving outside her window, but she wouldn't let anything deter her from going to see Tom today.

She hurried down the stairs, holding to the railing so that she wouldn't fall. In seconds, she was headed for the kitchen to talk with Gabrielle. She was turning the corner in the hallway when she bumped into Ron. She stood there for an instant. She wanted to smile but couldn't, knowing he hated Tom. She hadn't anticipated running into him, but he did live here. Now that she knew the whole story behind why he was in his wheelchair, she was unsure how to address him. He was the one who had ordered Tom to go after Gabrielle, and he was the reason Tom had gone to jail. Well, a part of it at least.

"Good morning, Mr. Rian. How are you today?" she said, politely trying to pass by him casually. He had abruptly stopped in the middle of her path, blocking her way. He was just staring at her, his eyebrows furrowed and his lips twisted in a scowl.

"What the hell are you doing back here?" he blurted out at her. Chantal opened mouth to answer him, but nothing came out. She was caught off guard. She wondered why he would attack her like that. She had never done anything to him. She took a step back and then stopped.

"Don't tell me you came back to meet up with that foul, vile excuse for a man who should still be in prison for putting me in this God-forsaken wheelchair and endangering my family. You should be ashamed to even associate with our family. You—you are going to get Gabrielle hurt. It will be your fault if someone from this family gets injured." His voice had risen as he went along. He was clenching his teeth.

It was obvious that Ron was angry. Chantal was taken aback for a minute. She looked at him with disgust, and she wrinkled her nose at him. She didn't want say anything, but then her anger took over. Chantal was going to give him a piece of her mind. She saw Gabrielle coming toward them, alarmed. She must have heard the shouting from the next room. Chantal wasn't going to let this man tell her what to do.

"Listen up, Mr. Rian. I have nothing against you, but let me tell you a few things. First, I would never hurt Gabrielle. I love her too much for that but you—YOU were the one who ordered Tom to destroy her. Or did you forget that? YOU were the one who started it all from the beginning because you couldn't accept her as an equal in your family. It's your own Goddamn fault you're in this wheelchair, no one else's. So accept it and move on. You really need a reality check!" She leaned toward him, breathing heavily. She could feel the heat rising from her neck to her face. She stared him down as he was doing to her. Her fear was gone. She stood there, and then she folded her arms in front of her chest.

"GET OUT of my house—you disgraceful girl! You are not welcome here. GET OUT!" he shouted at her. He lifted his arm and pointed his index finger toward the front door. Chantal saw Gabrielle run toward them.

"Ron, stop it! She's my guest, and she is welcome here. This is my home as much as yours," Gabrielle told him as sternly as she could without shouting at him. She now stood in front of him. Chantal walked past Ron and went to the entrance of the kitchen to wait for Gabrielle to return. She heard Gabrielle talking to him.

"Ron, she is right. You have to try to move on. Maybe you should think about forgiving him. I love you very much, but this hatred has to stop. Chantal is right. Now go and leave her alone," Gabrielle said to him softly, then walked out of the room, leaving Ron by himself to stew in the hallway. Chantal was by the counter in the kitchen. Her whole body was shaking. She looked down at her hands. They wouldn't stop shaking. She inhaled deeply and then exhaled. She had to get a grip on herself. It wasn't like her to blow up at anyone, but that man surely had deserved it. She wasn't one bit sorry.

She had only told him the truth, and he had to leave Tom alone. She heard footsteps coming toward her. She looked up and noticed Gabrielle coming toward her. She walked up to her and gave her a hug. Chantal could feel her eyes sting as tears threatened to overwhelm her, but she wouldn't give that man the satisfaction of making her cry. She blinked several times to get herself back under control.

"I'm so sorry you had to witness that. I was not very ladylike, was I? Sorry," Chantal said to Gabrielle when she let go of her. She bowed her head and quickly wiped the tears from her eyes.

"Hey! Don't worry about it. He deserved it. You didn't say anything to him that he didn't deserve. He still blames everyone but himself for what happened to him," Gabrielle told Chantal and then smiled at her to comfort her. She patted her arm to console her.

"I really told him, didn't I? Oh My God! I can't believe I just did that, but you know he deserved it. It wasn't entirely Tom's fault, and you know that. I'm so embarrassed," Chantal said to her friend as she flushed. She couldn't think straight anymore. She had to gain control again.

"I told you, it's fine. You kind of told him off, but he needed it," Gabrielle said, and then she laughed quietly with Chantal. She poured Chantal a cup of coffee and placed it in front of her.

"What are your plans for today?" Gabrielle asked while she grabbed her own coffee and sipped it. She walked back to Chantal, and they sat on the stools at the marble counter.

"I'm going to go find Tom and talk to him. I really don't know what I'm going to say, but I need answers," she said. She had stopped shaking, and her adrenaline was back to its normal level. She started to giggle and couldn't stop. Gabrielle looked at her.

"What's so funny?" she asked. Between laughs, Chantal explained.

"Who would of thought! That I, of all people, would stand up to such a rich and powerful man—and tell him off!"

They both looked at each other and laughed until Chantal had belly cramps. She had her arms around her stomach, holding it. Finally after everything was under control again, Chantal asked Gabrielle for Tom's home address. Gabrielle grabbed a pen and paper from the drawer and wrote it down. She passed it to Chantal, who looked at it and nodded.

"I'll have the car brought out front and have Steve bring you over. If you don't need him, send him on home," Gabrielle suggested to her and laughed some more.

"You are too funny. Shhh! Someone might hear us. It's not necessary. I can take a cab. It's nice to be chauffeured around town, but I also want to do a little shopping," she answered and then smiled at Gabrielle.

"Chauffeur, it is. And don't worry. Take your time." Chantal leaned over and hugged her one more time. Gabrielle went to the house phone and called Steve to bring the car.

***

Ron had sat in the hallway for at least five minutes, stunned. No one had ever talked to him that way. With the exception of his son Bernard, most people were afraid of him and were never so blunt or so honest. People usually sucked up to him—they always wanted something from him. His head spun, and he kept replaying the incident with Chantal and Gabrielle. He couldn't believe that he could be so wrong. He was never wrong!

Ron had been in his office for hours, but he couldn't stop thinking about the conversation with the girls. He sat by the window and gazed outside. Ron kept hearing what the girls had said to him with so much emotion. He began to realize that what they had said might be the truth.

Could they be right? Should he consider forgiving Tom?

His mind went back to the events that took place so long ago. What Chantal had said was true. He *had* started it all. At the beginning, he hadn't wanted Bernard to marry Gabrielle. He truly had thought that Bernard needed to marry someone who had the same social status as he did, but Bernard had fallen in love with Gabrielle.

It was correct that he had told Tom to discourage the union, but after Ron had found out that Gabrielle was pregnant with his grandchild, he had changed his mind. By that time, though, Tom had been set on follow-

172

ing through with the plan. Tom had tried to kill Gabrielle by blowing up her inn. Ron hadn't had any choice after that, so he had given Tom up to the authorities. Otherwise Tom would have been unstoppable. Ron was afraid of what Tom might have done to his family.

Tom had tried to get revenge against Ron for sending the police after him. He had infiltrated Ron's home and shot him. The bullet was still lodged in his back. Sure, Tom had gone to prison, but he hadn't been there as long as Ron had wanted. He wanted Tom to suffer just as much as he did every day that he had to sit in this wheelchair. His mind kept returning to Chantal dreadful words: *It's your own Goddamn fault that you are in this wheelchair, so accept it and move on.* He kept hearing it over and over. He placed his hands over his ears, as if doing so would block it out. He wondered if he wouldn't feel so angry every day if he forgave him and moved on.

He was so vexed with Tom sometimes that Ron sometimes wished he could kill him. Ron looked out down at the landscaped terrain and rubbed his arms. A chill ran down his back. He turned his wheelchair and decided he would rethink this subject later. He rolled his chair to the bar as quickly as he could and poured a drink. He swallowed it and then poured another. He was trying to drown out the voices in his head.

***

Chantal had decided to take advantage of Steve's assistance, since she had him for the day. She asked him first to drop her at Saks Fifth Avenue at Copley Place, a high-end retail store in downtown Boston. She wanted to buy a new outfit before she went to confront Tom.

"Could you pick me up about two hours from now? If I finish before, I'll call. Thank you, Steve," she said as she exited the vehicle, smiling at him after she had gotten out.

"Very well, miss. I'll be right here," Steve said. He took off to park the car.

She hurried inside the store to start looking at the fashions. She figured she could meet with Tom at his boarding house later in the afternoon. *What if he isn't there or he doesn't want to be with me?* she thought. But then why had he told her he loved her? She would find him. She now knew that she had heard him that morning. Maybe he hadn't wanted her to know. Uncertainties were creeping in her heart. She would be brave and face the challenges that were to come. She loved him more that anyone in this world. She would make him love her, or she would die without him.

CHAPTER 25

Tom sat on his bed in his room. He hadn't slept since he had seen Chantal arrive back in town. He looked at the unkempt bed and closed his eyes, wishing it was untidy because she had been in his bed. He was having a hard time focusing on anything else. He hated the emotions she had brought back. He really had thought he could go forward without her. He was debating whether he should try to contact her or not. He was afraid that if he met her, it would distract him from his plan. He wondered how it would feel to be loved unconditionally. He also sometimes wished that he could delete his whole past except for Chantal's love. She had given herself to him so freely and hadn't asked for anything in return.

He rubbed his face with both his hands, trying to erase her from his mind, but he knew it wouldn't be that easy. He stood and walked to the bathroom, hoping that a cold shower would wash away his sexual thoughts of her. He probably needed more than water, but right now he had to make an effort to forget her.

He walked out of the bathroom naked after his shower and threw on a pair of black jeans with a matching black hoody that he pulled over his head. He wanted to go back to the estate to see if she was still there before he went forward with his mission. He wouldn't endanger her.

A half-hour later, he had stepped out the front door, put his hands in his pockets, and walked to his truck in the parking garage. He drove down his street and passed a black sedan with tinted windows going the opposite way. He wondered if it was Chantal. It resembled the car that Gabrielle had sent for him when they had met at the pizzeria the day before.

"Shit," he mumbled. His gut feeling told him to stop and turn around. He couldn't keep driving. What if it was Chantal? An odd feeling surged through his whole body. His chest started pounding. What was he going to do if it was Chantal? You didn't see too many sedans driving through this part of the neighborhood. It had to be someone with means to have a chauffeur.

He pulled to the side of the street and quickly parked his vehicle. He adjusted his rearview mirror so he could see the person who stepped out of the sedan, but the only person that he saw was the chauffeur as he entered the boarding house. Tom watched anxiously. He held his breath and focused on the mirror. Tom waited.

Minutes ticked away; still no one stepped out of the car. Tom watched and tried to calm himself. If it was Chantal, why wasn't she coming out of the car? He noticed the chauffeur coming out. He walked back and got into the driver's seat of the sedan. He spoke to someone in the back seat, but Tom couldn't identify who it was. The tinted windows blocked his view.

The car now came his way. Tom scooted down in his seat. He absolutely didn't want to be recognized. Whoever was in that car was looking for him. He was sure of it. Ron was the only person he knew who had the means to send someone after him. He pulled himself up, grabbed a pair of dark sunglasses from the dashboard, put them on, tugged his hood down low, and pushed his vehicle in gear. He was going to follow them. He needed to know whether or not it was Chantal. He kept his distance, but he already knew whom the vehicle belonged to when they took the exit. It was definitely owned by the Rian family.

He backed away from the sedan a little. He didn't want to be right on its tail so when it turned into the Rians' driveway. He drove to the spot where he had parked the day before so that he could see who was in the car. *Damn it.* The car was going straight to the garage. It didn't stop at the front entrance. Now he wouldn't know who was in the backseat. Tom started his truck and headed back home. He wanted to know who had gone looking for him in the boarding house. Maybe the chauffeur had left a message.

He parked in front of the boarding house. He had no time to waste. He didn't care if someone saw him or not. He went up the steps two at a time, lunged for the door, opened it, and entered the house. He looked over at the woman at the desk. She was a woman in her late fifties who was stuck in the eighties, with her blue eye shadow and the big black puffy hair. She always dressed in tight clothes that looked like they had been made for a teenager.

Today he noticed her neon top that dipped much too low. Her push-up bra was working a little too well, and her breasts seemed to be popping out of her shirt. She also was wearing a pair of light-blue yoga pants. She really needed a makeover. She was known for not relaying messages well. He tried to slow his pace so he wouldn't frighten her; he wanted some answers. He caught his breath and gave her a sexy smile as he approached her.

"Hi, Stephanie! How are you today, sweetie?" Tom said. He sat on the corner of her desk, one leg dangling, the other on solid ground. He looked at her and grinned. She looked at him and sat up straight, bringing her shoulders back so that she could expose her chest at him even more.

"I'm good, honey. How about you?" she answered him. He needed the information, so he had to charm her in giving it. He reached over and touched her arm lightly. She smiled at him with teeth that had become yellowed and disgusting from smoking too many cigarettes. Tom continued. "The man with the sedan who was here a moment ago—what did he want?" he asked as pleasantly as he could, checking her out as he spoke. She noticed and gave him a broader smile.

"Why do you want to know, sweetie?" she asked him.

"Well, I just noticed him coming in. I thought that he might have been coming to see you, since you're so hot," he said in a low voice. She giggled, blushed, and looked away for an instant, but then she brought her chair closer to him. Tom could smell the revolting scent of tobacco smoke on her clothes.

"As a matter of fact, he was looking for you," she answered and tilted her head at him.

"Really? I don't know anyone that important. What did he want with me? Did he leave a message?" Tom was going to throw up if he had to keep this up any longer. He knew he had to make her think he was interested in her.

"No, he just asked if you were here, and I told him you weren't, so he said he'd came back later on. No message. Hey! How about we go out for a drink after I finish work today?" Stephanie asked him and gravitated toward him. Tom jumped off the desk and started walking as fast as he could toward the exit. He didn't bother answering her; he just wanted to get away from her. He heard her yell some foul words at him. He returned to his truck and drove off. It was time for him to go to the Rians'. It was now or never.

***

Ron sat in his chair near the entrance of the house. He had been watching the front door for the last hour. He was told that Chantal had gone shopping and would return shortly. He needed to talk to her about Tom. What she and Gabrielle had told him this morning had haunted him all day. He was going to try to make peace with Tom; maybe then he would be able to find the peace of mind he had sought for the last ten years. He now understood that being free of his anger toward Tom would take away some of his bitterness. Chantal was right. He had to start moving forward. It had taken a complete stranger to bring him to his senses. He needed to be happy again, and the only way was to let go of the grudge he held against Tom.

Every minute of every day for the last ten years, Ron had wasted his energy on his hatred toward Tom for putting him in his wheelchair, but now he wanted to let it go. Ron had once loved Tom like a son. While things couldn't go back to the way they had been before, Ron could forgive him. It would be a start. Tom had always tried to protect Ron's family when he had worked for him. Ron had hired men to follow Tom as soon as he had found out that Tom was out of prison, and Tom had never retaliated against him. "Maybe prison has changed him," he said to himself.

He had gotten the nerve to face him today. His chauffeur had brought him to the boarding house where Tom lived, but he hadn't been there. He wanted to tell Chantal that she was right. Tom might have repented since he had gotten out of prison. He wanted to tell her that he wished her the best with him.

Ron heard a car door shut and voices. He moved closer to the entrance. The front door opened, and Chantal walked in with several bags in her hands. She stopped immediately when she saw him there. Her mouth opened and then closed. Not a sound came out. She looked surprised to see him. "Chantal, may I have a word with you?" Ron said quietly.

"Sure, Mr. Rian," she said, still standing in the middle of the foyer. She was biting her lower lip. She looked worried, so Ron decided to be nice.

"Nothing too important. Why don't you get rid of your bags, then meet me in the library down the hall, and we'll have a drink." Ron pointed toward the room. He then he backed his chair so she could get by him. He smiled up at her.

"Okay, just give me a few minutes, and I'll be back. I'll put my bags in the bedroom." She nodded at him and walked past.

Ron watched as she went up the staircase. He then proceeded to the library, where he poured himself a glass of whiskey. He took a drink and closed his eyes as he felt it burn all the way to his stomach. He refilled his tumbler as he waited for Chantal to come and join him. He really hoped that this wouldn't end the same way as their encounter this morning.

***

Chantal was baffled by how nice Ron had been when she had met him in the entrance hallway. The difference in his moods was like night and day. She couldn't think what he wanted to speak to her about. The only thing they had in common was Tom, and she was not going to throw Tom under the bus. She would defend him and not listen to Ron's ranting against Tom.

She placed her bags on the bed, looked in the mirror to fix her hair a bit, and then walked downstairs to meet with Ron. Her stomach was in knots, but she kept walking. Midway down the stairs, she stopped and grabbed the railing. Her hands were trembling, her adrenaline level was high, and she was really nervous. Why on earth did he want to talk to her? Hopefully Ron wasn't going to harm Tom.

Her feet felt heavier with each step she took. She just knew Ron was going to discuss Tom.

When she arrived at the mahogany doors, she sighed and took the last few steps toward Ron. She saw him by the bar, drinking a cocktail.

"Oh! Good, you're here. Please join me. Would you care for a drink? Whiskey?" he asked while lifting his glass and smiling. He seemed in a good mood.

"Sure, I'll have whatever you're having," she answered. A whiskey might settle her nerves. She watched as he poured it in a tumbler.

"Ice?"

She just nodded at him. He picked up a few ice cubes, tossed them in, and passed her the drink. She grabbed it, her hand still shaking.

"Thank you." She brought it to her mouth and took a sip. It was a welcome taste, and it soothed her dry mouth.

"Let's go over here by the fire. You can sit and be more comfortable." She followed him without saying a word. Her legs were becoming rubbery. She would be glad to sit. What would such a powerful man want with her?

Finally she sat. She was grateful that she didn't have to walk any further. She bent her head down and stared at her drink. She kept telling her hands to stop quivering, but for some reason they weren't cooperating. She quickly glanced up at Ron and noticed that he was watching her. She felt the heat rise in her face.

"I asked you to join me here because I want to thank you and to apologize for being so rude to you this morning," Ron said. She couldn't believe her ears.

What had brought that on? "Thank me for what?"

"You were right. You made me realize that I was stuck in a rut and that it was time to move on and to try to forgive Tom. I thought it over, and I now realize that I have to let go of my anger toward Tom so that I can have peace again." He paused for a moment. "It wasn't all Tom's fault. I did have a part in all that happened ten years ago, and I'm going to try to forgive him," Ron said and then lifted his drink and took a sip. Chantal was speechless. She hadn't expected that from him. She was shocked that he would admit he was wrong. She felt herself calm down and noticed that her hands were no longer shaking. She just smiled at Ron.

"I just wanted to let you know, that's all. It took a stranger telling me off to bring me back to reality. Now, I'm going to try to make my life more tolerable. I have been preoccupied with my own grief for too many years.

Now I can see the other side. Thank you again," he told Chantal. She finished her drink, stood next to her chair, and looked down at Ron.

"I'm sorry I spoke to you so harshly, but I am glad you are going to try to patch it up with Tom." She walked to the bar and placed her empty glass on the counter. She turned toward Ron. "Thank you for the drink," Chantal said, and then she walked past him and left the library.

CHAPTER 26

Chantal needed fresh air, so she headed for the front door. She figured that a walk outside would do her good. As soon as she opened the door, the cool air calmed her. She inhaled the crisp, fresh scent of autumn. She was having a hard time understanding what had just happened, but she was optimistic that it was a good thing.

Ron had said that he wanted to forgive Tom, but she wondered whether Ron was sincere or was just pretending for her benefit. She decided to continue her stroll up the street before she showered and went to Tom's house. There still was time, and she wanted to clear her mind so she could face him. She didn't know what she was going to say, but she anticipated that he would be surprised to see her.

She walked down the street and admired the large homes of the neighborhood. The trees were starting to lose their leaves. The different colors of the leaves were breathtaking. As she strolled, she got a strange feeling that someone was watching her. She turned to look but didn't see anyone around, so she kept walking.

She noticed two vehicles that were parked not too far ahead. Someone was in one of them. She squinted so she could see better, but the man's face was partially covered by a hood. She felt a chill down her arms. She pulled her hands out of her pockets. *Don't panic*, she told herself. *It's fine. It's a safe area.* But the closer she got to the vehicle, the edgier she felt. It was as if she was drawn to him. *Chantal, turn around and get out of here. You're always the one who asks why people go places that they know are dangerous. Don't be an idiot,* she thought.

She was about half a block away from the Rians' house, but she didn't know what to do. Go forward, or turn and run? She stopped dead in her tracks. She wasn't going any further. She knew she wouldn't be able to lift her feet even if her life depended on it. A man stepped out of the truck and walked leisurely her way. His head was bowed just enough that she couldn't see his features. His hands were in the front pocket of his hoody. He came directly toward her. She started to tremble all over.

He was almost on her. *Dear God! Help me!* she prayed. *This is crazy,* she said to herself. *You are fine. Stop it!* She took a tentative step forward, and then another. The man was standing right in front of her. He lifted his head and nodded at her, and then passed her without saying a word.

She felt as if a load had been removed from her shoulders. She turned her head to make sure that he was still walking away. He was, so she went on her way. She felt stupid. It must be because she wasn't used to the big city. An hour later, she was back at the house and ready to face anything. She had totally forgotten about the incident with the young man.

***

Tom watched Chantal walk up the hill. He was crouched between the trees on the side of road with his 9-mm revolver. He saw her stop when she saw a young man come toward her. Tom had been ready to pounce on the guy had he made the wrong move. He had seen the fear on Chantal's face. He felt the need to protect her. What would he have done if he had shot the guy? This was insane.

He had to sort out his feelings for his woman before he proceeded forward. He crawled back into his truck, making sure that she didn't see him, and took off. Tom had no place to go. He felt alone. He had to reassess the situation. Should he talk to her? His body and heart told him yes, but his mind told him no.

He didn't want her in that house when he went after Ron. He had never thought it would come to this, but he knew he had to choose between her and Ron. He knew he couldn't have both. He had to make his decision soon. Every time he saw her, doubts crept into his mind.

He drove around the endless streets with no destination in mind. He turned into a park area and parked his truck. He jumped out. He needed to think. His strides were long and slow. He saw children playing on the playground to his right, their parents sitting on nearby benches and keeping an eye on them. He walked further in, following a jogging trail, and stopped next to a small pond. He saw a bench off the path, so he went and sat down to watch the ducks swimming in the water.

His mind wandered back to Chantal. Maybe he did have a chance with her. *Why had she returned to Boston? Has she really forgiven me? Gabrielle said she had, but is it true? Who had come to the boarding house today, looking for him? Had it been her?* He had asked himself these questions several times, but he still didn't have the answers.

He would have to take a plunge to answer his questions. It was now or never. He reached in his pocket and—without hesitation—dialed her number on his cellphone. He placed the phone to his ear and listened as it rang, once, twice, and then he heard her answer. His whole body tensed up, and his blood was pumping hard.

"Allo," Chantal answered.

He closed his eyes when he heard her voice. For the first time in years, he felt afraid. He was truly unsure and terrified the outcome of this conversation. He didn't even have the guts to face her. He had called her first. His desire for her came back the minute he heard her voice. He wanted her. He needed her. But—

"Hi, Chantal. It's John, or should I say, Tom." He was holding the phone so tightly his knuckles hurt. Unable to move a muscle, he waited for her to reject him. The cool wind whistled, but he didn't feel cold. A sweat formed along his back, and he wasn't breathing. He waited for the rebuttal of his life.

"Tom, is that you? Please, don't hang up! We need to talk. I'm in Boston." Chantal voice sent waves of memories crashing over him.

"I know." It was all he could say. His mouth was dry like the desert. He swallowed hard, but it didn't soothe his thirst.

"I want to meet you. Please, I'll come to you—anywhere," Chantal said. He could hear her voice quivering. He couldn't hurt her anymore. He had to agree to meet her one last time.

"Fine, meet me at the boarding house in an hour. Do you have the address?" he said. He was trying not to be too optimistic about this meeting. He had to be prepared for the rejection that was coming his way. He made his decision at that exact moment. He had to let her go. It was the only way. She needed to return home, to leave the Rians' house.

"Yes, yes, I have it. Tom, I—" He hung up the phone. He sat there dazed, immobilized. Not a thought or feeling was going through his mind. He just stared off at the water. A few minutes passed. He had to prepare for his best performance yet. He had to convince her he didn't love her and that she needed to go back home. This was his most crucial mission of all. He had to let her go.

He drove back to the boarding house and sat on the porch in one of the rocking chairs. He waited impatiently for Chantal to arrive. He still had half an hour to wait. It seemed like time had stopped. The minutes passed too slowly. He stood up and started pacing the length of the veranda, going back and forth. He kept his eyes on the street. He saw the black sedan approach. He knew it was Chantal. He watched as the car parked in front of the house. The chauffeur exited, opened the back passenger door, and then stood by the car.

Tom walked down the steps and approached the car. He ducked his head and peered in. Chantal sat gracefully on the seat. She smiled at him.

"Hi," she said and patted the seat beside her. He didn't answer her; he just slid into the seat and closed the door. He needed to be as cold as he could, otherwise she wouldn't leave. It was going to break his heart to pieces, but he couldn't show any emotion. He placed his hands on his knees. He didn't glance her way, looking straight ahead and hoping he could go through with what he had intended—to send her home.

"You wanted to talk? Then talk." he told her, stone-faced.

"Tom, I came back to Boston because I love you. I want us to be together. I know the whole story about your past, and it doesn't matter. I understand now why you did what you did. I just want you to give this relationship a chance. Please look at me." He felt her hand on his cheek, trying to turn his

185

face to hers. He let her move his head because the barest touch of her skin against his sent fire between his legs. He wanted her, but he had to fight it.

"I want you to go home. I'm not the right man for you. You will find someone else to love you." He looked into her eyes. They were filling with tears. His heart was breaking, but he had to do this.

"No, I won't go—I love you, and I know you feel the same way. Don't send me away. This relationship can work," she told him as a tear fell from her eye, but he didn't react. He didn't speak. He just took her hand and placed it on her knee.

"I don't love you. You need to return home. I won't see you again. This is the last time I will talk to you. I have other things that take priority over you." It took all his strength in his being to say those words, but it was for the best.

"Priorities! I'll give you priority. *I* am your priority. You are throwing everything away. Tell me what is more important than me. I know you love me." Her voice cracked, and she was now crying. Tears fell down her beautiful cheeks. He could feel her pain. He wanted to reach over and comfort her. He wanted to tell her he loved her more that anything in this world, but he would not. He needed his revenge.

"I'm sorry I misled you—I have to go." He turned to look at her, and the next thing he knew he had cupped his hands around her face and had pressed his mouth against hers. He wanted to taste her one more time. She wrapped her arms around his neck and pulled him closer to her. She opened her mouth so their tongues could dance together one last time.

He could feel her small breasts against his chest. He finally regained control and pulled away. She was an inch from his face. He could smell her perfume as he peered into her blue eyes, which were turning red as tears spilled down her face. The pain in his gut was unbearable, but he just said, "Goodbye, Chantal." He let go of her, turned his back, found the door handle, swung it opened, and stepped out.

As he was closing it he heard her shout, "No, don't do this! I love you! I will not let you go so easily!" Every step he took was like a spear through his heart. He never looked back until he was on the porch. He saw the chauffeur get into the sedan and drive away. He watched the car drive away until he could see it no longer. A tear fell down his cheek. He blinked it away, and he whispered, "I love you, too, Chantal."

CHAPTER 27

Chantal sobbed uncontrollably. Her tears burned her face. She had failed to convince Tom to be with her. Her love was gone. She might never love another man in the same way that she had loved Tom. Her heart was breaking to pieces as anguish pervaded her soul. How was she going to endure this? It was unbearable! What was more important than their love? What was the priority he had been talking about?

Halfway home she could no longer think straight. She looked into her bag, took out tissues, and then blew her nose. She was trying to regain her composure before she arrived back at Gabrielle's house. She wasn't leaving. She didn't believe a word he had said. She brought her fingers to her lips. The way he had kissed her a moment ago told her he still loved her, otherwise he wouldn't have kissed her so passionately. He hadn't been able to look her in the eye. That told her he still cared for her.

She was determined to win him over. She would try again. The car pulled into the driveway of the Rians'. She took a small mirror from her purse and examined her face. Her nose and eyes were still red, but at least she had stopped crying. She didn't want to face Gabrielle looking like this. She took her tube of lipstick and applied some to her lips.

She walked into the Rians' residence as quietly as she could. She really didn't want to talk to Gabrielle at this moment. She went up the stairs silently. When she arrived at her bedroom door, she sighed and then entered. She closed the door and went to lie down on top of her bed to rest and to try to sort this mess out.

She felt a headache building. She rubbed her temples to get rid of it. Chantal was confused. She didn't understand what Tom meant when he had said he had priorities.

I should be his priority. I love him. She turned on her side to face the window. All she wanted to do was to crawl into a hole and die. All of her expectations for this relationship had been shattered. She had to think and find a way to get to Tom to change his mind, but how?

Time passed. She had been in her room for about an hour when she heard a light tapping on her bedroom door. She sat up on her elbows and stared at the door. It had to be Gabrielle checking in on her.

"Come in," Chantal said, even though she didn't want to see anyone. She knew she would have to face Gabrielle sooner or later. The door opened slowly, and Gabrielle peeked her head inside.

"Hi, do you want company?" she asked her with concern in her voice.

"Sure, come in. I might as well tell you what happened." Chantal tried to fix her hair. She pushed her curls away, but they kept falling into her face, so she grabbed an elastic band off of the side table and pulled her hair into a ponytail.

"I brought you a cup of tea. I thought you might need it." Gabrielle placed it on her side table, then sat beside her and waited for Chantal to say something.

"Thanks. Sorry, I'm a mess. The meeting with Tom didn't go as I had planned. He told me to go back home and that he didn't love me, but I don't believe him." She started crying again. Gabrielle put her arms around her.

"Don't cry, Chantal. It will work out. We'll think of something. Don't cry." Gabrielle reached over to a box of tissues by the bed and gave her a few. Chantal blew her nose again and tried to stop the river of tears, but she was having a hard time. Finally, she gave Gabrielle a small smile.

"Thank you. You're a good friend."

"Tell me exactly what he said to you," Gabrielle told her as she passed her the cup of tea. Chantal held it carefully and sipped it, careful not to spill it. It warmed her, and she felt better.

"Well, first, I'm not convinced that he doesn't love me, because of the way he kissed me goodbye. There is no way someone kisses you like that when you don't love them. Second, he told me that he had priorities he had to attend to and that I should go back to Canada. What was that? Do you understand that?" Chantal looked to her friend for answers, who just shrugged.

"Priorities? What priorities?" Gabrielle asked, just as confused as Chantal. Neither said a word as they both thought. "What could be more important than you? And why does he want you out of here?" Gabrielle said to herself. She drew her breath in, her hand shot up to her mouth, and her eyes bulged.

"Oh! Dear God! I think I know what he is planning—what his priority is," Gabrielle blurted out.

"What? Tell me, because I'm clueless." Chantal looked straight at her, but Gabrielle rose and walked to the window. She didn't say anything for a minute.

"What? Tell me." Chantal waited. Gabrielle turned to face her.

"I think he is going to get his revenge for being sent to prison. He is going to try to harm Ron—or our entire family," Gabrielle said, as her face turned pale.

"What are you talking about? Why would he do that? You mean because Ron sent him to prison?" Chantal started to piece the puzzle together. Her face also lost its color. "I can't believe he would do such a thing," Chantal said. "No, if he did this, he would be sent back to jail." *Then what will I do?* Chantal stood and approached Gabrielle. Gabrielle placed her hand on Chantal's forearm and her eyes on her.

"You don't know this man like we do. At least he won't do anything as long as you are here. We cannot tell Ron. He will send an army after Tom to stop him. He will be killed." Gabrielle said. She looked down. "What are we going to do? We have to stop him." She paced back and forth between the window and Chantal. She rubbed her arms, cold despite the fact that the house was warm.

"Ron told me that he had forgiven Tom and that he was going to move on. He told me that he was sorry and that it wasn't all Tom's fault, but Tom doesn't know this. Ron only talked to me today. Maybe we can stop him?

I have to stop Tom from ruining his life and mine. There is no other way," Chantal said, determined to prevent Tom from getting into trouble again.

"How do you plan to do that?" Gabrielle said. Her voice was filled with panic and uncertainty.

"Let me think, OK? Let's keep this between us. Tom won't do anything as long as I'm in the house. That's why he wants me to go home. Of that I'm sure." Chantal had to find a way to convince Tom to not to hurt anyone, but how? "I know! I'm going to text him and tell him that I'm not leaving for Canada until next week and that I want to meet him again before I leave. That will give us time to figure out what to do and say. What do you think?" Chantal looked at Gabrielle for approval. Gabrielle just nodded.

"I suppose it's better that nothing. Are you sure it will work?" Gabrielle replied, unsure. Chantal nodded and then grabbed her cellphone from her pocketbook and started to text Tom. Her fingers flew over the keys.

"I'll make him change his mind. I'm sure he loves me. He'll do it for me." Chantal didn't know who she was trying to convince—Gabrielle or herself.

"Fine, let's wait and see if he answers," Gabrielle said and then walked to the door. She held the handle for a second and glanced at Chantal one last time. Fear was written on her face.

"For all of our sakes, let me know if he answers. I'll be downstairs." Gabrielle opened the door and left without another word.

I'll keep trying until he gives me an answer, otherwise I'm going to go find him. It will all be OK. It will be all right, Chantal kept telling herself while she typed away on her cellphone.

***

Tom had finished talking with Neil, and they were getting things ready. His arm was much better, and Chantal was leaving soon, so they would be able to move forward with the plan in a few days. He just needed to pick up a few more things from the hardware store before they were all set. His shoulder had healed sufficiently, and he felt that he'd be able to do whatever was necessary to defend himself should anything go wrong. After injuring his shoulder, he'd had to postpone his plans for weeks, but nothing was going to stop him now.

How difficult could it be to take down a few inexperienced security guards? He had professional training and could outmatch any of them.

After he said his last goodbye to Chantal, it had taken him a few hours to realize that it was the right thing to do. He was still haunted by the last thing she had said to him: "I won't let you go so easily." She was willing to fight for him. No one had ever done anything like that for him before. He'd always had to fight for everything he had wanted or needed. Nothing had ever been given to him.

Tom was about to leave his room when he heard a ping from his cellphone. He pulled it from his back pocket and looked at it. It was a text. Who would text him? No one knew this number except—no, it couldn't be. His chest felt tight, and he felt heat race to his head. He held his breath. It read:

> Tom, I am not leaving until we talk again. I love you, and I know in my heart that you feel the same. Meet me at tonight, Larz Anderson Park, on the small bridge overlooking the pond at seven o'clock. I'll be waiting for you.

Shit, he told himself. All of his feelings for her came rushing back. He loved her more that anything, but she didn't understand what he had to do. He had chosen to give her up for the sake of getting his revenge, but he knew that he couldn't face her again. He had to think this over. He couldn't let his feelings for her rule him. It would be a distraction he couldn't afford. Not when it meant life or death.

He wouldn't put Chantal in danger. He didn't know how it would go down with Ron and his security personnel. Ron was too unpredictable, especially after Tom had shot him. Ron wanted vengeance just as much as Tom did. Ron had already started by having Tom followed. Ron was no angel.

It would come down to who had the most devious plan and the strongest hand. Ron was never going to forgive him for putting him in that wheelchair. It was going to be him or Ron, and it definitely wasn't going to be him. He wouldn't be defeated in this fight. He'd have to wait for Chantal to leave. She had to return to Canada at some point, but when? He had waited ten years. He could hold off for a few more days. He was a very patient man.

CHAPTER 28

Time had never passed so slowly as after Chantal had texted Tom. She had held her phone for hours, but Tom had never responded. She just hoped that when she went to meet him tonight, he would be there so that they could patch up their relationship and be together. She had decided that she couldn't wait by the phone anymore because it was too painful and irrational.

She decided to take a shower to refresh herself. She stood under the warm jets of water. They massaged her tense muscles and washed the tears away. She shut the water off, stepped out, and wiped herself with a towel. She decided to let her curly hair air-dry. Tom liked it that way. She applied blush to her cheeks and lipstick to her lips and then pulled on her jeans and a sky-blue sweater.

She wasn't very hungry, even though she hadn't eaten since this morning. Her stomach felt as if someone was twisting it. She was so nervous that he wouldn't show tonight. Then what would she do? She walked down to the kitchen, where Gabrielle usually could be found either cooking or organizing the staff.

"Hi, did he answer?" she immediately whispered to Chantal. Chantal just shook her head as she took a seat at the counter. Chantal scanned the kitchen to make sure Ron wasn't around and then turned toward Gabrielle.

"I just wanted to let you know that I'm leaving to go to the park. Thanks for letting me borrow Steve again. I'll call you as soon as I know what's going on," Chantal said, then stood and walked over to her friend to give her a hug.

"Good luck. I say it not just for you, but also for all of us. I am positive I'm right about him. You're the only one who can stop him," Gabrielle murmured in her ear and then let go of her. Chantal nodded and then left the kitchen without another word.

***

Chantal sat anxiously in the back of the sedan as Steve drove. She kept looking at her watch. She still had at least fifteen minutes to wait after she got there. Steve parked the car in the parking lot and opened her door. She heard it shut behind her. Chantal shivered and started to walk away. She then noticed that Steve was only a few steps behind her. She turned to face him.

"Why are you following me?" Chantal asked him, puzzled.

"Sorry, miss, but I have my orders to not leave you alone until you return home," he answered, clasping his hands in front of him. This was Gabrielle being a mother hen. She wanted her security to keep Chantal safe, but Chantal didn't need it. She knew for a fact that Tom would never hurt her, but it was no use arguing with Steve. He wouldn't leave anyway.

"Fine, but could you stand a little further than two feet away from me?" she asked.

"Yes, miss," he said then continued following her until she approached the bridge. She halted and said, "Would you mind waiting on that bench over there, please?"

She hoped he wouldn't argue. He nodded and said, "I'll be right here if you need me." *Great*, Chantal thought. *He might just scare Tom away.* She took the final steps up the path and stopped in the middle of the bridge. She admired the view of the city skyline. She tapped her fingers on the railing of the bridge, sweeping the area for the man she loved. *Where are you, Tom? Will you show?* She just had to have faith that he would appear and that everything would work out. She would wait all night if she had to.

***

Tom had gotten to the park an hour and a half earlier. He had walked the grounds to make sure there weren't any threats to him or Chantal. He didn't trust Ron. He might have sent someone to apprehend him. He had found the bridge quickly and had established a hiding place about thirty yards to the right of it. There was a tree line that went back for about half a mile. The darkness had helped him to avoid anyone in the area until he was in position behind a large oak tree. The bushes in front of him concealed him even better.

He watched Chantal approach the bridge, but she was not alone—the chauffeur-bodyguard was with her. Why? Why hadn't she come alone? He could tell that she was searching for him. She turned her head every time someone came near the area. How beautiful she looked, with her curls flying in the wind and her red lipstick. He was getting sexually aroused just by observing her. He could feel the fire starting to mount between his legs and a bulge beginning to grow. He wanted to get up, envelop her in his arms, and never let go. *Stop it*, he thought. He couldn't risk a potential fight with the security guard. Not yet. He had to keep his strength for later.

She kept checking the time on her watch. He felt sorry for her. The time of the rendezvous had already come and gone. He wondered how long she would stay. *Why wasn't she leaving? Why had he bothered to come?* He knew the answer. He wanted to see her one more time before she left.

Two hours later, he watched as she wiped her tears with the palms of her hand. His heart broke. Agony shot through his chest, but he couldn't move his eyes from her. They were glued to her. He raked his fingers through his hair. He had to look away. Not being able to comfort her as she cried was too painful. He wanted to run up to her, wrap his arms around her to ease her pain, and tell her that he loved her and that it was going to be fine—but he couldn't. He had made his choice, and nothing was going to stop him.

His phone buzzed in his pocket, interrupting his thoughts. He reached for it and then looked up at Chantal. She had her phone in her hands; she was texting him again.

Tom, I will be on this bridge every night at seven until you come. Please do not do anything rash. I know what you are planning. Ron has told me he has forgiven you. Trust me. I love you so much.

He looked across the field. She was waiting for him to reply, but it wasn't going to happen. She walked away from the bridge. He couldn't move his eyes away. He watched her until she was out of sight. He bowed his head and rested his back against the tree. *I love you too—but not enough to fight for you.* He sat there for another hour, rereading the message she had sent to him.

How strange. He wondered what she meant by "I know what you are planning." How could she know? He hadn't told her anything. What shocked him even more was she had said Ron had forgiven him. He didn't believe it for one minute. Ron wasn't the type to forgive anyone. Tom would wait until tomorrow night. If she came alone, he would question her about what she meant and what she thought she knew. Better yet, he decided to send her a text. He pushed the buttons of the letters.

Tomorrow come alone.

Just three small words. He pushed Send, and that was it. He was going to keep a low profile until he met her again. He decided to visit Neil at the house in Ashburnham. No one knew him there, and he had less of a chance of bumping into any of the Rians or Chantal. Too many people now knew where he lived.

***

Chantal was unwilling to accept defeat. There would be another round tomorrow. If harming Ron was his priority, she was going to convince him to not follow through with it. She balled her fists tightly so she wouldn't cry. *Damn you, Tom. You have to trust me and stop pushing me away.* She wondered if Steve had scared him away. Tom knew Steve was Gabrielle's bodyguard. She would come alone tomorrow night. She was confident he would show. If he did not, she was going to go find him at the boarding house.

She was sure he had gotten her texts. He was just not responding to her. She had risked everything in her last one by telling him she knew what he was planning and that Ron had forgiven him. She just hoped he wouldn't run further away from her. She was willing to try whatever it took to bring him to his senses.

She closed her eyes for the ride back. She was mentally exhausted from the long day. She had almost drifted off when she heard her phone buzz. She fished her phone out quickly and read the three words Tom had sent. Her heart jumped for joy. She still had the opportunity to make it right. So he had been there tonight. She knew he would come. She had felt his presence. Now she was positive that he loved her, otherwise he wouldn't have been at the park. But where had he been hiding? It didn't matter. Tomorrow she would go alone.

Gabrielle must have been waiting anxiously for her to return home, because as soon as Chantal opened the front door, Gabrielle grabbed Chantal's arm and whisked her toward the kitchen. Chantal almost tripped along the way, Gabrielle was pulling her so hard.

"So, what happened? Why didn't you call me? I have been worried sick." Gabrielle stood in front of Chantal holding both her forearms.

"He didn't show," Chantal said quietly, then she went to sit on the stool. Gabrielle was right on her heels. She sat beside her and stared at her intensely. "What do you mean he didn't show? Now what? Why didn't he show?" Gabrielle hurled questions at Chantal faster than Chantal could answer.

"Shh! Let me speak. I'll tell you. I went to the bridge and waited, but he never showed. I think Steve spooked him. I texted him that I would be there tomorrow, and he answered back. He just said to come alone, so we are going to have to wait until tomorrow and see what happens," Chantal said calmly and then shrugged. "Now, I'm going to bed. I'm tired. I'll see you later." She bent toward Gabrielle, kissed her on the cheek, and marched out of the room. She had a plan on how to stop Tom, but she needed a little bit of help. She didn't know how she was going to manage it, but she was going to make it happen.

CHAPTER 29

Tom had gone to the house in Ashburnham the previous evening. He had slept like a log and gotten up late. He was well-rested. He had a hearty breakfast at a local diner and planned to make the last repairs to his fortress. He walked outside to the shed in the backyard, picked up his toolbox, and started fixing a few things. The first thing he tackled was the back door. It needed a new lock, so he had purchased one at the hardware store. He had neglected the house for the past few months while he had been staying at the boarding house. His accident hadn't helped the situation. Neil wasn't a very good handyman, so not much had been done, but at least he had kept the place clean.

His mind kept wandering back to Chantal. He had trouble concentrating on anything but her. He had to get back to what he had started in the first place and that was to get his revenge on Ron. He still couldn't get Chantal's text out of his mind. What did she think that she knew? He hadn't said anything to her except that he had priorities and that she wasn't on his list. Tom knew it must have hurt her, but what could he do? She was one of his prime concerns, but he had chosen his revenge first.

She must have talked to someone, but whom? It had to be Gabrielle, because Chantal did know the whole story of what had happened ten years ago. Gabrielle was the only one who would have been able to figure out what his priorities were. He put down his screwdriver on the counter. He leaned against the wall and then slid down it until he sat on the floor. He brought his knees up to his chest and just thought about Chantal. He was in a daze and at a loss about what to do. He did love her. He had never loved anyone this much. No one had ever loved him like she had. She loved him unconditionally.

Can I live without her? Will she still want me after I've gotten my revenge? He closed his eyes and reflected on how much he had wrecked his life. He once had the best job in the world. He had been head of security for one of the wealthiest men in the world. He had gone from that to being an ex-con with a janitorial job. How had it gone so bad so fast?

This wasn't how he had planned his life. Now he was preparing to bring down the man who had once given him a position of authority. He had taken it upon himself to destroy Ron's family. Why? Because Ron had chosen to accept his son's wife and baby but not him. Ron had swallowed his pride and recognized that it was for the best. Tom hadn't understood that love or the reason that his boss had betrayed him. Tom had never been able to comprehend the strength of Ron's love for his son—until now. Tom had a love in his own life now. It must have been difficult for Ron to accept Gabrielle, but he had. He had chosen her over Tom.

Chantal had said Ron had forgiven him. He didn't know if he could ever trust Ron again. Ron had treated him harshly and had betrayed him, but Chantal had confidence in him. Had Ron really forgiven him for shooting him, or was he just saying that? Maybe he was a better man than Tom. Could Ron really forgive and forget so easily? Tom wondered how it would feel to absolve someone of their misdeeds.

He had spent ten long years in prison while Ron had been free—free to roam the world, free to enjoy life as he pleased. But for all of his freedom, he had still been confined to a wheelchair. Tom had chosen to settle the score with Ron. Now he had to finish what he had started, or he would lose all self-respect. If he gave up, Ron would have beaten him. Tom wasn't a coward. He wasn't going to give up and let Ron win everything.

What about losing Chantal? Could he bear that loss? She was always in the back of his mind, encouraging him to give up his cause that he had worked for and dreamed of for so long. Tom couldn't escape her. He was always thinking of her. He missed Chantal's laugh and her gentle touch on his skin. She was what brought pleasure to his life. She was the only person who could make him forget the bad things that had happened to him. She brought joy and meaning into his life. She accepted him.

He rubbed his face with the palms of his hands, then passed his fingers through his hair. There would be time to love later, but would she still want to be with him after he destroyed Ron? He had to finish what he had started. He stood and finished securing the lock. He still had a few hours before he had to head back to Boston to meet Chantal. He had to convince her that whatever she thought she knew, she was wrong. He would tell her that he didn't love her and that she should go home. He also needed to ask her about Ron's forgiveness. How did she know this?

Ha! Tom smiled.

You couldn't believe anything Ron said. Tom knew the man too well. He could practically read the man's mind. This was just another lie or a trap to bring him down.

By late afternoon, Tom had finished most of his chores, so he jumped into his truck and headed back to Boston. He told Neil that he would be back in a few days. He just needed to stop by the boarding house to pick up the last of his belongings before he disappeared from the face of the earth.

***

Chantal roamed the halls of the mansion looking for Ron and Gabrielle. She had an idea on how to save Tom and Ron both at the same time. Chantal bumped into Gabrielle in one of the hallways upstairs. She signaled for Gabrielle to come with her. Chantal walked into one of the vacant guest rooms on the second floor. Gabrielle trailed behind her. The bedroom had a purple and green paisley comforter with matching throw pillows and wallpaper. There was a sofa in front of the window. Chantal directed Gabrielle to it. Chantal sat down and placed her hands on top of Gabrielle's and looked her in the eyes. She needed all of Gabrielle attention for what she was about to ask her.

"We need to talk. It's important," Chantal told her without blinking.

"OK, what about?" Gabrielle asked her.

"Are you sure that Tom is planning to hurt Ron?" Chantal kept her voice low so no one would overhear her.

"Well, I think so." Gabrielle frowned at her.

"I have a plan on how to stop Tom and save Ron without anyone getting hurt. When I go to meet Tom tonight, I'm going to invite him here afterward." Chantal said and then held her breath.

"Are you out of your mind? Ron would never allow him inside the house, especially not with Bernard away on a business trip. And what about Junior? It's too risky. You have to think of something else. Besides, what if he doesn't want to come?" Gabrielle questioned her. She drummed the armrest of the chair with her thumb.

"I'll make sure he comes. Don't worry, that's my job. You can send Junior to a friend's house for the evening, can't you? And you can help me convince Ron to invite him over or—" Chantal saw Gabrielle's mouth, but nothing came out. Chantal placed her hands together in a prayer gesture.

"Please, I can't do this by myself. And if we don't do something now, someone is going to get hurt down the road. Help me convince Ron," Chantal pleaded.

"You're asking a whole lot. I suppose I could send Junior to his friend's, but how in the hell do you think you will get Ron to allow Tom in this house? What if he won't agree? Then what? Now, that is the major obstacle," Gabrielle said to her as she scratched her head.

"No, listen. Ron told me that he had forgiven Tom and that he wanted to move on. We could tell Ron that he should let Tom know that he has forgiven him and that he wants a truce. No more bad blood between the two of them." Chantal said, but she wasn't sure that her plan would work. The only problem was whether Tom would forgive Ron. That was the big question, but Chantal was confident that she could turn him around. She had to at least try.

"I'm not as sure as you. What about Tom?" Gabrielle said. Chantal noticed that Gabrielle's leg was bouncing up and down. She placed her hand on top of her leg and rubbed it.

"Let me worry about Tom. Just help me with Ron, OK?" Chantal said. Gabrielle nodded at her. Chantal embraced Gabrielle tightly, and then they left the room hand-in-hand, looking for Ron.

***

Ron was at his usual spot in the library, going over company contracts. He shuffled papers from one pile to another. He had felt better this week than he had in a long time. He was eating well and sleeping much better. He didn't know why, but he had been much happier ever since he had forgiven Tom. Ron finally had realized that it wasn't all Tom's fault. Ron had started the whole mess. He should have done this a long time ago, but he had been too obstinate.

He had taken responsibility for what had happened ten years ago, and he had accepted his injury. It had been a long and difficult road, and he wished he had done it sooner. He knew he would still have bad days, but he would make the best of what he had today. His family was his whole world. His only desire was that Bernard and Gabrielle would have another child, but it hadn't happened yet.

It was late afternoon, and Ron was waiting for his grandson to run into his office to play cards or a game as he usually did after school, but instead he saw Chantal and Gabrielle walking into the room toward him.

They both wore serious expression, and neither smiled. They approached his desk with long strides him and stood in front of him.

"So, what are you girls up to? And where is my grandson? He's late today," Ron said as he kept making notes. He felt their eyes on him, so he stopped writing. Neither had said a word. Ron lifted his eyebrows at them.

"Anyone for a cocktail?" Ron asked as he directed his chair to the bar area at the other end of the room. *I shouldn't drink as much as I do,* he thought, but he still poured himself a scotch and lifted his glass to the girls.

"No, thank you, but you should go ahead," Gabrielle told him. Chantal just shook her head.

"Junior went to a friend's house for the night. Ron, we were hoping we could talk to you. It's a pretty delicate matter," Gabrielle said softly. She didn't so much as crack a smile at him. She was rubbing her hands together. He knew she was nervous. Whatever she wanted to talk to him about had to be important.

"Why don't you girls have a seat by the fireplace and tell me what's on your mind? I can see that it seems significant." He wheeled ahead of them and stopped beside the chair. "Now, tell me what's on your mind."

"Chantal told me you forgave Tom for what he did to you. We would like to know if you would consider telling him," Gabrielle said, then she reached over for Chantal's hand. He noticed how she tenderly she squeezed it and how they looked at each other.

"Tell him I forgive him? I never really thought it over. Why?" Ron scratched his chin and noticed that Chantal's head was bowed. For a moment everyone was silent.

"Mr. Rian, I love Tom with all my heart, and I know that he loves me, too, but we think he is focused on you. He told me I wasn't his priority. We think you are his priority," Chantal said sadly. The corners of her mouth were drawn downward, and her lip started to tremble. Ron was speechless. He'd been right. Tom was a threat, but could Ron change his mind and redirect his energy toward Chantal? He wasn't sure if he could do it.

"We hoped you could talk to him tonight. Chantal is supposed to meet him." Gabrielle took over. Ron knew it was because she didn't want Chantal to cry. Chantal's eyes were full of tears, and he felt his chest tighten. He hated to see a woman sob.

"Let me think about it," Ron answered. He couldn't give her a definite yes right now.

"I'll check with you before I leave later on. I'm meeting him at seven tonight," Chantal said and nodded his way. The girls stood up and walked out, leaving Ron alone to debate whether he should reconcile with Tom.

Ron was taken aback. He had never thought that he would ever talk to Tom again. All kinds of feelings, ranging from hatred to the fondness he had once felt for the man, ran through him. *She said she was not Tom's priority. She should be at the top of his list, not me,* Ron thought. He needed another drink. He polished the one he had and went back to the bar. He was holding his scotch as he thought about how he could make Tom understand. Ron was upset by the turn of events, but he had to help.

Tom was planning to hurt him. Well, he was going to be surprised. Ron was not going to allow himself to feel the way that he had felt before he had forgiven Tom. He had accepted his condition and forgiven him. It took him a long time—ten years—but he had missed out on a lot while pining for revenge. He hadn't been able to see that the most important things in his life were already right in front of him: his family and their love for him. He had to make Tom realize the power of love. Tom had a chance to be loved by someone. He shouldn't throw it away.

CHAPTER 30

It was almost time to go meet Tom. Chantal sat in a chair by the foyer door while she waited for Steve to bring the car in front. She had looked for Ron for the last half-hour but hadn't found him. She assumed it meant that he wouldn't help her with this situation. She felt sad, but she wouldn't cry. She had to be strong if she were to succeed with her plan. She was going to do it with or without Ron's help. She looked up and saw Gabrielle standing over her, extending her hand. Chantal wrapped her fingers around Gabrielle's. Chantal stood up and embraced her friend.

"I just wanted to wish you luck tonight. I hope everything goes well," Gabrielle said in a soft voice.

"Thanks. Did you hear from Ron? I haven't been able to find him. Do you know if he talked to Tom after we spoke to him?" Chantal asked.

"No, I haven't even seen him. I thought he was with you. I'm sorry it didn't work like you wanted, but try to convince Tom not to do anything rash. He loves you. He might listen to you," Gabrielle said, trying to encourage her friend.

"I'm going to do my best." Chantal saw the sedan pull up to the front entrance. Steve stood outside the vehicle with his hand on the back door handle, waiting for her to exit the house. She leaned over, kissed Gabrielle on the cheek, and then walked away. Steve opened the back door and she slid in, ready for what might be her final encounter with Tom.

***

Tom glanced at his watch. It was six forty-five. Fifteen more minutes before he saw her again. Fifteen more minutes before he could put his arms around her. He had his back against a large tree not far from the overpass where they were to meet. He had a good view of the parking lot and the bridge. He'd be able to watch Chantal from afar when she arrived. He noticed a black sedan pulling into the parking lot.

He waited with anticipation. His eyes focused on only one thing: Chantal. The driver exited and opened the back door. Tom's heart started pumping faster when he laid his eyes on her. She was alone. Steve was not following her. He had returned to his seat in the car.

Tom came out of his hiding place and started walking toward the bridge. He was on the opposite side of the pond, so he watched the reflection of her every step until they were about a foot away from each other. She gave him a smile that melted his heart. He was getting hard at the idea of touching her once more. She reached and placed her hands on his chest. She was intoxicating. He could smell her perfume as the wind blew it around him. Her curls were dancing in the breeze, and he couldn't help but lust after her. He wanted to hear her moan again. She bowed her head and laid it on his chest. He cupped her face and lifted it up. Her mouth opened, but no words came out. He brought his lips down on hers and inhaled as his tongue searched for hers. Her arms draped around his waist, and he lost all control. He had to pull away from her. He pushed her away so he could see her face, and then he grinned at her. In a sexy voice, he said, "I missed you."

"I missed you, too," she whispered and kept her hand on his arm. He needed to be firm and convince her to go home, but the kiss had not helped the situation. He turned away from her and placed both his hands on the railing of the bridge. He looked away from her and gazed out over the pond.

"Chantal, you need to listen to me. I don't want you to stay here. I want you to go back home to Canada. I will come meet you there when I can," he told her.

"I'm not going anywhere. I know what you are planning. Please don't do anything to jeopardize your freedom. Ron has forgiven you; you should do the same and move on. Do it for my sake. I love you, and I don't want you to go back to jail," Chantal pleaded.

"Chantal, you don't understand. That man sent me to prison for ten years. All I did was try to help him and do what he had ordered me to do. Am I supposed to forget that? He needs to suffer for what he did," he told her. He wouldn't look at her.

"Tom, he is suffering for his actions. You've already punished him enough. He'll be in a wheelchair for the rest of his life. He'll never walk again. He told me he doesn't hold you responsible anymore. He said it was as much his fault as yours. Believe me, he is paying dearly. He has moved on and forgiven you. Why can't you do the same? I love you, and I want us to be together, but if you—" Her voice broke. He glanced her way and saw her eyes water up. It broke his heart. He had to look away again.

"I've tried, but I don't know if I can forgive Ron," he told her.

"Tom, look at me. Answer me one question. Do you love me? If you do, please come with me, and talk to him. Do it for us. If he can forgive, you can too. Otherwise we don't have anything else to say to each other. We don't have a future together. I won't be able to live with knowing that you harmed him," she said and then started to walk back to the sedan.

Tom knew that the right thing was to forgive Ron, but he wasn't sure if he could. He didn't know if he wanted to pardon him, but he figured he should try for her. He loved this woman so much! The least he could do was to go see Ron. Maybe they could talk. He would listen to what the man had to say, and then he would make his final decision. At least he would have access to something he didn't have now.

"Chantal, wait," he said. She turned and looked his way, her hands on her hips as another tear fell from her eyes. He couldn't stand seeing her cry. It was stronger than he. "Fine, I'll try. Just for you. I'll try," he said. She held out her hand, and he took it in his and squeezed it. They started walking back toward the car.

"That's all I ask. That's it," she told him.

They were about ten feet from the vehicle when Tom saw Steve exit the car. He opened the back door to let them in. Chantal slid inside, and then it was Tom's turn. He peered in the backseat and froze. He grinned as he heard.

"Hello, Tom. Nice to see you again."

Tom sat beside Chantal and replied to Ron with a smirk, "Nice to see you, too." Tom reached for the handle as he closed the door, but his eyes never left Ron.

"I'm glad you agreed to meet. Chantal asked me if we could talk." Ron said as casually as he could. His head was starting to pound. He really didn't think Tom would meet him, considering the past that they had, but he was willing to discuss the possibility of a truce for the family's sake. Tom was as rooted to the spot like a statue. He didn't move a muscle, but his eyes took in everything. His eyes were cold.

"Go ahead, I'm listening," Tom said. He squinted at Ron. Ron inhaled, rubbed his hands together, and then laid them on his legs. He felt beads of sweat forming on his neck.

"First I want to say that I'm sorry. I no longer think that everything that happened was entirely your fault. I shouldn't have put you in that position. We both suffered but in different ways. You went to prison, and I'm paralyzed. I hated you for a very long time, just as you must hate me now. But Tom, I don't hate you any more. I have learned to accept what I cannot change and to try to make the best of it. I have my family, and you have this lovely woman who loves you. We should move past our disagreements and try to make peace. I have forgiven you, and I truly hope you will forgive me," Ron said and then waited for Tom to say something, but he didn't. Ron extended his hand, hoping Tom would shake it, but he didn't take it. Tom just stared at him. Ron pulled his hand back.

"Is that all?" Tom asked, not moving an inch.

"As a matter of fact, no. If you are willing to bury the hatchet and have peace between us, I will put in a good word for you so that you will be reemployed. That is, if you want. I hope you agree, because Chantal truly loves you and that only comes once in a lifetime. Don't throw it away. Now I'm done." Ron had tried his best, and he felt even better than before. He had done a good deed by trying to help him. He was just afraid that Tom might lunge at him and try to kill him. They locked eyes like they had from time to time when Tom had been his head of security. He felt like they had never lost touch, even after all that had happened between them.

"I'll let you know." That was all Tom said. He opened the door and stepped out. Ron heard Chantal say, "Tom, please don't do this." He shut the door and walked away.

CHAPTER 31

Tom was in a daze after he exited the car. He kept walking without feeling anything. His mind was blank until he sat behind the wheel of his truck. He couldn't get the image of Ron sitting in the sedan out of his mind. He still saw him sitting there in his fancy clothes. He clenched the wheel and held on tight. Tom tried to sort out his emotions. He couldn't believe that Ron had caught him off guard like that.

He'd had him. He could have gotten his revenge right then and there. But Chantal had been sitting next to him. He wouldn't put her in that position. He'd had the opportunity to grab Ron. He had been defenseless, just sitting there, but he hadn't wanted Chantal to judge him. What Ron had said had stunned him. Ron had forgiven him, but could he trust any word that come out of his mouth? He had wanted them to abandon their hostility toward each other. He had wanted a truce. Based on what? A handshake?

Ron had suffered. The change in him was obvious. He was no longer as domineering as he had once been. He had looked very frail. He wasn't as arrogant either. He seemed happy even though he couldn't walk. Ron had offered Tom his hand. Never in all the years that he had known the man had he shaken his hand.

Tom laid his head on the wheel. He was so confused. He didn't want to lose Chantal, and he knew if he attacked Ron, Chantal would never be by his side. She would never forgive him. She had changed him. He had never thought a woman would have the power to do this to him. He loved her. He now understood what Ron's family had meant to him when Ron had betrayed him so many years ago.

He started his truck and drove away. He didn't have a particular destination in mind. He rolled down his window. He needed fresh air before he suffocated. His whole body was shaking. He had to think things over, but all he could think about was how feeble Ron had looked. This man was no longer the man who, ten years ago, had ordered him to stop Gabrielle from marrying his son at all cost.

Tom had always put Ron on a pedestal. He had been unreachable. He had been and still was very powerful, but time had changed him. *What am I going to do?* He felt guilty. The Ron he was going after was not the Ron who had put him in prison. Tom reminded himself of that. *Or was he?* He had to decide whether to continue his mission or to forgive Ron and accept his confession that he was partially to blame.

How much time will Chantal give me? He had left her sitting in the back of the car without even saying a word to her. *What am I going to do? When will she leave to go back? In a day or a week?* His decision would change his life forever, but what would he choose? He had too many questions and no answers, so he decided to sleep on it—until tomorrow. He would see things differently after a good night's sleep. He drove back to the boarding house.

***

Chantal was crushed. She had tried to make Tom understand, but she had failed to make him change his mind. Ron hadn't said a word all the way home. It was as if they were headed to a funeral. Neither dared to say too much. Chantal had cried, but her tears were gone by the time they arrived back at the house. She was determined to go forward without Tom. It was going to be a painful for some time, but she wouldn't have part in his schemes. She would leave on the next plane to Canada.

As they came up the driveway, she looked at Ron and placed her hand on his. He turned toward her, but he waited for her to speak first. He smiled and then just nodded at her.

"I just want to thank you for at least trying to make things right," Chantal told him. She had grown to like this man. She wished Tom would have listened, but now it was too late.

"Chantal, you are a beautiful young person. You will find love again one day, and I must say, it was a pleasure to have you in our company. I hope you come again to visit us," Ron said and then tapped her hand.

"Thank you for everything you did." She was numb from pain but grateful they had tried to rectify the situation.

"I did nothing. You were the one that freed me and made me realize how wrong I was. Forgiveness set me free. I am so grateful to you for that." Ron leaned over and kissed her cheek. The car had crossed the driveway and they were now in front of the house.

"Now go. Steve will bring me in through the back entrance," Ron said. She slid out of the sedan when it stopped at the entrance of the house. She walked in, her feet heavy, but she marched straight upstairs to her bedroom to pack her bags. She no longer wanted to stay in Boston. She was going home tomorrow, and that was her final decision. Tom would always have a special place it her heart, but she wouldn't take part in his plans.

Morning came quickly. She was all packed and waiting for Steve to take her to the airport. Gabrielle stood next to her at the door.

"I hope you come back to visit. I am so sad it didn't work out as you had planned. It will be all right. You will see. Time heals a lot of things, and little by little you will forget the pain that you thought would never go," Gabrielle said to her and then gave her a final hug.

"Thanks. You are a great friend. Like they all say, give it time, right?" Chantal said. Her voice started to break, but she would be damned if she cried any more. She blinked several times to get control. She kissed her friend and reached down to pick up her bag before taking the last steps to the car.

"I'll call you when I arrive back in Canada. Love you. Bye." Chantal waved to her, and Steve took her bag as she went to sit inside the car. Chantal took one last look at her friend and waved. She would go forward now and not look back at what could have been. She rested her head on the seat, closed her eyes, and said a silent prayer for Tom.

***

Tom hadn't been able to get much sleep. He was trying to make the most crucial decision of his life. He needed to talk to Chantal one more time to try to resolve his dilemma. He had to go see her. He no longer cared what happened to him. He hopped into his truck and headed toward Gabrielle's house. He dialed her number and waited for her to answer, but she didn't pick up.

He continued driving since he was almost there. He turned onto Ron's property. He felt a chill fell run down his back. This was the first time he had been on the estate since he had gotten arrested ten years ago. He noticed security roaming the grounds as he drove up the long driveway. He parked in front of the house, and within a minute he was staring at three security guards who has surrounded his truck. He rolled his window down but stayed inside the vehicle, his hands on the wheel. He didn't want to provoke any of them. One of them approached his window, looked at him ,and bluntly asked. "What are you doing here? Do you have an appointment?" The guard's hand was on his handgun. "I'm here to see Chantal Arsenault." Tom glared at him. He didn't want to make any sudden moves because he could see in his rearview mirror that the other two guards also had their hands on their guns, ready to pull them out.

"She's no longer here," he replied. "Please leave the premises, sir."

Tom wasn't going to be intimated by them. He wasn't moving, and he wasn't afraid of them. He tightened his grip on the wheel and stared at the security guard.

"Where did she go, and when will she return?" Tom asked without flinching.

"I can't divulge that information. Now you will have to leave."

"I'm not leaving until I know where she went. I want to speak to Gabrielle Rian," he said, refusing to budge.

"Wait here." He watched as the guard motioned another guard to cover him. He spoke into his radio and then returned to the side of his truck.

"Mrs. Rian will be right with you. Don't leave the vehicle," he said as he stood next to the other guards.

A few minutes passed, and then the front door opened and Gabrielle emerged. She walked to Tom's window.

"What are you doing here? Chantal's not here," she told him. "She left this morning to go back home."

Tom couldn't breathe. She was gone. He felt as though someone had punched him in the stomach. He needed to find Chantal! He looked at Gabrielle in disbelief. He bowed his head, defeated. He was too late. He had let her slip out of his hands. What was he going to do now? He heard his name and turned his head toward Gabrielle.

"Tom, do you really love her?" Gabrielle asked, not taking her eyes off him.

"Yes, I love her," he answered without hesitation. Gabrielle gave him a small smile.

"You might still be able to catch her. She left about half an hour ago. Her flight doesn't leave for another two hours. She went to Logan Airport, and she's flying with Air Canada. You'd better not hurt her anymore. Do you hear me?" she told him. Tom glanced at Gabrielle. He could tell that she was serious. Her eyebrows were knit together, and her lips were tight. She stared at him.

"I won't. I promise. Thank you," he said as he started the truck, pressed the gas, and took off toward the city.

CHAPTER 32

Chantal had just left the ticket counter. She had checked her luggage, and she walked toward the convenience store to pick up a magazine for the flight. She really didn't feel like reading, but she wanted to try to distract herself from Tom. Her heart was broken. She would never forget him, but she couldn't agree with what he was about to do. How could he not choose her? The worst part of it all was the fact that he didn't love her enough to be with her. She would move forward. She had to. There was no other way. She randomly picked a magazine and went to the cashier to pay for it. She reached into her wallet, placed a $10 bill on the counter, took her magazine, and stepped out of the store.

She walked aimlessly, trying to find a place to sit. She still had time before she had to go through security. Finally she spotted an empty area, so she sat on a bench and closed her eyes. She tried to refocus her energy so she that she wouldn't cry. She took the magazine from her carry-on and pretended to read. Nothing was working. She couldn't focus.

She decided to watch the people who passed in front of her as they went to their designated gates. A tall man who was a little away from her caught her attention. He was dressed all in black, and his hair was slicked back. He scanned the passengers intently as he came forward. She'd know that walk and that body anywhere. It was Tom! Her chest pounded so hard that she couldn't move. Was he looking for her? What else could he be doing here?

As he approached, he locked eyes with her and stopped. He grinned and walked toward her slowly. She stood. Her magazine fell to the floor, but she held her ground. She watch his every move until he stood in front of her. He looked at her and bowed his head toward her. He placed his hands around her waist and pulled her against him. She didn't resist, but neither did she reciprocate his actions.

"Hey! You weren't going to leave without saying goodbye, were you?" He murmured. She was speechless. All she could do was look at him. She felt the heat of his body against hers. "I don't want you to leave," he whispered to her.

"I ... have to ..." She couldn't get the words out. The moment she peered into his eyes, she was lost. She couldn't think.

"I love you. Please stay. I'll do anything you want—even forgive Ron. Don't go," Tom pleaded. He brought his mouth down on hers and kissed her. Her arms flew around him in an instant. She couldn't pull away. She kissed him back. She felt him against her.

She pulled away. People were staring at them, but she didn't care. She just said, "I love you, too."

ABOUT THE AUTHOR

Ann El-Nemr was born in Boston, Massachusetts, but was raised in the quiet town of Cap-Pele, New Brunswick, Canada. She now lives in Shrewsbury, Massachusetts, with her husband and three children. Ann only started writing during the past few years—it's her new passion. She loves to travel the world to explore the different cultures of various countries and to learn about their history. Her first book, *Betrayed*, was released in January 2014; *Forgiven* is the sequel to *Betrayed* but can be read independently. Ann loves to hear from her readers—contact her at annelnemr.com, on Facebook, or on LinkedIn.

THE PLEDGE

On the one-year anniversary of a friend's death, Dalton receives a letter. In the letter, the friend reminds Dalton to honor his deathbed promise: to love and bring happiness back to his widow, Annette. Through his work, Dalton unexpectedly encounters Annette. He falls for her, so he breaks his current engagement—and he conceals from Annette the terms of his pledge to her former husband. When the scorned fiancée finds the posthumous letter, she becomes determined to win back Dalton at any cost—even death. Can Dalton protect Annette from his former fiancée's schemes? Will Dalton confess to Annette? Or will Annette leave Dalton because of his deceit?

CPSIA information can be obtained at www.ICGtesting.com
Printed in the USA
BVOW05s1205060614

355590BV00001B/1/P